Critical acclaim for James Humphreys

Sleeping Partner

'A splendid debut in crime fiction.
More, please, Mr Humphreys'
COLIN DEXTER

'A promising debut from an interesting writer'
Sunday Telegraph

'One of the more provocative and intelligent first novels in
some time . . . a genuine spellbinder'
Irish News

'A slick and gripping debut'
Guardian

Riptide

'*Sleeping Partner* was rapturously received by the critics . . .
Could James Humphreys do it again? He has.'
Birmingham Post

'Surprising, disturbing and exciting'
Scotsman

'An accomplished, intriguing story . . . A clever plot,
efficiently delivered, with a sympathetic central character'
Observer

Riptide

James Humphreys grew up in East Anglia and now lives in London with his wife and two young children. After working on environmental protection and European negotiations, he is now head of corporate communications in the Prime Minister's office at Downing Street. *Riptide* is his second novel, following the critically acclaimed *Sleeping Partner*.

Also by James Humphreys

SLEEPING PARTNER

James Humphreys

Riptide

PAN BOOKS

First published 2001 by Macmillan

This edition published 2002 by Pan Books
an imprint of Pan Macmillan Ltd
Pan Macmillan, 20 New Wharf Road, London N1 9RR
Basingstoke and Oxford
Associated companies throughout the world
www.panmacmillan.com

ISBN 0 330 48098 7

1 3 5 7 9 8 6 4 2

A CIP catalogue record for this book is available from
the British Library.

Printed and bound in Great Britain by
Mackays of Chatham plc, Chatham, Kent

Riptide

Prologue

They had left the noise and laughter and heat of the party behind. The late evening was cool and quiet, easing her headache, making her tiredness more comfortable.

They took the path through the dunes to the beach, finding their way by the faint starlight. The low sound of the sea was soothing.

On the beach, she drew her shawl closer against the cool breeze. She was grateful when he put his arm around her. And when she stumbled on the shingle and for a moment everything spun around her, she held his arm more tightly.

The moon came out from behind a cloud. They stopped to watch the sea, now silvered and sparkling. The deep rumble and rattle as each wave pushed the shingle back and forth was muted.

She felt detached from everything, entirely happy. On an impulse, she wrapped her arms around his head, drawing him towards her. At first he was surprised, and then returned her kiss too eagerly. She giggled, realizing her mistake. He was the wrong man.

Have I had too much to drink?

She slid from his arms and walked on, laughing to herself. The way the shingle gave beneath her feet was tiring and she was thankful to reach the next breakwater. She leant against the warm grey wood, studying intently the pattern of lichen which spread across it.

She could hear his footsteps approaching and the distant wash of the sea. Everything else was still and quiet.

On the other side of the breakwater the tide had left a patch of sand, smooth and dry. She lay down on it.

'Are you OK?' he asked, squatting beside her.

She found she couldn't speak. She waved one hand vaguely, to tell him she only wanted to rest for a minute.

Then, or later, she felt him take her hand and feel for a pulse. He pulled back her eyelid. She didn't mind but she wished he would let her sleep.

She woke again, seeing his anxious eyes.

'I'm going for help,' he said distinctly.

What a strange thing to say.

She listened as he tried to run across the shingle, back towards the car. The tiredness receded for a moment, and she half sat up. Against the lighter sky, she could see him start to climb back up the dunes, and then stop. Two other figures appeared in front of him. One grabbed his arms. She could hear angry voices, shouting, a struggle.

She sank back onto the soft sand. Something was wrong. She couldn't make any sense of it. But she was too tired to try to understand.

If she could only rest for a moment, everything would become clear.

She stretched out on the sand, her head pillowed on her arm, listening to the rise and fall of the sea.

A while later, the tide turned and began to creep slowly over the banks of sand and shingle. It formed pools around the end of the breakwaters, covered the patches of deep green seaweed and freed countless bubbles of air trapped in the sand.

The moon had set long before. A swathe of cloud came from the west, blanking out the starlit sky. The air grew colder and smears of mist began to form. By dawn, everything on the beach, living and dead, was painted with a glittering skin of dew.

Chapter One

As she lay in bed, gathering herself before getting up to make her tea, Rosemary Aylmer could already sense the change in the weather. The evening before had held some memory of the summer. Now she felt the cold and damp of an autumn morning, and when she pulled back the curtain she could see the field at the end of her garden was wreathed in mist, turning the hawthorn trees and gorse bushes into vague shadows. As she padded downstairs to the kitchen, her two Norfolk terriers following at her heels, she was grateful for her dressing gown. She would have to put the heating on for the first time since May, she decided.

Twenty minutes later, she was dressed in an old cashmere cardigan and thick tweed skirt with a waxed coat over the top, and walking shoes. She called to the dogs and set off for their morning run. Her house was the last but one along Beach Road, and like the others a gate at the bottom of her garden led across the fields to the dunes and then the sea itself. But she decided to take the road instead. Before it reached the dunes, the path crossed a field of high grass which would be sodden with dew at this early hour, and she preferred to keep her feet and skirt dry.

The dogs scampered ahead of her. There was no need to keep them on a lead as there was little chance of meeting anyone, and no car could travel at more than a crawl along the rutted and potholed road. The dogs worked together, sniffing along the length of the ditch to her right, searching the hedge to her left and running ahead to the end of the track. There they turned and grinned back at her, encouraging her to catch up. She waved an arm and they turned and ran out of sight.

She walked on, easing the stiffness from her right hip, enjoying the scent of moisture and the faint sound of water flowing again in the ditch after another dry spell. She found it difficult to sleep sometimes in the summer, with the heat and the short nights. The return of autumn, though she had seen it seventy times or more, was surprisingly welcome.

Beyond the last house was a flat expanse of turf cropped short by the same rabbits the dogs had sent scurrying for safety, where cars could turn. It was unusual for anyone to park here overnight, even in summer, as the road was private and the only people allowed down were residents, who each had their own key to the gate at the far end. But someone must have left it open, for on the far side was a rather flash little sports car.

The car's sharp outline and silver paintwork made a striking contrast to the soft browns and greens around. Rosemary went over, wondering if perhaps it had been stolen and abandoned, but as she examined it she realized she had no way of knowing what a stolen car might look like. It was locked, none of the windows had been broken and there was a coat and bag lying untouched on the tiny back seat. Then her eye was caught by a sticker on the passenger side of the windscreen. It was a staff parking permit for the Norfolk and Norwich Hospital; the 'N and N' as she remembered it from her own time working there as a ward sister.

She looked about her as if expecting to see a white-coated doctor appear from behind one of the clumps of gorse and bramble dotted along the dunes. But there was nothing except for the mist and the distant calls of the marsh warblers and redshank and, even more faintly, the sound of the sea.

Shrugging, she set off towards the dunes, thinking about her friends from those days, the very few she still kept up with. An image came to her mind, start-lingly clear, of a nurse standing weeping outside a linen cupboard because she had lost a patient, a student, they had all thought would recover. Rosemary could picture so clearly the cream-painted cupboard doors, and almost smell the stiff white sheets inside. She could remember the way the girl had blinked away the tears, wiped her eye with the back of her hand.

That must have been thirty years ago but it was astounding, she thought, how perfectly such things could return. She could recall the ward too, the long line of bays each with six beds, the clutter of trolleys and equipment, of portable tables and linen bags, light pouring in from the high windows patterning the worn lino and making the smiles of the relatives even more threadbare. It was satisfying that she could dredge up the name of the ward: Benton – named after a dreary village on the road to Ipswich. It had a reputation because it was the ward where the oncology patients were treated, and precious few of them survived in those days. People would lower their voices when they said *Did you know they've put him on Benton?* It was the medical equivalent of the last rites.

She climbed the line of dunes and stopped at the top. On a clear day she could have looked west to the distant golf course and the town of Hunstanton, and east along the line of Compton Spit. But everything was lost in the mist. It was a really horrible day, she thought, as she started off along the spit.

The sound of the sea was subdued, easily pierced by the excited barks of the dogs as they rushed up and down the waterline, but no less powerful for that. Every day, even a calm day like this, the sea was slowly gnawing at the beach. There were breakwaters every few hundred yards, built of massive baulks of wood and vast iron bolts, covered with mats of deep green slime and razor-sharp barnacles. But even they couldn't stop the sea from slowly washing the shore away grain by grain, to dump it further down the coast at Yarwell, or Blakeney, or on one of the many flats or sandbanks which lay just off the coast.

Rosemary turned to call again to the dogs but they were down by the sea, standing barking at the waves. She called out more sharply. She had kept dogs for years, even when she was living in Norwich, and though she understood that instinct would always show through – especially if there was a rabbit's trail to be followed or a rival to be seen off – she strongly disapproved of those people who could not control their dogs when the need arose. So she sighed and stepped carefully down the face of the dune and onto the beach itself, calling once more and waving their leads as a warning, but the two of them carried on barking at a bit of driftwood, half submerged at the edge of the water.

'Woody! Daisy! Come here!'

Daisy, the younger of the two, detached herself and ran a few yards towards her, but then stopped and turned again.

'Come here!'

But Rosemary's voice had lost its edge. She was looking more closely at the piece of wood – or perhaps it was sacking – which the waves were turning over and over. She went closer, and then, for one moment, everything seemed to stop: her heart, the agitated barking of the dogs. Only the waves carried on breaking and the thing rolled over again, showing an arm, a face and a patch of white shirt.

She could feel her heart beating, horribly loud, in her ears. She had her hand in front of her mouth. But inside a voice was telling her to stay calm, that she was more than able to cope and that it was only its unexpectedness that was shocking.

The dogs ran up to her, scrabbled at her, and without thinking she crouched down and clipped the leads onto them. Then she went to the very edge of the sea and looked again at the body sprawling in the foam a few feet from her.

It won't become any easier for waiting, she told herself, and she dropped the leads and stepped into the sea, gasping at the cold. Steeling herself, she took hold of one of the arms and tried to pull the body to shore. But though the water was little more than a foot deep, the corpse was too heavy, too waterlogged, for her to manage. She pulled again and again, grasping the icy hand in one of hers and the sleeve of the jacket in her other, leaning backwards to try to add to her strength; but it was no good. Rosemary noticed her breath was becoming faster and more shallow. She knew there was no hope anyway that this cold, dead thing could be revived by her or anyone else. It was beyond her to do anything unaided. The sensible thing was to go for help.

In the end, she overcame her instinct to keep trying even when hope was gone and with a shiver staggered back to the beach, feeling the cold biting on her legs and the horrible flap of the hem of her skirt wet against her knees and calves. She grabbed the end of Woody's lead, called to Daisy, and then walked quickly up the beach towards the dunes.

But Daisy would not follow. She was still running up and down further along the beach, trailing her lead and barking excitedly. Rosemary shouted to her, her voice close to a scream. She sensed how close she was to losing her grip. Another minute wouldn't matter, she told herself. She took a deep breath, wrapped Woody's lead around one of the beams of the nearest breakwater and, ignoring his outraged yaps, set off after the other dog.

Daisy was by the next breakwater, standing where the shingle was piled nearly to the top, almost at the edge of the sea and looking down at the far side. Rosemary reached her, seized the lead in triumph, shook her back with a grunt of satisfaction, and then glanced over the edge herself.

That was how she came to find the second body.

Chapter Two

The four officers had been sitting in the Transit van for the best part of an hour, but they were used to it and would sit there all day if necessary. Tony Collins, the inspector in charge, was further up the lane, talking to the farmer and the bailiffs, and assessing the situation. The police's job was to stay out of the way until called in or sent back to the station. Either way they would get their overtime and allowances.

They had settled down for a long wait, each one trying to find a measure of comfort on the narrow, rigid seats. Peter Lakofski had given up fiddling with the radio and was slumped as far down in the driver's seat as he could go. He was pale, with shadows under his eyes, but he looked contented enough, as if his Saturday night, though exhausting, had been well spent. Although he seemed almost asleep, he was watching his colleague Sarah Delaney from the corner of his eye. She was sitting with her feet up on the dashboard, passing the time by filling in an application form. She was fair, about his own age, and good-looking, too. She leaned forward to write something, and for a moment a glimpse of bare skin beneath the neck of her overalls gave him the pleasurable illusion that she might be naked underneath. But he had long

10

ago decided she wasn't for him. She was too serious. She didn't know how to enjoy herself. Not like Lisa, he thought, as he closed his eyes again.

Behind them, Greg Allott, by far the tallest of the four, was stretched out on one of the bench seats, his head pillowed on a protective vest, casually reading an old newspaper he had found on the floor. As usual, he radiated a positive satisfaction in being paid to do nothing. It was the youngest of the four, Darren Stevenson, who alone found it hard to reconcile himself to the inactivity. He was in the seat by the sliding side door, slowly wiping away the condensation from the window to allow him a better view of the mist beyond.

'D'you reckon there'll be any trouble?' he asked.

None of the others had a strong view but it would have been rude for no one to offer a reply.

'No,' Allott said after a while. 'They'll be on their way, if we give 'em long enough.'

'They won't want any trouble,' Lakofski added, 'in case they get a scratch on one of their vehicles. Have you seen? One of them's got a brand new Jeep. A Grand Cherokee. Brand new. That'll have cost more than I earn in a year.'

Sarah Delaney turned back to the form, put a line through the box marked higher education and started to fill in her previous employment. It didn't amount to much. A year waitressing at various cafes and restaurants in Yarwell. Another year there working as a receptionist at the doctor's surgery. Six months at Harfield Electronics in Diss. And a four-month gap just before joining the police which she hoped they wouldn't ask about at interview. Assuming she got that far.

'And God knows what they'll be taking with 'em,' Allott said, trying to keep the desultory conversation going.

'How d'you mean?' Darren asked, being new to the team and the set views of his colleagues.

'You know what they're like.' Allott put down his paper. 'Locusts. They'll have laid their hands on all sorts of stuff. Power tools, electrical stuff, you name it. There won't be any trouble with moving them on. But if we stopped them and had a look inside those caravans, there'd be trouble then soon enough, wouldn't there?'

'There's the filth too,' Lakofski added, helping out his colleague's education. 'Muck everywhere. And the way they let the kids play around in it – it's disgusting.'

'It looked pretty tidy to me,' Sarah said mildly.

'Yeah, well.' Allott wouldn't disagree directly. 'That's all about the face they put on, isn't it? Trying to make out they're put upon. That they're the victims. But you ask any farmer around here who the real victims are.'

He rustled his paper back into place to emphasize his final words on the subject. Sarah sighed, thinking that although what he was saying sounded ugly she wasn't sure she didn't agree in some way with him. It made her uncomfortable and she tried to concentrate on the application form instead.

A moment later, Inspector Collins rapped on the side door. While Darren slid back the door the others made some effort to look more alert and officer-like.

Lakofski struggled upright, Sarah took her feet off the dashboard and even Allott put aside his paper.

'We were just saying what an Aladdin's cave we'll be letting get past us, sir,' Allott said cheerfully. He had worked with Collins before and had a high regard for him – which was not returned.

'How's that?' But Collins' sharp tone passed Allott by.

'These gypsies, sir,' he went on. 'Bound to have some gear on them.'

'I need a volunteer,' Collins said, still ignoring him. 'DCI Blake phoned to say there's a body been found and they've no one left at the station they can spare. So who knows the area?'

'Delaney, sir,' Allott said confidently, happy to divert the possibility of work elsewhere.

Collins looked at the four of them briefly: Allott's self-satisfied repose; Lakofski, looking washed out, a shadow across his chin where he had failed to shave properly that morning, if at all; Delaney, her fair skin and hair scrubbed and fresh so he could almost smell the soap and shampoo; and Stevenson, staring back at him alertly, like a puppy hoping to be taken for a walk.

'Yeah? Right, Delaney, you take the patrol car and go and sort it out.'

He probably would have chosen her anyway. She had a reputation as a competent officer, and though he knew he wasn't supposed to think that way there was no doubt that a woman's touch was helpful if there were relatives to comfort.

'A Mrs Aylmer has found a body on the beach. Check it out, wait for the ambulance, take a statement. All of that. You know the score, don't you?'

She nodded, twisting around in her seat.

'Where is it?'

'Oh, yeah.' He glanced at the scrawled message. 'Compton. On Compton Spit. Know it?'

She knew it.

She wished she had asked Collins to send someone else. Driving towards the village of Compton as fast as the mist and her reluctance would allow, she felt the pain of old memories being disinterred. For three years her life had revolved around the place. In her last term at sixth-form college, her A levels finished, she had met Tom Strete at a party and fallen for him. His parents had a holiday home at Compton and his uncle owned the boatyard in Yarwell. Tom had a summer job there taking holidaymakers out to see the seals and she had moved to the coast to be with him and never left. Her parents, when they weren't wrangling with each other, had argued with her about giving up her chance of university but she ignored them. Tom's parents, his brother, sister and cousins, were like a second family, ready prepared for her. His friends were so much more interesting and exciting than hers. With him she had a complete life. One she loved.

And when it ended she was left with nothing. She could no longer face his family. One by one she had given up seeing their friends. She had never returned to the village or to the beach. Especially not the beach.

It only took a few minutes to reach the main road and turn towards Hunstanton. The road was slow, snaking through the narrow streets of Norton Staithe and Martlesham and cutting inland several times to avoid the creeks and estuaries which bit into the coastline. Strange shapes loomed out of the fog before resolving themselves into a hedge, a house or a parked car. She could only imagine the sea away to her right beyond the fields and the salt marshes and the long lines of dunes holding back the endless attack of the waves.

She tried to think of something else, like the coincidence that it was Blake who had called. He had been on her promotion board and given her a hard time. But then he had just been sidelined in a management shake-up: Jeremy Morton, one of the force's rising stars, who had once been Blake's sergeant, had taken the major crimes job from him. Blake had been made head of the drugs squad to compensate and had thrown himself into that in typically forthright style, but she felt for him as someone else whose face happened not to fit. She was too young for promotion while he was probably now too old to reach the top, too much the traditional copper with a legendary network of informants and a reputation for hard drinking on and off the job.

She slowed, turned off the main road and drove through the village, numbed by the way each twist in the lane brought back another painfully familiar sight, each one piling on the other. The White Hart, where they had spent so many evenings together. The recreation ground where they had hung about because there was nothing else to do. Then the riding school where Tom had persuaded her to ride a horse for the first time, a patient old barrel which had known the route onto the beach and back so well that it needed no direction from her. But the stables were ick and flint barns turned into holiday homes.

They had often walked across the fields to the village, from the Red House which stood at the end of Compton Spit itself. That was the holiday home where Tom and she had stayed so often, sometimes on their own, or with his cousins, or more usually with his parents. She could still picture the room she had always had, the broad blue stripe of the Regency wallpaper, the thin chintz curtains, the selection of old paperbacks that no one now would read.

Beyond the village a narrow lane ran first between massive hedges and then open fields to the beach. Again everything was familiar, but nothing had the poignancy of the village itself. She began to breathe more easily and wondered if maybe the worst was over. Maybe she should have come back and faced up to the past long ago.

At the end of the lane there was a car park, busy in the summer but now deserted. To one side a rough track followed the line of the dunes towards Compton Spit. This was Beach Road, and along it there were half a dozen houses, some let to holidaymakers, others with permanent residents who somehow managed to live with the glut of visitors in the summer and the isolation the rest of the year.

She stopped the car, surprised to find a steel gate blocking the way. It was heavy-duty, the posts set in concrete, nothing like the rotting wooden one she remembered which had always been pushed back into the lush grass of the verge. A metal sign, already rusting around the screw holes, read PRIVATE ROAD NO ACCESS TO BEACH.

She parked on the verge opposite and walked back to the gate, taking in the sudden silence with the engine turned off. She could hear the distant boom of the sea on the sands, the occasional call of the rooks in the trees behind her, the sounds of her own footsteps on the gravel, the rustle of her overalls. The gate was secured with a chain and a surprisingly stout padlock, and after looking helplessly about for any way past, she sighed and began to climb over.

It was exactly 6.40 a.m.

Chapter Three

Sarah walked though the mist, feeling the damp and the cold settling on her. To her right, the fields faded away into the grey. To the left, the houses along the road emerged eerily from the mist, resolved themselves for a minute or two as she passed, and then faded again behind her.

The roadway had once been properly made up with hardcore over a base of rubble, but years of frost and rain and cars had eaten away great holes in the surface, which were now filled with water and sharp rocks. She wondered why the residents didn't club together to sort it out. Maybe there wasn't much money around. Some of the houses had peeling paint, one had a broken-down gate half off its hinges. It wasn't only that it was the end of the summer season; there was a definite air of neglect. People wouldn't want to throw money at a house they only visited a few times a year, and if someone had retired here they might want to eke out their savings pretty carefully.

After the next house there was an empty paddock enclosed by a rough wire fence. Across the far side of the field was an abandoned railway truck, taken off its wheels and dumped there as a shed. A horse, standing nearby, raised its head from the grass to stare at her silently.

Then, further on, Sarah saw a figure standing by a gate, peering towards her through the mist. She was well wrapped up, dressed conventionally except for a bright green and purple anorak. Sarah could see that though she must be well into her seventies she was upright and vigorous and would certainly keep for a few minutes without collapsing or needing tea. She must be pretty tough to have found a body and to show so few signs of shock.

She introduced herself, immediately conscious that the older woman was surprised by her youth.

'Could you show me where you saw the body?' Sarah asked. 'That is, if you feel up to it.'

'I'll be fine,' Rosemary said firmly. 'The only thing is, I'm not sure they'll still be there. The tide comes in so fast . .'

Sarah glanced at her watch. The tide here would already be past its height. If the body had gone, she thought, it would be a hard job trying to find it.

'I'm sorry I wasn't here sooner,' Sarah said, listening to the outraged howls from Woody and Daisy, shut up in the house. 'The gate's locked at the bottom of the road.'

'We keep it closed in the summer. Otherwise there are far too many people coming down here thinking you can reach the beach.'

They started off, and Rosemary was glad of the company. It was still misty, with no sound except for the birds and the sea, and the faintest whisper of a breeze through the bushes and reeds along their way. She had made herself some tea and toast, but this didn't seem to have made any impression on the empty feeling deep inside her.

'Could you try and describe the body?' Sarah asked.

'Which one?' Rosemary replied, and Sarah stared at her. 'There were two of them,' she went on in exasperation. 'Didn't you know?'

Sarah took this in. The woman must have been too incoherent to explain properly to the control room, though she seemed pretty composed now.

'It must have been a mix-up,' Sarah said, thinking how weak this sounded. Perhaps Blake got the wrong end of the stick in passing the message on to Collins. She wondered what Blake was doing in the control room anyway, poking his nose in and messing things up. Typical of him, though.

But then the implications began to sink in. One body wasn't remarkable; every year there were drownings somewhere along the coast – holidaymakers cut off by the tide, swimmers or sailors who got into trouble – and the bodies had to come ashore somewhere. But two bodies didn't make any sense, unless they had both been swimming off the beach. Or maybe one got into trouble and the other went in after them. Or some freak of the tides had kept them together.

'It was the man I found first,' Rosemary went on. 'He was in his twenties or thirties, I think. Dark hair. Or it looked dark, anyway, but that could have been from the water. He didn't have a beard or a moustache or anything. I couldn't say how tall he was exactly, but perhaps just under six feet. Well-built. He was wearing a dark suit and a white shirt. And I think black shoes.'

Sarah stopped to make a brief note and then to call the control room. As she did so, Rosemary looked at her more carefully, noting the neat fair hair falling over her face as she leant forward, the nails on her hands cut sensibly short, and the careful way in which she wrote. She thawed a little towards the girl. She reminded Rosemary of one or two of the better nurses who had worked for her over the years, who had that same mix of competence and enthusiasm.

'The woman – well, the girl, really – she was a few feet away, by one of the breakwaters,' Rosemary said, before explaining about the dogs. 'Daisy wouldn't come, so I went over to fetch her. She was standing on the top of the breakwater where the shingle is piled up. There's a dip on the far side where the beach has been washed away. It's very sheltered and the girl was lying there.'

'How old would you say she was?' Sarah asked as they walked on.

'About your age,' Rosemary replied. 'Not old at all. Certainly no more than twenty-five.'

'What did she look like?'

'She had a sharp face and dark hair. Black, really. Again, about your length or even a bit shorter.'

'Which way was she facing?'

'Towards the breakwater. She was on one side, half curled up. She was wearing a black dress with short sleeves. What I'd call a party frock.'

'No jacket?'

'No. It was very warm last night.'

They walked on to the end of the road. It was the same as Sarah remembered except that a new sign had been put up on the dunes themselves. But the bushes, the long, sharp marram grass, the track continuing on to the Red House were all unchanged.

'Who owns that house?' Sarah asked, trying to sound casual.

'A family called Strete, but they never come here. I think the brother manages it for them as a holiday home though I don't know that they let it out very much. John Walton. He owns the boatyard in Yarwell. It's mainly his children who use it. I say children. They're all grown up now, of course.'

Even when Tom and she had their flat in Yarwell, just down the coast, they would still come here with the others for the weekend if the house hadn't been rented out. If the weather was even half-decent, there was swimming, windsurfing, even flying a kite. The boathouse was full of stuff. Then a barbecue on the beach or whisky in front of the fire, a huge meal in the kitchen, watching the remnants of the day fade over the sea through the windows of the conservatory.

'Is there anyone there at the moment, do you know?'

She had the horrible fear that the victims might have been staying at the Red House. Perhaps one of Tom's cousins, Nick or Andrew, or his sister Sophie. She wondered if Rosemary could hear the anxiety in her voice, and if so what she would make of it. But she gave no sign, instead shaking her head.

'I don't think so. I hadn't seen any cars going along. The thing is, it's mostly empty these days. It's too big really, and very isolated out there. I spoke to Mr Walton about it one time when he was about and he said they'd sell it except no one can get a mortgage. You know they've decided they won't repair the sea defences? Instead, they'll let nature take its course. Managed retreat, they call it, apparently. So it won't be long before the spit starts to shift or even break up. And the house will go with it.'

Sarah remembered the first time she and Tom walked along the shore of the spit. He had loped along beside her, grinning at what she said or just because she was there, letting his energy bubble out of him, sweeping his long brown hair from his eyes, waving his arms to help express something, so that the heavy woollen shirt he wore open over his t-shirt, like a jacket, flapped around him. For a moment she could remember her amazement that he should feel even a fraction of what she felt for him. That simply being with someone could push aside everything else.

That same visit his cousin Nick had been there too, with his girlfriend of the moment. She couldn't remember much about her except for frizzy hair and a slightly rabbity face, though she could picture so exactly the light of the day fading across the marshes, where they had sat in the pub, how they had planned her first trip out sailing the next day.

'We'll go out to Coldharbour Sand,' Tom had said. 'We'll take a picnic,' he'd added and laughed at her surprise that the sands should emerge from the sea at low tide, even miles from the shore. 'You get acres of it,' he'd gone on. 'It's an amazing sight. They used to play cricket out there in the old days, you know. Two innings before the tide came in again.'

She'd said she'd be frightened to get out of the boat that far from land.

'You'll love it,' he'd insisted. 'It's like your own magical place. Made just for you, for that one moment. Like Brigadoon. If you're lucky, there'll be seals too. They'll let you get up really close.'

23

That had been so typical of Tom – the mix of adventure and fun and tenderness. In contrast, Nick had then started into a story about helping to rescue a stranded yachtsman from one of the sandbanks. He was already one of the crew of the inshore lifeboat at Yarwell. The story had, she sensed, been polished to impress his girlfriend and, typical of Nick, her as well. He didn't realize that it was the person who mattered, not what they did. If Tom had been going on about morris dancing she would still have hung on his every word. She'd found it amusing that Nick should bother to try anything on while she was sitting next to the only man she had ever wanted to be with. Which was funny, given what had followed.

Rosemary and Sarah walked up the path to the spit, thinking of what lay beyond. Rosemary found she was quite calm, and again she thought back to her working life. She had seen so many dead people over the years that, however they had died and whatever had happened to the body, she doubted they could hold any terrors for her. Not like the girl walking silently beside her who seemed so preoccupied. She had expected the police to be a little more hardened than this.

In a few moments they had passed the car and reached the top of the dunes, and they stood side by side, looking out over the flat sea into the mist. It was high tide and the water was lapping almost at their feet. The breakwaters were nearly hidden and the margin of hard wet sand had dwindled almost to nothing.

With a cry, a seagull swept past them and hovered over a patch of sea, beating its wings and splaying out its legs before settling on the water. There it sat, looking around perkily, before snatching at some fragment on the surface.

Without saying anything, Rosemary and Sarah stepped down onto the beach, crunching through the mat of dried weeds and old pieces of rubbish thrown up by the spring tides to the water itself. They could see for a few hundred yards into the mist along the beach and out to sea; enough to see a couple of other birds walking about or riding the waves or, as one large black-headed gull was doing only a few yards away, sitting on one of the upright supports of the breakwater.

But that was all there was to see. The bodies were gone.

They walked to the next breakwater in case Rosemary was mistaken about which one the girl had been beside, but there was nothing there. So they climbed back up the dunes to return to their starting point by a post of rusted metal sticking out from the sand, twisted and looped. It was a relic from the last war when these open beaches, ideal for landing craft, had seemed menaced by invasion.

'Could you tell how long they'd been in the water?' Sarah asked.

'I've no idea.' Rosemary thought about it for a minute and then added, 'I'd say not long. A few hours, no longer than that. His skin was all wrinkled.'

'And the woman?'

'She hadn't been in the water at all.'

'Are you sure?'

'Yes, of course I am,' she replied sharply. 'That isn't the kind of thing I would expect to be mistaken about.'

Rosemary looked at the breakwater and watched another wave run along it in a welter of foam. She thought of the girl, lying in the shelter of the break-water seemingly only asleep. Except for the deathly pallor and the icy feel of the skin at her neck.

'It was the way she was lying,' she went on, more gently. 'As if she was asleep. I suppose that's why I put my coat over her. I know I shouldn't have done that. I didn't touch her because I knew by then that it was a police matter. But she looked so young and so lost, lying like that.'

She looked away, blinking.

'Anyway,' she said more briskly, 'that's when I went home and called 999.'

Sarah looked around, trying to understand what had happened.

'The thing is,' she said, 'if she hadn't been in the water then how did she die? I mean, one of them might have gone swimming or got into trouble and the other went in to help. Or they could have been cut off by the incoming tide, even. That would explain why they were fully clothed. But that can't be it, can it? Not if she had never been in the water.'

'Oh, but he didn't drown.' Rosemary said definitely. 'He'd been stabbed.'

Chapter Four

Sarah shivered. It was easy, at this time of year, to forget how cold it could be on the coast. Her police overalls were only cotton and the mist was starting to chill her. Definitely the mist, not the word which hung in the air between them and which she repeated, despite herself.

'Stabbed?'

Rosemary nodded, leaving Sarah to think through what this meant.

'Are you sure? Couldn't it have been a gash, say from a rock, while he was in the water? Or thrown against the breakwater. That's got sharp pieces on it.'

'He hadn't drowned,' Rosemary replied. 'There are signs, clinical signs, and he didn't have them.'

'You know what that means?'

'Oh yes. It means they were killed. I quite realize that. I worked it out while I was waiting for you.'

'I have to ask,' Sarah said as gently as she could. 'Are you sure about what you saw?'

Rosemary turned to her, suddenly feeling tired.

'I was a nurse for almost forty years. I've seen more than enough of death in my time.'

The girl nodded, apparently satisfied, and while she called the control room again Rosemary wondered if she was suffering from delayed shock. She felt shivery, unsteady; and she stumbled a few paces and rested gratefully against the comforting bulk of one of the breakwaters.

The policewoman was still making her report. In a way it was worse now that the authorities were there and taking it seriously. It was no longer like a dream. Rosemary had to acknowledge that two people were dead – had been killed, in all probability. All less than half a mile from her own house. Perhaps the killer was still about. If so, the girl wouldn't be much use. She wasn't armed of course; Rosemary had never approved of armed police but she didn't even have a truncheon or handcuffs. How could she be a match for someone with a knife who had overpowered a fit young man and presumably the girl as well?

And there was the question, growing ever more urgent, of who had done this. Rosemary told herself that the idea that anyone in the village or one of her neighbours could be responsible was preposterous. Helen Sutton, taking a break from painting her insipid watercolours, to turn to murder? Or Alastair, killing them because they weren't supposed to be on the beach? Surely there was no one local who could have done a thing like this. One would know if they were capable of it.

But how? How could she know?

With these thoughts gnawing at her resolution, she was relieved when Sarah finished her call and announced that a team of officers was on its way.

'We should go back to your house, if that's all right.'

'Might you give me a hand?' Rosemary asked. 'I'm not sure I feel quite up to it.'

Rosemary was grateful for the arm supporting her, and grateful too when they paused at the foot of the dunes. She sat on one of the wooden posts which prevented anyone driving onto the dunes themselves while Sarah examined the car parked there, calling into the station with the registration details, peering in through the windows. Then the policewoman pulled on some gloves and tried the door, eventually managing to work the lock open with a piece of wire. She got the bag from the back seat and sat it on the bonnet, quickly skimming through the contents. It was a small black rucksack, the kind all the girls seemed to have nowadays, Rosemary thought, and so much more convenient than a handbag, if less elegant.

After a moment Sarah came over, holding open a small plastic wallet.

'Is this the girl you saw?'

One side of the wallet held a cash card from behind which a couple of £20 notes showed. In the other side was a hospital identity card showing a young woman with black hair and a sharp pretty face, staring evenly back at the camera. She read the name: Nicola Page.

Rosemary could picture her so clearly lying on the sand, her legs tucked up almost underneath her and her head resting on one arm. From the photo she could see she was naturally pale, and perhaps that was why, in death, she had seemed as if she was only sleeping.

'Yes, that's her,' she said.

Once she had escorted Rosemary back to her house and was standing outside again, by the gate to the neat garden, Sarah looked again at the photo pass, at the face of the missing woman, and tried to puzzle out how she had died. Perhaps she was killed in her sleep. Rosemary had said she had looked peaceful. Or maybe she was woken by a noise, looked up still half-asleep, still warm and confused from her sleep, only to suffer a horrible moment of realization before she died.

She shut the wallet, put it carefully in her pocket and headed back towards the beach. The sea was starting to retreat, leaving a growing expanse of shingle. Further out, a patch of broken water showed white against the grey of the sea where the waves were breaking on a sandbank.

She noticed a sign on one of the breakwaters warning people to keep off. She thought about them being left to fall apart. Eventually the whole spit would be washed away to be dumped by the sea further along the coast. Like the bodies. She could already think where they would have to look: Blundell, Blakeney Point, even as far as Sheringham. Or maybe they would be found on one of the sandbanks further out.

She turned her back to the sea, looking out instead across the fields and the marshes towards the woods which hid the village of Compton. Only the tower of the church showed where it lay. Below her, a path crossed the ditch that ran alongside Beach Road via an iron bridge and then headed across the fields directly towards the spire.

She thought of the last time she and Tom had sat in the pub and could even remember the heavy sweet taste of Southern Comfort which she had taken to drinking because he did. A quiet night spent chatting, making plans, talking about a film they had seen. Then, afterwards, they had walked back down the narrow rutted track that led past the church to the path across the fields to Beach Road. One of the last nights of her old life.

She looked intently at the tower, blinking back the tears. She could picture the church so clearly, though it was three years or more since she had been there. The massive tower set off by the delicacy of the stonework, and the tracery of the windows. The foundations rooted in the midst of smooth turf. The weathered headstones and dripping yews that clustered around. The sense of peace – and of loss.

It was where Tom was buried.

It had been a day much like this when Tom went out for the last time. He was a fine sailor who knew the coast intimately and though there was mist around he should have been safe. But something had gone wrong: he had misjudged where he was and run at full speed onto one of the shifting sandbanks, tearing off the boat's keel. It had sunk in moments. And he hadn't had a life jacket.

It had been six days before they found his body. She had waited by the sea's edge for every waking moment, either at the boatyard in Yarwell where Tom worked, or here at Compton. She had watched the sea roll back and forth, accepted cups of tea she didn't want and didn't drink, eaten sandwiches only because it was easier to take them than to argue that she wasn't hungry. From time to time she had been taken back to the flat she and Tom shared only a few yards from the harbour to try to sleep, and then to give up and sit cold and shivering, looking through the window over the jumble of red-tiled roofs towards the sea.

She remembered the moment she had first learnt he was missing. She had been in the café, about to take an order over to one of the tables. Nick had come in looking for her. She had known at once that something was wrong, appallingly wrong, from his look and the tone of his voice. He had only had to say two words: 'It's Tom . . .' But she had still taken the plates over, ground black pepper over the pasta, smiled, returned with the bread the man wanted, and only then said quietly to Jan, the owner, that she had to go out.

She had watched the yard's own boat return as night fell, empty. Then she and a few others – she couldn't remember who now, though she could recall exactly what the people in the café had ordered – had gone out to the lifeboat station at Yarwell Point. The inshore boat was part of the search, but later it too came in having found nothing but wreckage.

The night had been beautiful, warm and calm without the slightest breeze to trouble the thin mist. The lights had danced merrily on the water, the buoys marking the channel into the harbour had winked red and green, and once in a while a yacht or fishing boat would motor past, its engine struggling against the tide and the currents.

She had stood there as long as she could, watching and waiting, shrugging off any words or gestures of comfort though she had known from the start, from the very first moment in the café, that he was dead.

Now she heard a crunching sound from behind as a dark blue car nosed its way slowly along the track. This would be Morton, arriving to take control.

Chapter Five

Morton was thin, like a long-distance runner, though with his fair hair and steel-rimmed glasses he looked more like an academic than a senior policeman. He was also young for his rank, and looked even younger today because he was dressed in jeans and a jacket rather than his usual grey suit.

He was still on the phone as he got out of the passenger seat of the car. Andy Linehan, his sergeant, had driven him and now came around the car to greet Sarah. Like Morton, he was in his late thirties but rounder, more relaxed, with the flushed, full cheeks of a trumpet player. As always, he was looking for amusement.

'One body not enough for you, then?' he said.

'Gives you something to do,' she replied. But she couldn't manage a smile in return.

'And now you've gone and lost them.'

'If you'd been a bit quicker . . .'

'Oh yeah?' He pulled out a pack of cigarettes. 'You don't, do you?' He lit one and puffed the smoke far over his head, towards the swirling mist. 'Could it be an accident, do you reckon?'

'Could be, but the woman who found them is

adamant the man was stabbed. And that there were two of them, whatever Blake said.'

'Oh right. Blake's blaming the operators. He's spitting blood about it so everyone at the station is in hiding.'

'I can imagine. Blake was on the panel when I sat the sergeant's board and was his usual charmless self.'

'Yeah? He can be a right bastard when he's in the mood. One time I had—'

But by then Morton had finished his call and was coming over. Andy pinched out his cigarette resignedly and put the end back in its packet.

'Hello, Delaney,' Morton said. 'Still no sign of the bodies?'

'None, sir, They were both below the high water mark. I doubt they'll show up here.'

'OK. We'll need to sort out a search. Any witnesses?'

'Only Mrs Aylmer. She's the one who found them. There's a car parked by the beach. It's registered to a Chris Hannay, who lives in Reepham, and there's a staff parking permit for the Norfolk and Norwich Hospital on it as well. I got the car open and there's a bag with ID for a nurse who works there, Nicola Page. Mrs Aylmer's pretty sure it was her she saw.'

She felt reluctant to hand the photo card over. The woman seemed too young and too ordinary to be part of an investigation; to be docketed and filed, to be handled by world-weary detectives and brought before a coroner's court. She glanced at her photo as she passed it to Morton, imagining this Nicola Page laughing about how bad the picture was with her friends, in the pub after work.

'Just our luck if Hannay turns out to be a senior consultant or something,' Andy said.

'He's listed as Mr at the DVLA,' Sarah said. 'But he might be a surgeon. She was a junior sister, according to her security card.'

'How junior is that?' Morton asked.

'It means you take being a nurse seriously. As a career. You'd be a junior sister after five years, maybe, and a senior sister in your early thirties. If you're good.'

'You seem to know a lot about it.' There was something in Morton's tone, but Sarah couldn't tell if it was encouragement or doubt.

'My father's a doctor. And my brother.'

'Fair enough. Maybe you could go over there later and see what you can find out. Is that OK?'

'Of course. I was going to ask if you wanted me to stay on.'

'Yeah, could you? You'd better start by showing me where they were found.'

The three of them walked up to the dunes and stood at the same spot, looking at the same patch of water, grey except where the waves broke along the breakwater. Sarah pointed out where Rosemary had seen the bodies but after that there was nothing else to say. The tide was clearly on the way out again. She wondered if there would be anything left behind.

'Do a lot of people use this beach?' Morton asked.

'Not really,' Sarah replied. 'The beach is all shingle so people tend to go to Hunstanton instead; it's only a couple of miles up the coast. The coastal path goes inland here too, on the other side of those marshes. You might get the odd birdwatcher, but not on a day like this.'

'No, I guess not,' he said, wiping the fine drops of rain from his glasses.

'There are only a few people live here all the time. Mrs Aylmer is in the second house from here. There's a couple more residents further along, she tells me. And a wing commander in the last house by the gate. The rest are weekend homes or holiday lets. She doesn't think anyone was staying this weekend.'

Morton looked about him, taking it all in.

'Where does that track go?' he asked, pointing along the spit.

'There's a house at the end of the spit. It's called the Red House. It's a holiday home.'

'This Mrs Aylmer; did she say how the woman died?'

'No. She said she was hunched over, so she might have been strangled or stabbed, I suppose.'

Morton pondered on this for a minute.

'If there's anything in this,' he said, mainly to Andy Linehan, 'the most likely thing is some kind of domestic dispute. Murder and suicide by one of them, or a third party. So we'll need to start turning their lives over. At work especially. But we'll have to go carefully.

'I'd like you to sort out a search for the bodies,' he said to Sarah. 'We'll need to find them as soon as we can. Put together some search parties if that's what it needs. You've got the best local knowledge of all of us for this. But liaise with the coastguard and the lifeboats, of course.

'One other thing: could you go out to that house and check everything's all right? If it's empty, fine, but if there's anyone staying there get a statement from them. OK? You'd better walk. I don't want any more vehicles up that track, if we can avoid it.'

Morton smiled briefly and then headed off towards Rosemary's house.

'Nice to have someone local around,' Andy Linehan added with a smirk before he followed Morton up the road. 'Enjoy your walk.'

It took her half an hour to sort out the search parties, speak to the maritime rescue centre in Yarmouth and write up her notes. Finally, she couldn't delay going out to the Red House any longer. She wondered about phoning Nick Walton and asking him if there was anyone staying there. He still worked at the boatyard, running diving courses and the seal trips. He was one of the Yarwell lifeboat crew as well and she couldn't think of anyone better placed to help. But she wanted to put off speaking to him. Searching for bodies along the same coast where Tom had died was bad enough without having to have his cousin by her side.

So she started up the track. The spit was never wider than a few hundred yards, made of dunes held together with marram grass and a narrow belt of pine trees, and shored up by the old wooden breakwaters. The track ran along the leeward side with mudflats stretching away towards Martlesham. Between the track and the trees were brambles, banks of straggly nettles and vast brown spiky bushes of a species unknown to Sarah. Some were ten feet or more across and rabbits had burrowed into the sand around the thick roots. The PCs would hate it but she guessed each one would have to be searched inch by inch.

The track continued to curve gently, and now through the trees she could see the house. It was surprisingly large, with a high-pitched red tiled roof, neat mullioned windows, and mellow brickwork patterned with timber beams. It would have seemed unremarkable on a leafy road in the Surrey commuter belt but here, with the sea close on three sides, it looked bizarre. Instead of rose bushes and laburnums, it was surrounded by a chain-link fence enclosing an expanse of rough springy turf dotted with dandelions, clover and daisies. It gained some thin shelter from the wind by a line of old Scots pines. These were bare in places, like a child's moth-eaten toy which had lost patches of fur.

She could see at once that it was empty. There were no lights on and the curtains were drawn back. There were no towels and swimming costumes forgotten on the clothes line, no wellingtons or deck shoes left to air by the porch and no car parked outside. To one side of the house was a pair of weather-beaten kayaks sitting on bricks, turned upside down. But these would be overspill from the boathouse which stood beside the house and looked, with its wooden doors, like a half-timbered garage. It must still be crammed with bikes, bits of boat, sun loungers and the like, as it had been when she used to stay.

There was no reason to climb over the padlocked gate and peer in the windows of the house. Only curiosity.

She walked cautiously to the door, conscious of the isolation, the blank windows staring down at her. No one answered her knocks and she followed the concrete path around the side of the house to the conservatory, peering in at the tiled floor, the long pine table, the kitchen in the background, the passage to the pantry, the back stairs and the study. Hardly anything had changed except that the paint, the kitchen units and the sofa by the far wall all looked more shabby than she remembered. Perhaps it wasn't worth the time or money to do the place up. It was huge, isolated and unlikely ever to be rented out more than a few times a year. And if Rosemary was right about the spit being abandoned, then within a few years it might not be here at all.

The back of the house was showing signs of neglect as well. The paint was flaking from the window sills and in places the wood was splitting, dark and swollen with moisture. The windows badly needed cleaning where spray from the sea had left a scurf of salt. Her feet crunched on the fragments of a roof tile dislodged by a storm to fall and smash on the path.

She stepped back, looking at the upper rooms, the small bare bedroom where she had stayed when Tom was here with his family. Early on, they had been careful about what his parents would think. They'd had separate rooms, and Tom had showed her which floorboards creaked and which doors needed to be opened slowly, so that she could creep around the house silently. He had explained about the Yale lock on the back door from the pantry which he had oiled to ease their escape, and the way to climb onto the flat roof above the kitchen and flick open the bathroom window, so they could return after their time out on the dunes.

She smiled at the thought of it. Surely his parents knew they were sleeping together. They must have suspected that some farcical proceedings were going on under their roof. They might even have suggested separate rooms just for the amusement of seeing how subtly Tom and she would get around them. It would have been so much in character; they had both shared his slightly manic sense of humour, though in their case mellowed by the years.

She smiled, enjoying for a moment the unexpected warm feelings the sight of the house brought back. Until she thought of what had followed, what she had found out about Tom after his death. Then she turned, climbed back over the gate and onto the track without a backward glance.

Sarah returned to the car park, where a couple of scene of crime officers in their bright white overalls were looking over Hannay's sports car, and a handful of detectives in their own uniform of jeans and jackets stood apart, chatting, waiting to start their formal house-to-house enquiries. It wouldn't take long. She'd be surprised if there were more than ten people to see along the whole road.

Andy Linehan appeared and waved to her.

'That's good timing. Morton's got a job for you. Could you go to the hospital and get this checked out?'

He handed her a polythene bag which held a half-dozen brown glass bottles with oversized white caps and printed labels. Each of them held a few pills, except for one which had had a small bag stuffed into it.

'We found them in the glove compartment.'

'What's so suspicious about that?' she asked. 'He is a doctor.'

'No, he's an anaesthetist. They wouldn't ever need to prescribe stuff to people.' So much for her pretensions to being an expert on doctors, she thought bitterly. 'Morton wants you to take this to the dispensary at the hospital and get the pills identified; to check that they are what they say on the labels. But don't lose the bottles or let them handle them.'

'Fingerprints?'

'No, continuity of evidence. I don't want any suggestion the pills could have got mixed up. Get them to take one out, check it and put it back before looking at the next one. Write a note afterwards to say that's what you saw them do. And whatever you do, don't lose this one.' He stabbed at the bottle with the bag inside. 'It's got a white powder in and Morton and Blake both reckon it's probably cocaine.'

'But that could mean—'

'It could mean lots of things,' he cut in. 'Don't start answering their questions, though. Now the other thing Morton wants is for you to dig up some background about Hannay and Page. The relationship, girlfriends, boyfriends and so on. Don't say they're definitely dead, nothing about murder, only that they're missing and we're anxious to trace them. Make it sound routine.'

'Sure.'

'It doesn't need to be in detail; we'll be going over there later today to do it properly.' He must have realized this sounded insulting because he went on, 'It would be excellent to have your first impressions, though.'

'Right.' She thought about it. 'It's all right to ask about relationships and so on? I can always say there's

41

a chance they've run off together. We'd want to know so we can scale down the search.'

'Yeah, that sounds OK. But play it safe, won't you? Not only for the investigation. Morton likes to try out people with things like this when he hasn't worked with them before. It'd be a good chance to impress. But don't try too hard, eh?'

Chapter Six

Sarah had never been to the new hospital. It lay on the outskirts of the city on the side of a hill, a long stretch of low buildings which looked more like an office complex or a high-tech factory than a hospital. She'd arranged to be met at reception by Tim Baldwin, one of the administrators, a bouncy man of about forty who seemed surprisingly cheerful about her visit. Perhaps it was being surrounded by death which made him unusually relaxed, even when it came a little closer to home.

'I've checked our records,' he said, leading her along a bright deserted corridor. 'I've done you a printout – when they came here, previous employment, references, where they lived, next of kin, that kind of thing. And we also have a picture of Chris Hannay,' he added, handing her a professional portrait photo with a flourish.

She looked at the print, surprised at how different he looked from the image she had of him. She had pictured him as younger and more vulnerable. In the photo, Hannay looked confident to the point of arrogance, with his well-fed face, his sharply-combed hair and his expensive-looking shirt and tie. There might be a weakness around the eyes and the mouth but it was the kind that invited distrust rather than pity. She supposed she had imagined a victim. What she had was the photo of a real person.

'Is that any good?'

'It's excellent,' she assured him. 'Just what I need.'

'I'm only sorry we don't have anything like that for Sister Page. We had all the doctors done earlier this year. I can't remember why now. A brochure, perhaps.'

They walked on, occasionally passing a patient who ignored them, or a member of staff, who glanced at them covertly. Sarah guessed the news of their colleagues' disappearance would be all over the hospital by now.

'I've also got their pay and NI records,' Baldwin went on. 'Though I don't suppose you'll need them.'

'It all helps.'

'Right. I see.' He thought about this while he ushered her into a lift. 'Mr Hannay lives off site and Sister Page has a room in the St Stephen's Annexe. That's in the city centre.'

'Perhaps I could go there later?'

'Sure. I can fix that up. And they said you wanted to see where they worked. As it happens, Mr Hannay doesn't have a single place of work because he works in theatre. But he shares an office on the third floor and there's the doctor's mess room.'

The office was modern, crammed with papers and files and two desks facing away from each other. It took Sarah a moment to realize that the room had no windows.

'Do you know which is Hannay's?'

'Sorry. I've no idea.'

The desks provided a stark contrast: one silted up

with Post-it notes, pens, paper clips and a pile of medical journals mixed in with gardening magazines; the other almost empty, with any personality tidied away. Even the mug sitting cleaned on one corner gave nothing away about its owner, being a gift from a drugs company.

It was only too predictable that the desk packed with hints as to the character of the owner belonged to another doctor and that Hannay's was bare of any clues. Though forensics would probably need to examine it more closely, there was nothing obvious here – no address book or photos or letters.

'Who does he share with?'

'Dr Greenwood.'

'Is he likely to be in today?'

'She. It's possible but I doubt it, on a Sunday. I can bleep her for you, if you want?'

She thought it best to wait, and Baldwin, who had watched in fascination as she pulled on her gloves and skimmed through the contents of Hannay's desk, happily locked the door of the office behind them and led her towards the ward where Nicola Page had worked. There he introduced her to two of Nicola's colleagues, Carol Banks and Amina Lewis, who had heard the rumours and looked both worried and excited, as she would have expected. But all they could say was that they couldn't believe it and were sure she would be all right. She had been off work with a fairly serious illness and had only been back a week. Neither had known her all that well.

'She was a bit stand-offish,' Carol said, perched on the end of her desk.

'Well, more reserved than stand-offish,' Amina

added, putting down the tray of equipment she was carrying. 'She was always friendly. But very quiet.'

'Maybe it was the illness made her that way,' Carol conceded, as if remembering to speak well of the dead. 'It takes a while to get over something like that.'

Amina thought that Nicola had a boyfriend working overseas but couldn't remember more than his first name: Mark. There was nothing more to learn there so Tim Baldwin took her along to the dispensary where the pharmacist, seemingly unable to say more than a few muttered words, pulled out a huge ring-bound folder containing hundreds of pictures of individual pills of every imaginable colour in all kinds of sizes and shapes, and with different symbols incised upon them. It seemed impossible to pick out a single pill, but with the same skill as a botanist or birdwatcher the pharmacist had soon identified each one.

'Are they what they're supposed to be?' Sarah asked.

'These are exactly what they say on the bottles; these aren't,' he said, holding up the guilty bottle. 'They look similar but they're definitely the wrong pills.'

'So what are they?'

'Diazapam. But they're labelled as Coproxamol.'

'Is that unusual?'

'It's absolutely extraordinary,' the man said looking at her for the first time, clearly shocked by what he'd found and by her inability to appreciate the enormity of it. 'I can't understand a doctor of all people mixing drugs up in this way. It's so dangerous.'

'Should he have had them at all?'

'I couldn't say,' the man replied, cautious again.

Conscious of Tim Baldwin's curious looks, she put

away the bag. Just then, a loud patrician voice called to them from behind.

'Ah, Tim. Found you. Excellent.'

They turned to face a man in his fifties, dressed in a dark suit and broadly-striped shirt, and an equally bright but well-coordinated tie. Even without his white coat he couldn't be anything other than a senior consultant.

'Are you from the police? My name is Collingwood. I'm the Director of Medical Care and I'm also on the Board of the Trust. I suppose in a way both Chris and Sister Page work for me, though I didn't know her at all well.'

They shook hands, and she took in his large squared-off head and bushy eyebrows. Like Rosemary, he didn't look too impressed as she introduced herself.

'Could you fill me in on what this is all about? Something about them going missing?'

He looked a little worried behind the easy mask of authority, but not upset. She wondered how closely he had worked with Chris Hannay. Not so closely that the suggestion Hannay might be dead upset him much. Maybe he didn't believe it. Or maybe he hadn't liked him.

'We've had a report of two bodies being washed out to sea and both Dr Hannay and Sister Page are missing. Naturally, we're anxious to trace them both so we can eliminate them from the search.'

It was an easy, comforting lie. As Collingwood knew, she meant confirm they were the bodies they were searching for.

'Ah. I see. Are you questioning any of the staff?'

'Only in passing. If it comes to the worst, there are

other officers who'll take formal statements and so on. But if you have any information, I'd be very happy to pass it on to Chief Inspector Morton straight away.'

'I see.'

As she'd hoped, he wasn't sure how to play this and it took him a moment to reach a decision.

'Right. Let's go back to my office and have a quick word. You can fill me in on what you know. And I'll do the same.'

She trailed along behind him, sure that he planned to gain far more knowledge than he gave away. They went up a flight of stairs and into a corridor of offices. Collingwood's turned out to be surprisingly modest though it had a wide view over the fields to the west.

'I'll be next door,' Baldwin muttered and left them to it.

Sarah decided she had better take the initiative rather than let the man drag all kinds of information out of her which Morton might prefer to keep to himself.

'I'll tell you everything we know,' she lied. 'A woman reported two bodies on the beach at Compton this morning. We don't know how they died because the tide took them away before we got to the scene but both Dr Hannay and Nicola Page are missing. His car was parked nearby. And the woman has made an identification. It's too early to be sure but I'm sorry to have to say there's a strong chance they're both dead.'

She waited while he digested this, doodling on the blotter on his desk as he did so, but as he looked up she came in with a question.

'Is either of them married as far as you know? Or in a long-term relationship?'

'What has that to do with it?' he asked cautiously.

'Another explanation for their disappearance would be that they're conducting some kind of affair. If either were married there'd be more reason to keep it hidden, or even to go off like that. It's a long shot but we need to be sure one way or the other.'

To Sarah, it sounded pitifully thin. But Collingwood seemed convinced.

'Well, I can see that, I suppose.' I've no idea about Page; but as to Chris Hannay, I don't think he is, er, seeing anyone. I had a barbecue thing over the summer and he didn't bring anyone to it. I don't remember any talk about anyone. But there are others who would know better than I.'

'Sure.' She paused, catching up with her notes before starting on the next line of questions; ones she had a feeling he wouldn't like at all.

'What kind of doctor is Dr Hannay?'

'How do you mean?'

'Well,' she went on, waving her hand to show the various kinds there might be. 'What kind of medicine does he specialize in? Is he good? Would you let him operate on your children?'

'He's an anaesthetist so I certainly wouldn't want him operating on anyone. But that said, he's a very efficient and competent doctor.'

'Has he ever been involved in any kind of professional difficulties? An accident, medical claim, that sort of thing?'

'No. Not as far as I know. Certainly not at this hospital.' He might as well have said out loud that, even if Hannay was dead, he was still one of them.

One of the medical brethren he was duty-bound to protect.

'Would Dr Hannay, in his professional duties, ever handle Class A drugs?'

'Well, given he was an anaesthetist and given that most anaesthetic drugs are based on different formulations of opiates, you can assume that he does.'

'What kind of drugs, exactly?'

'I don't know. It would depend on the operation, the patient. Propofol and pethadin mainly, I would guess. And diamorphine.'

'Would he have any reason to use or handle diazapam?' she asked, managing not to stumble over the unfamiliar name.

'I've no idea.' But the look that went with his reply showed Collingwood was curious, if not more.

'Do you hold stocks of these drugs here at the hospital?'

'I'm sure we would, yes.'

'But controlled, of course.'

'Of course. I don't see exactly what this has to do with . . .' He broke off, looked down at his folded hands and then at the ceiling above, making a show of choosing his next words carefully. 'Dr Hannay would only have access to opiates or other drugs in theatre, and all drugs administered would be recorded and checked by the theatre staff.'

'How about opportunities to make off with drugs, perhaps to sell rather than for his own use?'

'I doubt it would justify the risk. Had he been caught he would of course have been struck off. And prosecuted too, in all likelihood.'

'But could such a thing happen?'

'As I said,' he replied with a slight show of impatience, 'everything has to be recorded. The drugs aren't drawn off by the anaesthetist at all but by the ODA or the theatre manager. And everything is double-signed.'

'What about if he were in league with the theatre staff?'

'They change from week to week. And everything is triple-checked. Either he would have to record he was giving patients more than they needed or he would have to record the right dose and actually give them less than they needed. Either way, there would be the danger of being caught. I doubt you could make very much from it, and if he had to pay off the orderly as well . . . No, frankly I don't think it stacks up.'

'What about other drugs? Could he have wandered onto a ward and made off with some left lying around?'

'If you'd ever been on a ward here, you'd have seen we do not leave drugs "lying around". Everything is accounted for, secured, locked up. He would not have a key for any cabinet on the wards. The whole thing is preposterous.' She tried to put her next question but he talked her down. 'From your line of questioning, you obviously have some reason for thinking there is a link between his death and drugs. Far be it from me to teach you your job,' he said as he stood up, signalling that as far as he was concerned the interview was over, 'but all I can say is that in Chris Hannay's case it would have been completely out of character.'

As Sarah and Baldwin crossed the atrium at the entrance to the hospital, a voice called out her name from above. She turned to see a figure leaning over a balcony and waving at her: a man about her own age, fair-headed, oddly familiar despite the white doctor's coat, though she couldn't think who he was. He gestured to her to stay where she was before he disappeared from sight.

'Do you know Dr Woodford?' Tim Baldwin said in mild surprise.

Of course, she thought. Alban Woodford, a friend of Tom's. He'd just taken his first medical exams in the summer when Tom died and now here he was, qualified and let loose in a hospital. He'd been the most caustic and cynical of all Tom's friends; always amusing but not kind or forgiving. She wondered whether the years had mellowed him at all and what he could want to say so urgently.

He emerged from a side door and hurried across, his coat flapping open.

'My God. Sarah Delaney. It must be . . . I don't know. Three years?'

'Four,' she said quietly.

'Yeah,' he said, clearly thinking back to Tom's death, the funeral, the last time they had all been together. 'Someone told me you joined the police; I didn't believe it.'

'As you can see,' she said, gesturing at her uniform, 'it's quite true.'

He stood looking at her, amazed, pleased, unsure what to say next. Tim Baldwin muttered something about returning in a minute and disappeared.

'So what are you doing here, anyway? You're not hurt, are you?'

'No, but there's been some sort of accident. Two

people drowned. There's a possibility they worked here.'

'Shit. Who is it?'

'Chris Hannay. And Nicola Page.'

He had been looking concerned in a conventional way. But now he turned pale and stared at her with something like horror on his face.

'You're joking.'

'I'm not, believe me. Do you know them?'

'I don't believe it,' he said, shaking his head. 'I saw them last night. At the ball at Mantlesham Hall. You must've got it all wrong.'

'I hope we have. But Chris Hannay's car was found nearby.'

'Near where?'

'Compton Spit.'

He looked so stunned by the news that Sarah guided him gently to the nearest bench and sat beside him.

'What happened to them?' he asked. She felt he was clearly too deeply involved with one or other of them to be fobbed off as the others had been.

'We think they may have been swept out to sea,' she said, which was true in a way. 'Late last night or early this morning. So they might have gone there afterwards, on their way home.'

'I told him about Compton,' he said in a low voice. 'This was weeks ago. He wanted to know the best beaches to go to. The quiet ones. He knew I grew up around there.' He shook his head. 'But it's not dangerous. Not really, unless you're stupid enough to go swimming. Do you know what happened?'

'I don't,' she said truthfully. 'We've got search teams out.'

'So they might be OK?' he said, hope in his voice.

'They might. There's always hope.'

'God, it's so awful. Are you sure Nicola was there? If it was Chris's car, she might have got a lift back with someone else, or something. She'd been ill recently and was looking pretty tired.'

He was talking himself into a more cheerful state of mind. She hated to break the comforting illusion.

'We're not sure but we think she was there. Look, we might need to take a statement from you as well. If you can explain why they were there. Will you be all right to do that?'

'I'll be fine,' he said, nodding and sitting up straight. 'It's just a bit of a shock.' He tried a weak smile. 'I mean, you get used to bad news here, breaking it to other people, but you don't think it'll happen to people you know.'

She saw Tim Baldwin returning.

'Well, look,' she said, standing up, 'I've got to go but someone'll come back later. And as soon as there's any news, I'll let you know.'

'Yeah. Yeah, you'll do that, won't you? You can get me through the switchboard. They can bleep me. Day or night.'

'I'll do that. And I'm really sorry to come with bad news like this.'

'Yeah,' he said, nodding. 'Like the last time we met.' He winced. 'Sorry. That wasn't a nice thing to say.'

'It doesn't matter.'

'Look, I . . .' He ran his fingers through his short fair hair, so that it stood up on end. 'The thing is, there's a chance that they've decided to stay at the cottage. It's—'

He broke off to answer his bleep.

'Shit,' he whispered. 'I've got to go. Could you give me your number? So I can call you?'

'Sure,' she said, and as soon as she'd scribbled the number on a scrap of paper he'd grabbed it and was gone.

Chapter Seven

Half an hour later Tim Baldwin was showing Sarah into St Stephen's hostel in Norwich city centre. It took up an entire row of Victorian terraced houses, converted years ago, long before the hospital moved out and the old buildings on the other side of Cromer Road were sold off for housing.

He led her down a drab grubby corridor lined with doors and floored with a pattern of carpet tiles in different shades of brown. Once or twice Sarah had visited friends who'd gone to university and lived in halls of residence. This had the same atmosphere, the slightly musty smell, the same signs of people leading careless lives: scuff-marks on the walls, plates and pans piled soaking in the sink of the communal kitchen, a bike half-blocking a passageway.

'This is her room.'

She looked around and knew at once that there was far more here to reveal the occupant's character than in Hannay's aseptic office. There were books lined up neatly on the shelves and clothes and magazines scattered over the floor as if Nicola Page had enjoyed a busy messy life but still cleared up properly every few days. Sarah imagined a long tiring day on the wards, maybe drinks after work with her colleagues or with friends in town, and then back here to crash out until her shift began again.

The sheets were rucked up on the bed, the pillow still showed where her head had lain. The whole room had a faint but clear smell: a mix of spray and dust and body and soap and a hundred other scents that had made up a living person.

Sarah swallowed and started on her task, trying to be the professional. The curtains were drawn – perhaps because Nicola Page had been working night shifts – and she had to resist the temptation to pull them back and throw open the window, to make the place less intimate. She glanced at the line of books and at the CDs on the shelf below, next to a small stereo, and beneath that a desk on which lay a few textbooks and a couple more glossy magazines. There were clothes hanging in the wardrobe and more on the shelves, all neatly separated and piled.

She found the search upsetting. They would have enjoyed the same music, perhaps, even read the same books. She could imagine her going to the same cinemas and cafés, drifting through the same clothes shops, choosing the same meal at Pizza Express.

To one side of the desk was a small cork board which had a few photos pinned to it. Several showed a young man, thin and fair, smiling at the camera with a shy grin that stayed the same whatever the background – a skiing scene, a party, a sunny beach. Another showed him standing behind Nicola who was sitting in a chair. He was still smiling, but she looked more solemn. She guessed this was Mark, the boy-friend.

'I've got to make a couple of calls,' Baldwin said,

and Sarah was relieved when he'd gone. It was much easier working without being watched. It made her feel less like a thief, rifling through the remains of this unknown woman's life.

She checked the drawers of the desk and eventually found a pile of more photos. There were several of Nicola including one where she was actually smiling, even if a little faintly, and many more where she was one of a group. Her colleagues would have fun tracking down all these people and finding out exactly what their relationship to her was, and what light they could throw on the crime.

She was about to shut the drawer when she noticed a tiny cassette nestling almost at the back. She took it out and turned it over but there was no label on it. She guessed it was from a video camera and, though there was no camera in the room itself, she felt she deserved some good fortune and that it must have some footage of the dead woman on it.

'Are you from the police?'

She hadn't heard the door open and she turned with a slight sense of guilt. Standing in the doorway was a nurse in her twenties whose eyes roved around the room as if to ensure that Sarah wasn't trashing the place or making off with any valuables. She introduced herself as Suzy, a friend of Nicola's. She was the first person Sarah had met who had used that term.

'Is it true, then?'

'Nothing's certain,' Sarah said, closing the door. 'But we are worried about her. Do you know how well she knows Chris Hannay?'

'They worked together a bit. And they were together at the ball last night, the hospital's charity do at Martlesham Hall. But it wasn't that they were . . . you know, going out. She had a boyfriend. Hong Kong, I think.'

'Is that where he is? The boyfriend?'

Suzy shrugged. She seemed calm and competent, standing with her hands resting lightly on her hips. Or maybe it was the uniform and the sensibly-plaited hair which made her seem so. There was something behind the eyes that suggested that she was upset, though controlling it well.

'Was she looking forward to this weekend?' Sarah asked. 'Did she seem anxious about it?'

'It's hard to say.' The nurse sat on the end of the bed and began to smooth out the duvet. 'She's been ill a lot recently. Off work for a few weeks. She had some kind of kidney infection, I think, though she didn't talk about it and I didn't pry. She was on all kinds of medication; couldn't drink, couldn't work. It's left her feeling really down. She hadn't gone out for ages, so I think she was looking forward to it.'

'Was she back at work?'

'Yes, for this week. She looked very tired on Friday but she still wanted to go.'

Sarah couldn't think of any more questions. Instead, she went back to looking through the wardrobe, at the shelves of neatly piled clothes: jeans, tops, trousers and long woollen skirts, drawers of sensible underwear, piles of shoes at the bottom. There were a few dresses hanging up and a single formal suit in black wool.

It reminded her of the way Rosemary Aylmer had described Nicola lying curled up on the beach, seemingly asleep. The image held none of the lurid horror of Hannay awash by the water's edge with his pallid skin and staring eyes. Except that the same wind that ruffled Nicola's hair so gently would be piling up the sand against her, burying her by imperceptible degrees. And the seagulls, perched on the piles of the breakwater, their hard glassy eyes fixed on her, wings held out for flight, would soon gain the confidence to go closer, to start to peck, and then tear at the exposed skin.

Sarah closed the wardrobe door, wishing she could shut out the image as easily.

Suzy was still watching her. Sarah straightened herself and tried to find a suitably serious and business-like expression. She wondered if this was something Nicola herself had done, facing a terminally ill patient or trying to cope with her own sickness.

'Do you have a photo of Nicola? A really clear one?' she asked.

'Maybe. I suppose so. What do you want it for?'

'We need to organize a search for her.'

The woman looked at her sharply, with a trace of bitterness.

'You mean a search for her body, don't you?'

Chapter Eight

Once Sarah had left the nurses' hostel and was back in her car, she took out the list of drugs the pharmacist had given her. The names meant nothing to her but her older brother Patrick was a doctor. She ought to call him anyway to let him know she wouldn't be over later as planned but he might also be able to tell her about the drugs.

When he answered the phone she could hear voices and shouts in the background, and smiled as she pictured the scene in the kitchen: Sam in one high chair learning how to feed himself; and Lucie in the other refining her technique for flicking beans against the wall.

'Bad time?' she asked, hearing Patrick's wife Julia trying to reason with Sam, followed by a squeal of outrage.

'Not as long as you don't mind me breaking off to do a bit of riot control.'

'That's fine with me.'

'But this had better not be you trying to get another prescription off me. You just take some aspirin and go to bed 'till you feel better.'

'It's work, actually. We've got a missing person, a doctor. Only we've found some medicines in his car and wondered if they meant anything. I mean, whether they were illegal drugs. Maybe he'd put them in an old bottle to disguise them, something like that.'

'What a nasty mind you have.'

'So if I told you what they were, could you tell me what they do?'

'I can try.'

'The first one's Triludan.'

'That's an anti-histamine,' he said promptly. 'Your doctor is probably a hayfever sufferer. It's prescription only but fairly common.'

'And Diazapam?'

'That's a sedative, quite a powerful one. Again, you'd only get that on prescription. Not that I'd ever want to prescribe it.'

'Why not?' she asked, sensing something more cautious in his tone.

'I wouldn't want the risk of them getting into the wrong hands.'

'You mean on the black market?'

'Well, there'd be people prepared to pay good money for them.'

'Like benzedrine?' The only time Sarah had ever found drugs on a suspect it had been a few grams of benzedrine.

'No, quite the opposite,' Pat replied, happy to tease her with his superior knowledge.

'Why's that?' she had to ask.

'Benzedrine is a stimulant and Diazapam is a sedative. That's why people want it. It knocks you out quickly and leaves no trace so it's a very effective date rape drug.'

She called Morton next but the information about the pills didn't surprise him. Fortunately he seemed happy with her hesitant description of her conversation with Collingwood, which she had come to realize hadn't exactly matched Linehan's instructions. But if he was in any way impressed, he still didn't ask her to do any more detective work.

'It's the search that really matters now,' he said. 'Until we have the bodies there's little real progress we can make. So I want you on that full-time. OK? At least until I've got a sergeant I can spare to put onto it.'

She knew she now had no choice but to phone Nick Walton. He answered on the first ring, as if he had been waiting for her call.

'How the hell are you?' He sounded unchanged, still full of life and energy.

'Fine, Nick. I'm fine.' She explained as quickly as she could what it was she wanted.

'Helping the police with their enquiries?' he said with an audible smirk. 'Well, of course. What can I do? I'm not on duty today so I'm free later if you want a chat.'

They arranged to meet at the harbour in Yarwell. That done, she sat back in the seat, trying to relax, amazed how tense she had been calling him. She wished the day was over already, or that she could go home and forget all about the search. But by now there should be four teams beginning the task of scouring the beaches and inlets to the east of Compton Spit. If this was going to be her only task, she had better see how they were doing. She decided to go to Blundell from where she could head back towards Compton and meet up with one of the teams heading east on the way. At least she would see what the search parties were up against.

Away from the coast, the mist had thinned but the clouds still hung low, seeming to suck the colour from the fields and trees, the passing cars, even from the garish hoardings of the petrol stations she passed. Blundell, too, was melancholy. In the summer, the place would have been full of people on their way to the beach, and the ice cream van that usually parked by the gate would have been under siege. Now there was no one around, except for a single officer standing patiently by a police van, watching her arrival.

The constable she knew: a local man, heavy and greying though only in his early forties and seemingly resigned to his poor prospects of promotion. Maybe waiting for early retirement so he could set himself up as a taxi driver or publican, like so many of their colleagues. She remembered his name – Paul Taylor – after stalling for a moment by rummaging for her notebook.

The only time they had worked together was the Julie Stanforth case the year before. He had been in charge of the party that had found the body, which wasn't something to reminisce over. He seemed cheerful enough in a gloomy sort of way, and she guessed he was called in whenever local knowledge was helpful or when there was a nasty job which needed palming off onto someone. He would have seen plenty of drowned bodies before; in the last year or so there had been a woman fished out of the River Glaven and a man swept out to sea from the harbour at Yarwell.

Taylor explained that he was waiting for the search

party to finish here, and then they would move further along the coast. She found herself saying that she would walk out to meet the group, only to be faced with an expression of faint pity at her enthusiasm and keeness. As she left him, she could hear him whistling a tune in a sad, slightly off-key way: *Oh I do like to be beside the seaside.*

The path wound through a belt of pine trees which framed the edge of the beach, then opened out to reveal the sand spread away in front of her, flat and empty. There was the faint suggestion of a stronger light in the distance, as if the sun was trying to burn through the mist. But she felt more strongly the damp, the dismal drip of dew from the branches of the trees and bushes, and she wondered what she was doing searching for two dead bodies when she could have had a normal job and been at home in her own warm bed, looking forward to seeing her nephew and niece for a family Sunday roast.

She headed straight towards the distant sea and soon all she could hear was the wind blowing around her and the faint sound of dry sand sifting around her feet. The teams were supposed to check anything that might be out of the ordinary or looked like it had been cast ashore in the last few days. They must be cursing, she thought. Every few yards there was something out of place – a plastic bottle, a shoe, some orange netting, pieces of wood and chunks of polystyrene. If they collected everything, these would be the cleanest beaches in the country.

She turned over yet another boot. The rubber sole had cracked and the plastic upper had faded, so she let it lie there but wondered how it had come to be in the sea. Perhaps thrown overboard because it had worn out. Or washed over the side. Or maybe the wearer was lost too, another corpse to be fished out or end up as food for the fishes.

After a while she reached the sea itself and stood there for a moment, watching as the waves ran slowly across the ridges of the beach, slowly filling and emptying thousands of individual dips and hollows imperceptibly claiming them back. She had wanted to see the difficulties involved and now she knew they were immense. They were probably wasting their time. A single helicopter could go along the beach low enough and slow enough to spot a body and still finish the job in an hour or two, if only the weather would clear. Something smaller they might miss. But what better chance did someone on foot have?

In any case, it seemed impossible to believe that a body could be lying on the clear brown sands. The only thing one could imagine finding was a pile of shells or the remains of a sand castle. She started to wonder if Rosemary could really have seen what she had said. At the time, Sarah had found her very convincing but out here it seemed incredible.

The slight curve of the bay led to a short promontory, and Sarah followed the line of the tide around it, her eyes flicking from the wrack at her feet to the horizon and back again. From here she could see almost as far as Charnham Head. Another few miles from there was Compton Spit.

Now, in the far distance, she could see a small group of figures dressed in dark clothes and bulked out by their anoraks, spread out in a line. She waved and one waved back, and then, just in time, she stopped.

Almost at her feet was the body of a seagull. It was quite fresh though the sea had battered it as it was cast ashore. The wind ruffled the feathers gently.

She shivered and walked on.

The search party had found nothing except rubbish thrown up by the tide, and a call to the incident room confirmed that none of the others had yet had better luck. There was no point in going there and in any case it was almost time to meet Nick. She hoped he might have a better idea of what to do.

Driving into Yarwell had some of the same power to stir up the past as revisiting Compton. She had lived here for two years with Tom and every shop, every street, each pub and café had its own set of memories: Where they had browsed for second-hand books or listened to the few pub bands the town could produce, or sat and recovered from their hangovers with a relaxed Sunday morning pint; the café where she had been a waitress and the boatyard where Tom and Nick had both worked.

The flat she had shared with Tom was only a few yards from the harbour, up one of the narrow lanes – hardly wide enough for a single car – which ran from the quayside to the main part of the town. It had an attic bedroom running the whole length of the building and they'd had the bed at one end and a huge squashy old sofa at the other in front of a gas fire. There were windows set into the roof which let in the sunlight in the morning and the smell of the harbour day and night – a mix of salt water, seaweed and fish, with hot tar as well in the summer. The place had been too run-down to rent out to holidaymakers, and the couple who owned it and the gallery on the ground floor were fortunately too hard up or too idle to put in central heating and a proper kitchen, or to block up the draughts.

She drove along the quay, feeling a pang at having left the town for good. Out of the tourist season, nowhere she knew had the same mixture of charm and reality – pretty whitewashed cottages, the fine flint church and the shining spread of the harbour beyond, mixed with the stink of fish and the noise of the boatyard. Though a holiday resort, complete with arcades on the front and a holiday camp on the point, it was still a working port. From the windows of the flat they could see the boats pushing their way out to the fishing grounds, sometimes hear them landing their catches in the early morning. It had only taken a few minutes for her to walk up to the café and even less time for Tom to reach the family boatyard.

The cluster of drab wooden sheds that made up the yard was unchanged, though she could see a few smaller improvements: the launch had been replaced by a more modern craft and she guessed the new Mercedes parked in front of the main offices belonged to John Walton, Nick's father.

Nick wasn't at the boatyard, or the harbour master's office, or the sheds, or hanging around on the quayside. In the end she tracked him down to the Harbour Café, catching sight of his bulky shoulders through the misted windows. She thought of all the times that she and Tom had come here when he was working in the boatyard across the road. Most lunchtimes of course, and quite often in the afternoon as well, if the weather

RIPTIDE

was poor and there were no groups to take out to see
the seals or go diving off the sandbanks, or to learn to
sail or windsurf in the safer waters of Norton Staithe.

'Time for another coffee?' Nick asked, smiling up
at her as she came in. She glanced at her watch. 'It's
OK,' he went on. 'High tide's not for another four hours.'

'Sure,' she replied, sliding into one of the plastic
seats opposite him. He called his order over to the
woman behind the counter who shouted something
back which was lost in a burst of steam from one of
the machines.

'I guess you've eaten,' he said, wiping a last piece
of toast around his plate. 'You'd know to stoke up on a
day like this.'

She hadn't, but she didn't feel like it and didn't
want to waste more time. Instead she let him finish
his last mouthful, studying his grinning face, the sandy
hair, the freckled skin becoming florid with the years
and the slightly anxious look that lurked behind his
hazel eyes. Maybe he was thinking back to the time
when they had split up. Maybe he felt bad about it,
though that was hardly his style.

'Where's the best place to start?' she asked, trying
to be businesslike.

'I've had a look at the charts and a bit of a think.
The timing's all-important. When they went into the
water, that is. Can you be any more exact?'

'Not really. Around six thirty this morning. The
man maybe ten minutes before, the woman ten
minutes after.'

'Well, assuming that, they'll have gone out here,
towards Sumner Sand, then carried out into deeper

69

water. That's probably where they are now, or maybe more towards the east.'

'Is there any point going out to look?'

'None at all. The thing is, it's all guesswork. But there's more chance of finding them when they come ashore. A body in the water – well, you probably know how hard they are to see.'

She did. But she wondered how Nick could be so stupid as to say it. It was as if Tom was a distant memory, an historic curiosity rather than his cousin whose loss he must surely still feel. Unless it was she who was out of step, for not moving on, not forgetting.

'Much better to wait for them to come ashore,' he went on. 'The currents may bring them inshore, into Blundell Bay. That's the best chance. Otherwise there's no chance of them coming ashore this side of Blakeney. Maybe even round past Sheringham.'

'Would that take long?'

'Days. Of course they might never come ashore. If they end up in the Missel Hole, for instance, there's no chance. It never lets anything go,' he added with a hint of relish.

She sipped her coffee while he asked what the police were doing already.

'We're searching all along the beaches. Walking the high tide mark and looking out over the sands. That way, if there's anything light like a bag or a shoe we'll be right on it, because it'll definitely be at the high water line. And if there's a body, even further away, it should show up against the sand.'

'And if the fog lifts, you can put up a helicopter to look further out,' he added.

'Right.'

'So what do you want me to do?'

'Could you show me the most likely places to look? Then we can sort out the search parties to go there this afternoon or first thing in the morning.'

'Fine by me. Shall we start?'

He stood and grabbed his jacket, leaving a few pounds for his meal. She offered to pay for her half-finished coffee but he waved her money away.

'The thing is,' she said, 'until we find the bodies there's not much to go on. In fact, I was going to ask—'

Just then the door opened with a crash. An old man in a verminous-looking jacket came in and at once clapped Nick on the shoulder.

'Hello, son. Not disturbing a romantic meeting with the young lady, I hope.' And he winked at Sarah.

'Greg. Just the man,' Nick said, shaking his hand. 'We need your advice about something.'

'Do you now?' The man's eyes were watery with age but still looked shrewd enough. 'What would that be about, then?'

'Will you be in the Ship later?'

'I might.'

'There's a pint or two in it for you.'

'Ah, well maybe, then.'

'The thing is, this is Police Constable Sarah Delaney,' he said, relishing the title as if he couldn't quite take her career seriously. 'We're organizing the search for those two bodies which were lost this morning. I thought you might be able to help.'

The man shrugged his shoulders. 'Always glad to help.'

'Have a think about this.' Nick leaned over conspiratorially. 'Two bodies lost off Compton Spit at six thirty this morning, just before high tide. Where would they come ashore?'

The man scratched his chin.

'Who's to say?'

'I thought you knew these waters. Maybe I was wrong.'

'You don't get me that way,' he cackled. 'I can see you coming.' But still he thought for a moment, his eyes far away. 'Course, there's a pull all along there as far as Blundell. But with the tide setting they'll be further out. Could catch on Blundell, but not for a day or two. Maybe as far as the overfalls.'

'Or Dead Sand?' Sarah asked, despite herself.

'Could be,' he said carefully, watching her closely.

'Have a think, anyway,' Nick interrupted. 'I'll see you later.'

They turned to leave but the man stopped them. 'There's one sure way to find out. It's what I was always told, anyway.' He waited, milking their interest.

'What's that, then?' Sarah had to ask.

'You throw in a loaf of bread. Into the sea. Same place. See where it goes. Where it turns up, that's where you'll find 'em.'

'Does it work?'

'Course it works,' he snorted. 'Stands to reason. If it didn't work, why would they say it did?'

There was no arguing with that. As they left the man called after them, 'Mind it's not sliced, eh?'

His laughter followed them out of the door.

Chapter Nine

They took Nick's old Land Rover and headed back towards Compton. He drove quickly despite the fog, and Sarah had to hang on as he took the corners far too fast for comfort. All the time he chatted on, shouting over the noise of the engine, though at least he kept his eyes on the road.

'Last time we spoke, you were up for promotion.'

'I didn't get it.'

He slowed down a little as they clattered through Norton Staithe, the noise from the engine bouncing off the hard flint walls of the old part of the village.

'What next?' he went on. 'With your career?'

'I'm thinking about leaving. But I don't know. If I do stay, I'd try for a move into CID, if I can.'

'More exciting?'

'More interesting. More varied. And fewer shifts, too.'

'That's good, is it?'

'Messes up your social life less,' she replied and then regretted it, and looked out of the side window at the hedges, still wreathed in fog.

'You ever go sailing these days?'

'No.'

'Why's that?'

She wondered why he should ask as he knew the answer as well as she did herself. *Because Tom died out there. Because I think about him still, every time I watch a boat go out.*

'I don't like getting cold,' she said. 'Or wet.'

He laughed.

'You should do what I do and have a boat with a cabin, an engine and a bloody big heater.' He changed down a gear and sped past a van, almost touching the verge on the far side. 'But then, if you like sailing, cold and wet don't matter.'

'No.'

She liked Nick, despite or probably because of everything in the past. He was usually good company, always with a story or a bit of gossip to pass on, or a new gadget to show off proudly. But for once she found it hard to think of anything that wouldn't sound stilted or be read the wrong way.

'What do you think happened to them?' Nick asked. 'This dead couple.'

'I've no idea. I suppose it's possible one of them killed the other and then themselves. But you'd have to be pretty out of it to stick a knife in yourself.'

'So a third party? Love interest maybe?'

'I suppose so. Or a psycho. Or it could be something to do with drugs.'

'Drugs?' he said sharply. 'Like smuggling?'

'I suppose so. I was thinking maybe Hannay was buying or selling. A drugs deal gone wrong. We found some in his car. Stuff he probably shouldn't have had.'

Outside, a break in the hedges gave a glimpse of the dark, cold fields beyond.

'Don't mention that to anyone, will you?' she added.

'Don't worry,' he said grinning. 'We're a team, remember? Batman and Robin.' His smile made crinkly little lines around his eyes. 'By the way, if it helps I could take out one of our launches later. There's a couple of places where the currents can catch things up, out on the sandbanks, places you couldn't reach from the shore. May be worth me stooging around a bit and having a look.'

He slowed down a little as they approached a blind bend but Sarah still had to hold onto the dashboard as they cornered.

'Are you sure?'

He laughed. 'I'm serious, you know. For me any excuse to get out to sea. I spend too much time in the office these days. It's all spreadsheets and business plans and crawling to the bank manager. But if it's a public duty, and you were there too . . .'

'That would be great,' she said cautiously. 'But I don't know if I'll still be on the case.'

'Well, I'll insist you are. I don't want to be lumbered with some dull plod for the day.'

What should she make of this? When they had got together it was just after Tom's death. She had felt lonely, restless. She had wanted her mourning to be over. She had found out that Tom had betrayed her, had been seeing someone else. And Nick had been there.

She had tried to work out, once it was over and she and Nick had drifted apart again, who had used the other more. She knew she had wanted to hit back at Tom, to hurt him in the same way he had hurt her so deeply. Though it hadn't occurred to her at the time, doing it with Nick had been a form of revenge. If Nick had taken advantage of her when she was vulnerable and lonely and upset, that was only life. She couldn't blame him for that, any more than she blamed Tom or blamed herself. It was all a long time ago now.

He wasn't exactly attractive, she thought, watching his profile as he drove. Brown hair that was almost ginger, in tight short waves that were almost curls. A pronounced widow's peak, that suggested his hair would soon start to recede. Red mottling on his cheeks from the outdoors and the self-indulgence. The tiny vanity of the ring on his little finger.

Not a man to grow old with. But now, in his prime, fit and full of energy, he had a a childlike directness and immediacy, a love of life, a sense of fun which she found attractive. It was so different to the cynicism of so many of her colleagues, the wariness that came with the job.

She couldn't believe he was completely unattached. He would enjoy himself too much for that. He might have a one-night stand in mind but she didn't think so. They had too much of a past together for that.

'If I had a doubt,' he said after a while, 'it would be about how they died.'

'Really?'

'Well, it's most likely to be an accident, isn't it? Mucking about on one of the groynes. He fell off or something. Don't you think it's possible?'

She thought about this for a while. She could picture the scene with Hannay having had too much to drink, wanting to show off, to impress this girl. Ignoring the warning signs, or not seeing them in the dark. Standing on the groyne, pacing along it like a high-wire artist with Nicola perhaps shouting at him to come back. Surely not encouraging him. He then walking on above the waves which are louder, nearer and perhaps a little more frightening than seen from the shore. Making for the steel pole at the end, but then a foot slips on some seaweed. For a moment he's balanced, one arm outstretched, a dark figure caught in the moonlight. Then he falls, bashing his head, tearing a wound in his front on one of the iron fastenings.

But what about Nicola? How did she then meet her death? It didn't make sense. However clearly she could imagine it, she knew it had never happened.

'You've only one witness,' Nick went on. 'Couldn't she have got it wrong?'

'She seemed certain when I spoke to her.'

Nick turned the car off the road and down a narrow track hardly wider than the car itself, still driving far too fast.

'Interesting about the drugs, though, isn't it? Maybe they had some bad stuff.'

She looked at him again, noticing the wrinkles on his forehead, the razored lines of his sideburns, the muscles on his neck. He could be surprisingly sharp, she now remembered. His suspicions seemed to be heading the same way as hers.

'I think—'

He cursed and slammed on the brakes. Sarah was flung forward as the Land Rover slid to a halt a couple of feet from the front of a tractor advancing up the lane. Its lights glowed in the mist and she could hardly make out the driver leaning in the cab high above them.

'Great brakes these things have,' Nick said, laughing, as he backed up the lane to a passing place. 'What car do you have?'

'A Renault,' she said, still trying to catch her breath.

'Yeah? Do they last well?'

'Mine has.'

The tractor pulled past them, and then Nick set off at the same speed or even faster.

'No chance of meeting anything now,' he said as they sped around another sharp bend.

'Is this for my benefit?'

'No.' He sounded truly surprised. 'You know I always drive like this. Boring, otherwise.'

They reached the end of the lane without any more alarms. In front of them was a turning area and a steel gate blocking access to the marshes themselves. A drainage ditch ran sluggishly in front of them, and along one side was a track barely wide enough for a car. Nick pointed out where the search team should start and which of the creeks they could safely ignore.

'I used to go beachcombing here as a kid,' he said quietly. 'I knew all the places to go to find stuff: wood, bottles, boxes, shells. Fish boxes were the best. They paid good money to get them back.'

'I didn't know. It sounds like a lonely way to make some pocket money.'

'Comes of having three brothers. This was before Andrew went into the army. I quite liked the chance for a bit of peace and quiet. Plus my dad's always been keen on us pulling our weight. We've always had to bring in the cash; no freeloaders in our family.'

It was raining now. Sarah thought of coming out here again hoping to find the two corpses, and fearing it too. Fearing how much or how little would have been left by the sea. Then the job of telling the family. She was sure that was going to be the sting in the tail of this particular task. The thought of that, on top of the long day, made her sick of the whole thing.

'We should go,' she said suddenly.

'Yeah?' He looked at her, trying to read her mood. 'OK.'

They walked back along the sea wall, watching the birds stalking over the mudflats or wheeling above, black against the grey of the sky. Despite her coat Sarah felt even colder than she had that morning. She wished she'd had something to eat.

'I ought to get back to the incident room. See what's happened. Let them know what the plan is for tomorrow.'

'Of course. Shall I run you back there?'

'If you would,' she said with a smile. 'That'd be really kind.'

'Then I'll go and hunt up Greg, the man we saw in the café. If anyone really knows where to look, it's him.'

During the ten-minute run back to Compton neither said anything. Sarah was too tired and it was already well into the afternoon. She hoped there wouldn't be much more to do.

'Would it help if I was around tomorrow?' he asked as he dropped her off outside the station.

'If you could that would be great,' she said, wishing she didn't sound so tired and that her words held more enthusiasm. But he just smiled and drove off.

Chapter Ten

Morton had set up an incident room in the training suite at the back of Frampton police station and already had the desks and computers in place. A couple of officers were staring into screens, tapping away. Andy Linehan was standing at the far end of the room, drawing on a whiteboard.

'Hiya,' he called over.

Coming closer, she saw that photos of the two victims had been stuck to the wall and were already surrounded by Post-it notes with various odd scraps of information about them. Alongside were large-scale maps of the area and a series of photos of the beach itself.

'Jeremy's not here, if you're looking for him. He's gone to the hospital. You know the drugs in Hannay's bag? It was cocaine. Medical purity too, so probably lifted from the hospital.'

'Cocaine? What do they have that for?'

'It reduces swelling, would you believe? Get hit on the nose in a fight, they give you cocaine. Good thing no one knows about it, eh?'

'How much was there?'

'Enough for a very good weekend, I'm told. But it was probably a sample.'

'He was selling it, then?'

'Who knows? Jezza thinks it's a crime of passion and Blake's chuffed because we've found someone who saw a strange-looking man in Compton at about the right time, which helps his theory that the killer is some kind of stalker or psycho. I, on the other hand,' he said, holding a finger aloft, 'I still reckon Hannay was meeting someone on the beach, and that he and the nurse were in it together. We were over at the hospital earlier and they explained how it works. Apparently it's hard for one person to buck the system for handling controlled drugs in hospital but two people working together makes it much easier. And Hannay and Page had worked together before. Maybe they had a lot more stuff with them and the dealer decided to kill them both and make off with it without the bother of paying.'

'But why kill them? They could hardly come to us and complain about it.'

'That's what's so worrying. That amount of violence doesn't make sense. Which means we've got to catch them quickly before they do it again.'

'Do you know what Morton wants me to do next?' Sarah asked. 'He said concentrate on finding the bodies, but I've set up the search parties and spoken to the coastguard and lifeboats and so on and there's nothing more I can do until after high tide.'

'Yeah, well . . .' Andy looked a little uncomfortable. 'The thing is, we've got the serious crime team in place now so we don't really need anyone else. It's been great you being able to help out, but that's it really. For now.'

'Right,' Sarah said, hoping her disappointment

didn't show too much. 'I'm supposed to be on leave from tomorrow anyway.'

'There is one job, though. We need someone to act as witness liaison. You know, keep them informed on the progress of the case, look after them if they need it. Would you be willing to take that on? You know Mrs Aylmer already.'

'I could. I hadn't got anything planned.' She was supposed to be helping her mother clear up the house ready for the removals people later in the week. Anything would be better than that, even if witness liaison was little more than public relations.

'You get a trip to London out of it anyway. To go and collect the witness we've dug up. I spoke to her earlier and she sounded OK. A bit put out at the idea of a local busybody taking down her number. I can see her point, though. Range Rovers aren't exactly unusual around here. Anyway, here you are. A Miss A. J. Mabbott. Lives in Shoreditch, wherever that is.'

She could picture the woman already: tall, with long fair hair and an annoying drawl. 'A' would be for Amanda, Sarah guessed, or even for Arabella, given she was a Londoner with a four-wheel drive car.

'So could you go down tonight, take a statement, and if it sounds promising then bring her back here first thing in the morning? She could look at some mug shots and look around the area. See if she can spot the man she saw.'

Sarah brightened up at the thought of a jaunt to London. She could stay with her friend Justine, maybe go out for a meal, catch up with her gossip. It would be good too to have the chance to get away from the coast for a few hours. Put some distance between herself and all the memories the case had stirred up.

Andy must have noticed her cheerful expression.

'You're OK to do that then? And off to London tonight?'

'Fine.'

'Staying with a friend?' he asked.

'That's right,' she said, hoping she wouldn't blush at his suspicions.

'You've kept that quiet,' he said. And then added with a smirk, 'Don't oversleep, will you?'

Sarah was just about to leave her flat, her overnight bag already packed, when Nick called to ask if she was OK, how the investigation was going and then to suggest a drink.

'Tonight? I can't. I'm off to London.'

'Are you off the case?'

'It's just to pick up a witness. I'll be back in the morning.'

'Tell you what,' he said. 'Why don't we meet tomorrow after you finish work?'

'Sure. I don't know when I'll be done, though.'

'Doesn't matter to me. Look, let's meet in the pub in Yarwell, and then if you're late or you can't make it, it won't put me out.'

'OK.'

Yarwell had several pubs to choose from. She and Tom had always gone to the Mariners or the Ship, but she'd still know too many people at both for a quiet drink. There was the Lord Anson, but that was more a hotel than a pub though like the others it had nautical

memorabilia on every wall. Only one pub, the Rose
and Crown, turned its back on the sea. That was the
one she suggested.

'Whatever you say.'

'It's a bit quieter than the others. It'd be easier to
talk about the search.'

'Sure,' he said. 'But don't feel you've got to. We can
just talk.'

There was no mistaking what he meant. She knew
she should stop it there, tell him it was business only.

'See you there around nine, nine thirty, then,' he
said.

'Yeah. See you then.'

Chapter Eleven

After falling asleep on the train Sarah found Liverpool
Street station a shock of bright lights and rushing, set-
faced people. She made her way to the underground
adjusting to the London crowds, moving faster, keeping
her eyes away from others and adopting the look of
sullen suffering of the other tube passengers. But for
the first time in a while she got a buzz from the change,
from the sense of action, the anonymity. She could be
anyone, go anywhere. She wasn't on duty as she would
be in Norfolk. She was free to sink without trace.

Ms Mabbott had arranged to meet her in a sports
centre in Hoxton, and from the spectators' gallery
Sarah could look down on the various games in progress, each somehow making sense of the over-lapping,
multi-coloured markings on the floor. A woman with
long fair hair loosely bunched behind her playing
netball almost directly below came closest to her image
of the Range Rover driver. Her side was clearly losing;
the opposition were much more of a team, more professional, their sharp calls echoing under the high steel
roof.

A shortish man wearing the green polo shirt and
black cycling shorts which seemed to be the staff
uniform came over and asked what she wanted.

'I'm waiting to see one of the players,' she replied, ignoring the slight aggression in his voice.

'Who's that, then?' he said.

'Miss Mabbott.'

'Does she know you're here?'

'Oh yes,' Sarah said, conscious that there was something here more than an ordinary feeling for security. 'We're going to go off for a quick drink and a chat.'

The man relaxed, smiling for the first time.

'I'm sorry about being so heavy,' he said, 'but I didn't know you was a friend of hers.'

'That's all right.'

'The thing is,' he went on, clearly concerned he had caused offence, 'I thought you was a reporter. We've had a few of them hanging around.'

'Why's that?'

Her question was blunt enough to make him pause for a second.

'Well, because of that stuff a year or two back.'

Sarah smiled, she hoped disarmingly, and admitted she hadn't a clue what he was talking about.

'I've only known her a short time, you see,' she said. 'I don't know anything about her work, or anything.'

'Don't you know who she is?'

'I don't even know what she looks like.'

He pointed towards the winning team.

'She's the captain. She's wearing an armband.'

'The one on the far side?'

'No.' The man laughed. 'The one by the net.'

The woman was in her late twenties, black, and as far as Sarah could guess from her vantage-point above the court, about six foot tall. But she was still fast, even graceful, as she threaded past the defenders, then held the ball high out of reach of her opponents.

'She's very good,' Sarah said.

'This is only a knockabout for her.'

The next point saw the losing team rally, only to be bundled out of possession when about to score. The fair-headed woman was left sitting on the floor from where Mabbott helped her to her feet.

'So what happened last year?' Sarah asked the man, amused by the way he was still watching Mabbott. She could understand why any man might be impressed by her.

'If you don't know,' he replied, with a return to his original suspiciousness, 'I'll leave it to her to tell you.'

With that he left. Sarah shrugged it off and finished her coffee. The other team were looking resigned and she guessed it was almost the end. As they moved slowly back to their positions, Mabbott looked up at the balcony, noticed her and stared a little longer than anyone would from ordinary curiosity. So when she came up to the café a few minutes later there was no need for introductions though they still shook hands rather formally. Mabbott carried a bottle of water and had a sports bag slung over one shoulder.

'If you want to have a shower first, I can wait,' Sarah said.

'That's OK. I didn't get into much of a sweat.' For the first time the other woman smiled and Sarah relaxed a little. 'Do you play? I saw you watching.'

'Yes,' Sarah said. 'Sometimes. But I'd make sure I was on your team.'

'Yeah, we did all right, didn't we?' She leant back

in her plastic chair. 'So what do you want me to tell you?'

'About what you saw last night. You say what happened and I'll write it up and ask you to sign it. As a witness statement.'

'Like you'd use in court?'

'That's right.'

She nodded and drank some of her water, and Sarah took the chance to study her more closely. She had a broad face and straight black hair cut short which emphasized the muscles in her neck and shoulders. Her expression gave nothing away, but there was a glint in her eye, as if she could sense Sarah's scrutiny. Sarah looked down at her notebook.

'Ed – he's my boyfriend – Ed and me went to the seaside for the day, a kind of spur of the moment thing. We went to somewhere called Hunstanton. D'you know it?'

Sarah nodded.

'In the evening we went to a pub to eat. Then, maybe about eleven at night, we left and went to have a last look at the sea. We got a bit lost. Not my fault,' she said, smiling. 'Ed had the map. I was driving. Anyway, we never found the beach but that's when I saw this man.'

She took another swig of water, still watching Sarah as she did so.

'OK. Can I take some details? Your full name and address?'

'Atlanta Mabbott. No middle name. I live in Shoreditch. Forty-six St Chad's Street.'

'Can I ask what you do for a living, Miss Mabbott?'

'Atlanta,' she corrected. 'I'm a designer.'

'A clothes designer?'

She laughed.

'Not me. I work on brochures, company reports, internet. Stuff like that.'

'Where do you work?'

'It's a company called ATC Design. In the City.'

'D'you like it?'

'It pays well. Lots of night work.'

'Better than magazines?'

'How do you mean?'

Sarah hadn't meant anything; she was only making conversation to put the other woman at her ease. It seemed to be doing the opposite.

'I don't know,' she ploughed on. 'I suppose I'd guess it'd be more interesting to work on one of the big glossy mags. Er . . . *Vogue*, maybe?'

'Not many black people work in magazines,' Atlanta said. There was nothing much Sarah could think to say in reply.

'Er . . . you mentioned you went with your boy-friend,' she went on. 'Could you give me his name and address?'

'Ed Denton. He lives with me at the moment. He's got a flat in Hackney he rents out, if you're interested.'

'What does he do?'

'He runs a club, mainly. It's called Spanish Town, on Mare Street. You should go sometime.'

Atlanta said this deadpan but Sarah suspected that inside she was laughing at her. Maybe because she was a country bumpkin who didn't know her way around London. Or because she was from the police.

'Do you think I'd like it?' Sarah asked.

'Maybe.' Atlanta smiled and leant back. 'Shouldn't you be asking me more about yesterday?'

'All right. Let's start with this man you saw.'

'Well . . .' She shut her eyes, making a show of trying to remember. 'We were looking for the beach and going down some crappy little road with no lights. We went past a church, then got to a gate and we stopped. Ed went on to see if he could find a way through to the beach. He reckoned he could sort of sense it was there. Anyway, I was sitting there waiting for him when this man came along and looked in the car window. He looked really scary. He had a funny round hat and stubble and staring eyes. I think I must have shouted out because he vanished again.'

'Did you see where he went?'

'No. I wasn't planning on getting out and looking either.'

'Or where he'd come from?'

'No. Like I said, I didn't know he was there until he had his face up against the glass.'

'Do you know what time this was?'

'It must've been about midnight.'

'And at the time you thought he looked weird?'

'Definitely. Really weird. He seemed to come out of nowhere and he looked at me in this strange way. It freaked me out.'

'Could you have another go at describing him?'

'He was pretty tall. He had this dark stubble and I think his hair was reddish-brown. But it was the eyes I noticed most. They were so strange.'

'And his clothes?'

'I think he had a coat on. It might have been green but it's hard to tell in the dark. It was a bit shiny. And a sweater. I could see that because the coat was open. It was like they have in the army. Knitted, with ribs. With patches on the shoulders and elbows.'

She patted herself to show what she meant.

'Not that I could see those of course, because of the coat. But it was that kind of sweater.'

'I know the kind,' Sarah said.

'And a hat.' Atlanta was becoming more animated. 'It was round, like a flowerpot. With a kind of rim all round it.'

'A fly fishing hat?'

Atlanta didn't know what such a hat would look like but thought she could draw what she had seen. She looked about her for some paper. Sarah handed over her notebook and pen and watched as the other woman leant over and began to draw. She sketched the hat in a few bold strokes, wrinkling her nose with the effort of remembering, holding the page flat with her long fingers and grasping the pen lightly and far from the nib with her left hand. Sarah wondered if she might have found the ideal witness: one who had a clear memory but could also draw her own picture of the suspect rather than having to rely on a police artist.

'Something like that,' she said, turning the page around.

'That's great,' Sarah replied. 'Would you be able to come and see for yourself? See if you could spot the man again?'

'What? Go back there?' She made it sound like the far side of the world. 'I don't know.' She shook her head and looked doubtful. 'I don't think I could do much.'

'It's so important to us, though. Any chance is worth it. If there's a madman going around killing people then we need to do anything we can to find him.'

She still looked reluctant.

'He could do it again. Any time. That's what they do.'

She shrugged and said, 'When would you want me to come?'

'Tomorrow? We'd pay expenses and so on.' Atlanta was lost in thought. 'Also, we could try to do a photofit or an artist's impression.'

Atlanta had folded one leg over the other and was picking at the lace of her trainer. Sarah wondered if it was work or not wanting to have anything to do with the police that was making her so reluctant. But then she looked up and nodded.

'OK. But I'll need to talk to my boss. And to Ed.'

She took a mobile phone from her bag and went off to call. Sarah wasn't surprised she wouldn't talk in front of her but she wondered if she would ever get used to the way people were so suspicious and reserved once they knew she worked for the police.

It was nearly eight and she wondered what to do with the rest of the evening. Justine had been happy to lend Sarah her spare room but she was going out for dinner with her new boyfriend. So no chance of a heart-to-heart. Her disappointment was made more galling by having missed out on an evening with Nick.

She looked at the drawing again. Atlanta had shaded it in to give a three-dimensional effect, and the hatching was the same check pattern as the hat would have had. It seemed more tangible evidence than the words Sarah had written down. She felt excited, as if she was making real progress. As if she had found the hat itself lying under a hedge in Beach Road. A clue that could lead them to find whoever it was had killed the two medics.

Atlanta came back into the café, weaving easily between the empty chairs.

'Everything's sorted,' she said.

'That's great. Do you want me to fix up a ticket?'

'I'd rather drive, if that's OK. I can give you a lift if you want.' She picked up her bag before Sarah could reply. 'Are you hungry? I need to eat.'

'Er, no. But . . .'

'I'm seeing Ed in a minute. Round the corner. Come and have a drink. We'll sort everything out for tomorrow.'

Sarah meant to say no but she had no other plan for the evening and it would save seeing Ed another time. After all, Morton had told her to stick close to her witness.

It was cold outside and their breath misted as they walked along, though Atlanta didn't seem to feel it. The street was quiet except for the sound of traffic passing at the main road ahead.

'You always been in the police?' Atlanta asked.

'No. Just two years.'

'Thought so,' she said with satisfaction, and Sarah realized the other woman was trying to wind her up.

'Have you always lived in London?' Sarah asked.

'Yeah.'

'You wouldn't want to move?'

'Nah. I like it here. Why d'you ask that?'

'Some people come up to Norfolk looking for somewhere to live. They like the idea of getting out of the city.'

'Not me,' Atlanta said laughing, her head back. 'No way. I hate the countryside. I only went because Ed was going on about it. It shows I was right too, doesn't it?'

'How do you mean?'

'Well, look at it, right?'

She stopped and waved her arm around at the shuttered shops, the youths hanging around by a phone box, beanie hats pulled down over their ears, and the three beefy men in leather jackets standing outside a minicab firm.

'It's supposed to be rough round here – right? Shootings. Stabbings. Well, I've never had any trouble. I don't know anyone who has. But I go to the country and I almost run into a crazy killer. See what I'm saying? It's weird in the country.'

They walked on a few paces and then Atlanta turned down an alley, saying something about a short cut. There were no street lights and Sarah found it difficult to keep up and pick her way safely over the puddles and the spilling sacks of rubbish. She guessed, as their route twisted around more back streets and then cut through an estate, that Atlanta was playing some game; trying to frighten her or make a point. Atlanta herself seemed a little more wary although she chatted on happily.

'I spoke to a friend of yours,' Sarah said. 'I think he works there. He pointed you out.'

'That must've been Franklin. He's cool. Looks after me.'

'That's nice,' Sarah said, but Atlanta chose not to explain. They walked on in silence until they could see the main road only a few yards away. There was a bar on the corner, and Atlanta opened the door for her. There was a flight of stairs heading down, the walls painted in red and black, and then another door at the bottom. Even from outside, Sarah was struck first by the noise and then the warmth. A muffled burst of laughter came floating up, reminding her of the sounds from the café below her flat.

'You coming?' Atlanta asked, when Sarah hesitated.

'I'd better get back,' she replied. 'I ought to call in as well. Tell them what you told me.'

'Fair enough. I'll see you tomorrow, then.' She waved and headed down the stairs, and the door gently closed in Sarah's face.

Morton's first thought was to insist Sarah come straight back to Norfolk with Atlanta. It was only when she stressed the early start and the need not to antagonize such an important witness that he relented.

'And she's clear about what she saw?' he said insistently.

'Very clear.'

'Well, like I said, you stick with her. Look after her, make sure she's OK, keep her away from any other witnesses, that sort of thing. And keep her sweet so she'll testify. The more you can get to know her, the better. If she really saw the killer, she's the most important lead we've got.'

'Right.' Sarah felt buoyed up by Morton's enthusiasm.

'We should also get her to do a photofit,' he went on. 'Or get one of the artists in.'

'We may not need to,' Sarah said, explaining that

Atlanta probably had the skills to draw an impression of the man herself.

'Really? We could do with a lucky break,' Morton said.

'So has anything more come out this afternoon?'

'Nothing.'

'The drugs?'

'Blake checked those out. The hospital's adamant they couldn't have lost anything like the quantities which would make dealing a realistic prospect. They just don't use that much of any of them.'

'So that doesn't take us much further.'

'No, except to suggest the sort of man he was. Which may mean there's some link there. It's still possible they arranged to meet a drug dealer there on the beach that night, and in some way it went wrong. But I have to say Graham Blake isn't convinced by that either.'

She felt she ought to say something intelligent or at least reassuring. But all she could manage was a question about the weather.

'Still foggy,' he replied. 'Someone said it might clear later tomorrow or Tuesday.'

They chatted on for a few minutes, more because Morton was feeling in the mood than because he had anything else to say. After he had gone, Sarah wondered if the case was starting to get to him. There was so little to go on, but that wouldn't stop people from blaming him if it went nowhere.

Later, lying in bed in Justine's flat, listening to Justine and her boyfriend trying and failing to go to bed together without making a noise, Sarah's mind filled with the images of the day. She thought of Rosemary and wondered if she too was lying awake, perhaps listening for every sound, wondering if it was the killer returning. She thought of Collingwood and the calculating way he had sifted every word he had said to her, as if it was all just part of his job and nothing to do with the death of his colleagues. She imagined Nicola lying on the beach, and though she knew the bodies would hardly be recognizable if they did turn up, in her imagination the girl was much as she was in the photo, as she would have been had she simply fallen asleep.

It was odd that Mrs Aylmer had put it that way – that the girl looked asleep rather than dead. Sarah had heard enough about violent death to know that people rarely curled up and drifted into unconsciousness; there was too much blood and pain and fear for that. So something else must have happened, something which had to be significant.

Then there was the man Atlanta had seen that night, and the drawing she had made of the hat. The more Sarah thought of it, the more the hat seemed immensely sinister, like an everyday object turned into a piece of evidence: the stained clothing, the hammer used as a murder weapon. And why was the man walking along the path at all? Maybe it meant he had no car and lived on Beach Road or in Compton itself. That would mean there was a limited number of people it could be. Easy enough for Atlanta to spend a few hours in the area to see if she could spot him again.

She wondered if the staring-eyed, hatted, waxed-jacketed killer would now pursue her in her sleep. But in the event she slept deeply, without any dreams.

Chapter Twelve

Atlanta's flat was in a converted warehouse, a square block of whitewashed concrete and glass at least five storeys tall running along most of one side of a narrow street. The block had a video entryphone, the front door to the flat was triple-locked and strengthened with steel, and there was another camera set in toughened glass looking down at her. But the man who opened the door smiled at her warmly.

'You found us OK, then,' he said, shaking her hand. 'I'm Ed. But you guessed that.Come on in,' he said over his shoulder, and she followed him into an open-plan living room with a desk at one end, a group of chairs and sofas in the middle and a gleaming kitchen along the far wall. There was space for a dining table as well as the breakfast bar, where a pot of coffee and a bowl of fruit stood perfectly judged to give colour to the cool surroundings. The room was made even larger by the windows running down one side. Beyond them was a balcony in the same vaguely nautical style, with steel rails painted white and deck chairs in striped canvas. Sarah had never seen such a spacious room in a London flat.

'Atlanta's still getting ready,' Ed said, walking over to the kitchen.

'Fine,' Sarah replied, wondering how much the place must be worth and where the money had come from.

'She said you might want to ask me a few questions,' he added.

'If you wouldn't mind.'

'No worries.'

Ed was shorter than Atlanta by an inch or two, and he looked younger too. There was something boyish about him despite or perhaps because of his razor-sharp haircut. Maybe it was his eyes, Sarah thought, or the way he seemed ready to find everything amusing. Whatever it was it made him attractive.

'First off,' he said, 'would you like some coffee? Breakfast? Anything like that?'

'I'd love some coffee,' she mumbled.

'Great. Chuck your bag down here and take a seat.'

He waved her to a stool on the other side of the breakfast bar and pushed a mug of coffee in front of her. It smelt fantastic.

'Fire away, then.'

She started on her standard questions and he answered them easily, confirming his address, his job and how he and Atlanta had decided on the spur of the moment to go to the seaside that weekend. They chose Norfolk because neither of them had been there before.

'We didn't think it'd take so long to get there, though. So we didn't have much time before it got dark.'

'Did you go straight to Compton?'

'Is that where it happened? No, we went into Hunstanton first off, had a look around. Not much going on.'

She watched him as he moved around the kitchen, fetching milk, fruit juice and cereal, and reaching up to a shelf for a clean bowl. With his easy smile, his bright red T-shirt and his toned body he looked straight out of an advert.

'Yeah, so we had an ice cream, walked about a bit, then decided to find somewhere to eat. We set off along the coast and stopped in a pub. I don't know where exactly. When we'd finished it was dark but not too late, and Atlanta said she wanted to see the sea before we went back. See a proper beach.'

'Right,' Sarah said, sipping the coffee.

'So we went on until there was a sign to the beach. But then the road was blocked off by a gate. We stopped for a while. And then we went off again . . .'

'What time would this have been? When you stopped.'

'No idea. Before midnight, definitely. But we weren't thinking about the time. You know what I mean?' He saw her puzzled look and grinned.

'You know how it is, the moonlight, the summer evening. One thing leads to another . . .'

'Atlanta didn't mention that you'd, er . . .'

'She's a very modest woman.'

'And when you were, er, what shall I say?' she asked, her pen hovering over her notebook. 'Relaxing for a bit?'

'Nice one.' He laughed.

'You were in the car?'

'No. We went for a walk.'

'So when did you see this man?'

'I didn't. Afterwards, Atlanta said she was feeling sleepy and I still wanted to see the sea. So I went on to see if there was a way through to the beach and she stayed in the car. When I got back, she told me she'd seen this weirdo. At first I thought she was making it up. She's like that. Trying to freak me out. You know, the whole thing was like a horror film. The trees, the dark, then this weird man walking all alone down the road. But she told me straight up there was this man, staring eyes, a hat like you'd have to be a killer to wear it.'

Sarah had no more questions but felt there was something more to learn.

'Do you mind if I ask if you have a car?'

He took another mouthful of cereal and chewed for a bit before replying.

'Why's that?'

'This might seem like a stupid question, but most men I know would have expected to drive.'

'You don't know the right men, then,' he said, laughing. 'The thing is, I don't drive at the moment.'

'Really?'

'Yeah. As it happens, I lost my licence last year.' He looked a little shamefaced, and took his bowl over to the sink and started to rinse it out. 'Anyhow, she's a better driver than me.'

'Not many men would say that.'

'No, she is, believe me. It happens to be true. She's very calm, she doesn't get het up if someone cuts her up. Not that they do, though. Not in that Jeep of hers.'

'That's a comfort. She's driving me back to Norfolk.'

'Yeah. Anyway, I've got to get ready,' he said,

heading for the bedroom. 'Help yourself to more coffee if you want it.'

While she waited Sarah wandered around the room, looking at the shelves of books and the paintings and tapestries on the plain white walls. The whole thing was beautiful, though a little like a gallery. The only unexpected object was a modern javelin hanging on the wall over the front door, crossed with an older throwing spear with a wooden handle and a broad steel blade.

'They'd be good if someone tried to break in, wouldn't they?' Ed said, coming back in. He'd changed into a deep blue suit and was buttoning up a crisp white shirt; he looked very businesslike.

'Are they Atlanta's?' she asked.

'Yeah. She was in the British squad, you know. Three or four years in a row. Hurdles first, then hepta-thlon. She did really well.'

'Doesn't she compete any more?'

'No. She packed it in a few years back.'

'She wouldn't have been that old.'

'No.'

She thought of asking him more but his mood had changed again, so instead she ran through the last of her questions.

'I meant to ask . . . Did you ever reach the beach?'

'No. I got as far as this bridge over a stream, and went back again.'

'And why didn't Atlanta go with you. Wouldn't she have liked the walk?'

'I don't think so,' he said, laughing again. 'You don't know Atlanta. She won't walk anywhere if she can help it. Born lazy and got worse, her mum says.'

He finished adjusting his tie and was shrugging himself into his jacket as Atlanta came in, still in her dressing gown but now rubbing her wet hair with a white towel. She looked tired, as if she had a hangover. She wondered how late they had stayed up, after she'd left to go back to Justine's flat.

'You still here?' Atlanta said to Ed, seemingly offhand. But as she walked past she put her hand on his shoulder, and he took it and kissed it. It was all so natural Sarah could have missed it. But it made her heart turn over, thinking of how she used to do exactly that with Tom.

'I'm going, woman. Anyway, I've been looking after your new friend.'

There was something else they said silently to each other as Atlanta tweaked his tie, but Sarah couldn't tell what. They held each other for a while, and then Ed kissed her on the forehead.

'Take care of her, eh?' he said to Sarah as he left.

Atlanta hardly said a word before going off again to get dressed. Sarah tried phoning Morton only to find he was busy.

'He'll be back by lunch,' Andy Linehan said. 'He said to bring your witness in to see him this afternoon. And we had a message for you from one of the people you met at the hospital, Dr Woodford.'

'Sure,' Sarah said, scrawling a note of the number. 'Any other news?'

'Yeah. We've got a good lead at last.'

'Spit it out.'

'We found some stuff hidden in the dunes, including an empty hold-all. It was brand new and can't have been there more than a day or so. I can't say any more over the phone.'

'That big? Or is this a wind-up?'

'You'll find out later, won't you. When'll you get here?'

'Before midday, if the traffic's not too bad.'

'OK, I'd better go. I'm supposed to phone the forensics people every hour until they cough up their report.'

'See you.'

Sarah was too impatient to sit still and read any of the magazines lying around on the table, wanting to get back to Norfolk where the investigation was moving at last. Instead, she turned to examining a series of arty black and white prints along one wall, several of which looked like Atlanta's family. There was only one of Atlanta. It showed her on a running track, bent over, hands on her knees to catch her breath, but looking up so that the camera had caught her expression of inner satisfaction. A smile for herself and no one else. Sarah could understand why she had kept it – but why no others? And where were the cups and medals she must have won?

Atlanta emerged from the bedroom, wearing a black polo neck and black skirt and carrying a pair of black suede boots to complete the effect. She caught Sarah's look and smiled.

'You think I should wear something else?' she asked. 'Only I'm not planning on walking in any fields.'

Atlanta went past her towards the kitchen, treading carefully in her stockinged feet on the slippery maple floor.

'How long have you lived here?' Sarah asked. 'It's a lovely flat.'

'Five years.'

'It's really amazing.'

'Yeah? It was a wreck when I got it. It took a year to do up. You want anything else?' she asked, pouring herself some juice.

'No thanks. Ed gave me some coffee.'

Atlanta drained the glass, put it in the dishwasher and then wiped down the surface where it had stood, though Sarah was sure there was nothing spilt.

'We've got time for breakfast, if you want,' Sarah said, but Atlanta said she didn't feel hungry.

'I'll have to be back by Wednesday afternoon,' she went on. 'I'm booked in on a job and my boss'll kill me if I let him down.'

'We should be finished by tomorrow at the latest.'

'Did Ed tell you everything you needed to know?'

'He did. He might still be able to help us if he could take the time off work to come and look around.'

Atlanta nodded, then asked unexpectedly, 'You got a man?'

'No,' Sarah said, surprised into answering without thinking first. 'Why do you ask?'

'No reason,' Atlanta said, smiling to herself. 'Just wondered, that's all.' Sarah didn't rise to the bait, so she went on, 'Only you've come a long way for us to have to go straight back there again. I thought maybe I wasn't the main attraction.'

'You're right about it being a long way. We should get moving.'

'Oh yeah, right. Sorry I overslept.'

'That's all right.'

'I expect you're angry because I stayed out late.'

'I'm not angry,' Sarah said, trying not to get annoyed. 'It's really good of you to agree to help us anyway.'

'The thing is,' Atlanta said, unconcernedly, 'I work better at night. And I was up late doing you this.'

She went over to the desk at the far end of the room and brought back an art pad. She sat back on the sofa and opened it up on the coffee table.

'What d'you think?' she said with an air of indifference.

Sarah came and sat beside her. The picture was drawn in pencil, a mixture of bold lines and careful shading, and showed the head and upper body of a man aged around forty, with a heavy lined face and blank eyes staring out from just beneath the rim of his fishing hat. He was wearing a waxed jacket, open to show a military-style pullover beneath. The man's shoulders were bulky but he stood slightly slouched.

It was a powerful image. Atlanta had managed to capture something of the look of indifference, of deep lack of imagination, which made the idea of someone killing another human being randomly, in cold blood, more believable.

But it wasn't that which made Sarah shiver. It was the feeling that she had seen the face somewhere before.

Chapter Thirteen

Atlanta drove very well, just as Ed had said, and Sarah enjoyed the way they passed so quietly and smoothly past the rows of video stores, corner shops and off-licences. The Jeep was high off the ground and gave the same pleasurable sense of safety and superiority which Sarah remembered from the Land Rover her father had owned for years. He'd used it as a second car, claiming he needed it for his rounds in the winter or when the flood waters were up. It must have been twenty years old even then and was noisy and uncomfortable with a constant breeze coming through the side windows. Nothing like this warm, sound-proofed interior.

Soon they were on a viaduct, high above the surrounding houses, passing under the sky-blue motorway signs.

'I used to live over there.'

Atlanta hadn't spoken much since they had started off and Sarah looked at her in surprise. The woman's face was set, concentrating on the road and the other traffic, but she waved beyond the spread of grey-brown terraces to Sarah's left, the patch of green, the timber yard, all flashing by, to where a line of tower blocks stood in the distance.

'Hackney,' she went on. 'Well, Homerton, more like. My mum still lives there. Off Morning Lane.'

'I don't know Hackney,' Sarah replied lamely.

'I went to school just over there.'

There was no sign of a school, and when Sarah tried to picture it she came up instead with memories of her own school. The chalk dust in maths setting her teeth on edge. The ruthless way they had tormented Mrs Chelmer during French, turning each lesson into such chaos that she was surprised that any of them had passed the exam. The temporary classrooms where they had studied history, seemingly always in midwinter, with bright fluorescent lights, the windows reflecting the room and everyone, even Mr Powlesland, wearing their coats against the cold. Seven years ago, she realized with surprise.

'Was it a good school?' Sarah asked.

'It was OK. There were a couple of really great teachers. Especially for art. So I was lucky; I ended up with A levels in Art, English and French.'

'French?'

'A boy,' Atlanta replied cryptically. While Sarah pondered this the road curved round to the right and instead of houses there was a bleak open space, empty except for a road cutting across it and a man walking a dog.

'My brother still plays football here every Sunday.'

Sarah wondered vaguely what point Atlanta was trying to make and guessed she was talking more to herself.

'Do you go back much?' she asked.

'When I can. I've still got a lot of family and friends there.'

'That's good.'

'I may even move back. We've been thinking about it. Maybe a bit closer to my mother.'

Sarah couldn't believe she'd give up her flat to move back here, but before she could find a polite way to say this Atlanta was asking about where she'd grown up.

'You're not a Londoner, are you?' she asked, with a hint of mockery.

'No, I'm from Norfolk.'

'And you still live there?'

'Yeah. I live in Frampton now but I grew up in this place on the Suffolk border. A town called Diss.'

Atlanta found this highly amusing but wouldn't explain why.

'So why did you join the police, anyway? You're not like my usual image of what that fine body of men and women is like.'

'Maybe not.'

'So why did you join?'

She'd answered the question a hundred times before and always the same way. Now it almost felt like the truth.

'I didn't want to move away. My father was a police surgeon and had lots of friends in the force, so I knew what it was like. And it's a good career, really, especially if you haven't got a degree.'

'You haven't? You surprise me. Why was that, then?' But Sarah didn't reply and Atlanta chose to say no more.

For the next hour or so, as they left London far behind, they exchanged more snatches of conversation. Sarah learnt that, after school, Atlanta had gone on to do a part-time course in graphic design. She had thought about university but the chance to be in the team for the European athletics championships had won out.

'You want to keep at it. It's about seeing how good you can be. And you feel you owe it to people, right? Like your coach, the club, the people you train with. With a part-time course, I could do both.'

'Sounds like hard work,' Sarah said, remembering Ed's comment about her supposed laziness.

'It doesn't feel like it. I mean, don't get me wrong. There are days when you're sick to death of it. But when it's going well there's nothing like it. Not clubbing, not . . . well, nothing, anyway.'

She seemed less reserved than before, as if she'd forgotten Sarah was a police officer. They passed the sign marking the Norfolk border and Sarah tried again to think where it was she had seen the face that Atlanta had drawn. It could have been anywhere. In a police cell, on the street even in the papers or on TV. But there was nothing she could associate with it except her own conviction that it was the face of a killer.

'Did it take you long to do that picture?' she asked.

'No, not really. A couple of hours.'

'It's very good.'

'You can't be sure, can you? Not until you find him.'

'That's not what I mean. It's . . . assured. You know what you're doing. Do you ever do illustrations? For books?'

'I've done a bit. It doesn't pay so well. Plus you have to know people to get the work. What I do, someone else gets the work and I just do it.'

'Why's that better?'

'Oh, lots of reasons. It's not so lonely. Even if I'm in overnight there's other people around, and—'

Sarah's phone rang and Atlanta broke off while she answered it. It was Sarah's mother asking whether she'd still be able to make lunch on Wednesday.

'Patrick's coming over with the kids. You haven't seen them for ages.'

'I'll be there if I can. It's just with this case . . .'

'It'd be sad if you couldn't' her mother said, in the same tone she used about all her disappointments, from the time that Sarah had given up the chance to go on to university onwards.

'How's the move going?'

'Oh, it's awful. The packers are coming in tomorrow and I'm nowhere near ready. Everything's all over the place.'

'That's the point, though, isn't it?' Sarah said, smiling as she pictured her mother cleaning and polishing everything that was about to go into storage. 'They're supposed to sort everything out for you.'

'If only you knew . . .' She started to catalogue the incompetence of the removals firm but Sarah could hear someone calling out in the background and her mother rang off. She sat back in her seat, suddenly realizing how tense she had become. She glanced at Atlanta, sensing her amusement at the exchange, but the other woman was staring unconcernedly at the road.

'Your mother,' she stated after a minute.

'That's right.'

Neither said any more but Sarah again felt she'd come off worse in some way.

'How did you and Ed meet?' she asked, wondering if she might find a way of irritating Atlanta in return.

'He is sweet, isn't he?' was all she said in reply.

'How do you mean?'

'Nothing.' Atlanta paused while she overtook another car. 'Only I thought you might be wondering if he had a brother.'

Sarah decided to give up on the small talk for a while.

A few minutes later Sarah's mother phoned back.

'It's about the boxes in the attic. We've got them down but you'll really have to decide what you want done with them.'

'I will. Honestly, I will.'

'If you want us to throw them away . . .'

'No, I ought to look through them.'

The boxes held the possessions she had stored since leaving home for the last time: a series of battered dusty cardboard boxes stuffed with books, games, toys, photos, clothes, tapes and a thousand other relics from her childhood, from school. Holiday souvenirs, letters and postcards from friends. From Tom.

When Tom had died she had gone back to her parents, taking only a few clothes and books from the flat they had shared. And when she had found out the truth about him, she couldn't bear to return. Her brother Patrick had cleared out her stuff from the flat. He wouldn't have known what was hers or what was Tom's. In any case, they had bought so much of the furnishings together, hunting them down in the junk shops of Yarwell' upper town. And all of that must be in those boxes too.

'Couldn't you pick them up now? Sam and Lucie are here. They were sorry to miss you yesterday. And Alex will be over later. He can give you a hand.'

'I can't come now. I'm working. And I'm not in my car.'

'Don't worry about that,' Atlanta cut in.

'What?'

'If you want to pick something up on the way, that's fine with me. Plenty of room in the back.'

'We can't do that!' Sarah said in desperation, hoping her mother hadn't heard. 'It's miles away.'

'Your choice,' Atlanta said.

'That sounds like a very kind offer,' Sarah's mother said. 'Where are you now?'

'Mildenhall.'

'Oh well, that's no distance. Come off at Thetford and take the A1066.'

'I know the way,' Sarah said in exasperation.

'I'll have some tea ready,' her mother said, ignoring her. 'And maybe a sandwich. Have you eaten?'

'Yes we have.'

'Tea would be nice,' Atlanta called out.

Sarah sighed and closed her eyes, furious at the way she was being manoeuvred so effectively, embarrassed at the idea of her professional and personal life being mixed, even for half an hour.

'It's straight on at the roundabout,' she told Atlanta. 'Towards Thetford.'

*

Her mother's welcome had been a little too effusive, Sarah had felt in her supersensitive state. She had plied them with tea and cake and little elegant sandwiches, and Atlanta had played up to her, admiring everything, amazed by the age of the fireplace and showing a winning mixture of enthusiasm and humility in her questions about the porcelain ranged around the drawing room.

Sarah had taken the twins, who had stood staring up at Atlanta wide-eyed, seemingly on the edge of tears, off into the dining room. There she had helped them arrange their toy farm, distracting them when they argued over the horse, and sweeping them both into her arms when Sam took a tumble and banged his head.

Then Alex, her younger brother, had arrived, and after chasing the twins around the dining table for a while, he had taken the opportunity of their mother making more tea to start to chat to Atlanta. She listened politely while he went on at length about Yarwell: the harbour, the upper town, and what he called the nightspots. Listening from the dining room, Sarah had been surprised he hadn't gone all the way and asked Atlanta for her phone number.

Now he was giving Sarah a hand loading the half-dozen cardboard boxes into the boot of the Jeep while their mother finished showing Atlanta over the house.

'So how long is, er, Atlanta up here for?' he asked.

'Don't even think about asking her out.'

'I wasn't going to,' he protested.

'She's got a boyfriend. He's very large and works out a lot.'

'Honest. It's just a bit sad if she's left on her own. Not knowing anyone.'

Alex had the kind of charm that had won over several of Sarah's friends down the years. He'd become used to a certain amount of attention. It might be good for him to be slapped down with the kind of sarcasm Atlanta was sure to hand out.

'What's in these boxes anyway?' he said, tapping one with his toe.

'I don't know. Stuff. I'll sort them out at the other end.'

She was holding a sagging cardboard carton which had originally held forty-eight cans of soup. The top was folded shut but the contents rattled a little with the distinct hard plastic sound of cassette cases. Tom had made her several compilation tapes and she'd assumed they were lost long ago. They were probably inside and she wondered what else might be there. All kinds of private things of Tom's, perhaps: letters, diaries, anything. Stuff from Kelly's perhaps. She remembered a party – one of the chefs at the café had asked them all back to his room – and how Tom had been on a sofa beside her and Kelly had sat cross-legged on the floor next to him, fiddling complacently with her long dark hair, leaning back lightly and so casually against his leg, stretching her arm back to attract his attention, to ask him something, all done with a casual possessiveness. Would there really be nothing to find?

She could, she thought, simply throw the boxes away as they were. She'd done without them all these years. She could take them down to the council tip, heave each one into the huge steel bins, watch their contents spill out and join the rubbish of a thousand other lives. Then the bins themselves would be taken away and dumped into the landfill, mixed in with sacks of rotting food, old bottles and cans, stained newspapers, torn clothing. And eventually they would cover them all over with a layer of dark clean earth, ready for the next layer of trash. It felt right. Her memories had been ruined by what she had learnt about him afterwards. She didn't want them back.

'You OK, Sis?' Alex asked, concerned.

'Fine. I'm fine. Just working too hard,' she said, dropping the last box into the back of Atlanta's car.

'Yeah, right, tell me about it,' he said, nodding in understanding. But as he was still a student, taking in just enough lectures to keep the university authorities happy, she thought with a touch of malice, it wasn't likely that he understood at all.

Sarah had expected Atlanta to be full of questions, or of slightly snide comments. After all, she had been interested enough in Sarah's private life to help engineer the visit to her mother's house. And there was the bonus of Alex bouncing around her like an eager puppy. But in the event she was silent as they headed north towards Norwich until in an everyday voice, nothing like her usual lazy amused tone, she asked if Sarah had ever been attacked on duty.

'A couple of times,' Sarah replied, surprised. She had no idea why Atlanta should ask this, of all the questions she might put to her about the police. She tried to follow the path that Atlanta's thoughts must have taken, perhaps from something her mother had said about worrying about Sarah's job. 'There was only once that was really bad,' Sarah went on. 'Usually you can talk your way out of trouble.'

'How do you do that, then?' Atlanta asked.

'I don't know. It really depends on the situation. Sometimes you can calm people down by talking to them. Sometimes it's about making them back down; you can intimidate them a bit with the uniform and the back-up. And then sometimes that doesn't work. It was one of those times and I got caught. I was stuck against the side of a car and this bloke had my head and bashed it against the bonnet a few times.'

'God, were you all right?'

Sarah grinned.

'You'd be surprised how thin the metal on cars is. It left a huge dent but it didn't hurt that much. But then I fell and he kicked me a few times on the ground. That hurt like hell for weeks after. I had two broken ribs. But the worst of it was knowing how close I was to being really smashed up. If he'd got my face or stamped on my head.'

'Would he have done that?'

'He might. I'd turned towards him just before he hit me the first time and I remember his eyes were all glazed over.'

'Weren't you frightened?'

'It was all over very quickly. But yes, for a moment, I thought I'd had it.'

Chapter Fourteen

They reached Frampton by midday and Sarah introduced Atlanta to Andy Linehan, noting his momentary
surprise that Atlanta wasn't a typical Norfolk visitor.
He recovered quickly, spread on some charm, and
invited her into one of the interview rooms to go
through the first batch of mug shots.

'It'll take about an hour,' he said to them both. 'Then
if you could be available, Sarah, to show Miss Mabbott
around the area? See if she can spot the person she
saw that night.'

Sarah wondered how much chance there was of
this working, but knew better than to question her
superiors' instructions in front of a member of the
public. And it kept her in the investigation, she told
herself as she breezed into her own office. There David
Tollington, her Inspector, was frowning over a thick
file.

'Hello. How are you?' he said, surprised and
pleased to see her.

'Fine.' Sarah dumped her bag and scanned through
the papers on her desk, the Post-it notes, the phone
messages. It could all wait, she decided.

'How's your case, then?' he asked, leaning back in
his chair, waiting to be entertained. He was in his

forties, another refugee from a northern city force. He had an amazing fund of stories about his time on the beat and was always looking for new tales he could polish and adapt to his own style of telling.

'Fine,' she said airily. 'Routine. Just another murder.'

'I don't suppose you can tell us anything?'

'Sandwich?' she suggested.

'Not the canteen.'

There was a café a few minutes' walk away. It boasted a handful of tables on the pavement outside where a few pale-skinned office workers were shivering in the late September breeze. They went inside, where the condensation was building up on the windows, and hunched conspiratorially over their table as Sarah filled him in on the investigation. He asked her a few questions about the victims, the woman who found them and the chances of finding the bodies.

'Not good,' she said definitely.

'Is it the weather?'

'In a way. It's calm, and at this time of year that means there's a lot of fog off the coast which makes searching difficult. But if the weather breaks and the seas get up, the bodies'll be carried further and be harder to spot. And if it gets bad enough the boats won't go out. Worst of all, they won't be in such good shape when they do come ashore.'

'Why's that?'

'Well, the rougher the sea, the more they get bashed about.' She waved her hands to show the action of the waves. David looked pained.

'Tell us more about your witness,' he growled, pointing at the remains of his lunch, 'before I sick this back up.'

Her sandwich gone, she ate the cream from the top of her cappuccino with a spoon before starting on her slice of cake. David wondered how she stayed in shape.

'She's pretty difficult,' she said thoughtfully. 'She treats the whole thing like a massive joke. Not on the surface, but underneath. She keeps making sarcastic little comments. And she specializes in looking unimpressed.'

'Sounds like a right cow.'

'No, it's not exactly like that.' Sarah couldn't think how to explain. 'She's quite funny at the same time. It's like she's trying to wind me up but not in a nasty way.'

'I don't think I'd be splitting my sides. Doesn't she know two people are dead?'

'Yeah . . .' Sarah wished she hadn't mentioned Atlanta at all. 'I wonder if part of it is wanting to get back at us. At the police. After all, she's black. She's probably had loads of hassle over the years.'

'From the Met, maybe,' David said, before disappearing to order another couple of coffees. Sarah was left to mull over what might lay behind this particular prejudice of his.

'Are you still thinking about leaving?' David asked when he returned.

'I've filled the forms out but I'm still not sure.'

'Where was it again?'

'Peterborough. A firm called Summertons. They want an outdoor clerk. It's not much different from what I'm doing now. Serving papers, taking statements, looking after witnesses, that kind of thing. But they'd let me take time off for studying.'

'Is the money any good?'

'Not really. And it would mean leaving Frampton as well.'

'Could be time.'

'Also, I shouldn't build my hopes up,' she said, side-stepping his comment. 'I know it's an outside chance. But maybe I need to move on. I think . . .' She looked out of the window, not wanting to put what she felt into words.

'I'd better go,' David said after draining his cup. 'But think about this. It's easy to make a really big mistake if you're feeling down or you're hacked off with things. I'd hate you to do that. So if you want a chat some time, you let me know.'

An hour later, and Sarah and Atlanta were heading towards the coast. Apart from commenting that Norfolk seemed full of ugly people – if the mug shots were anything to go by – Atlanta said nothing until they were almost at Hunstanton. There they stopped at a service station and Sarah took the chance for a breath of fresh air, or as fresh as the fumes from the petrol pumps and the passing traffic would allow. While Atlanta took a surprising time to pay, Sarah wandered almost to the edge of the forecourt where she could look over a wooden fence into a ditch and fields beyond. The water in the ditch shimmered with a film of oil and the nearest field was cold bare earth, turned ready for sowing. Even in the few minutes she was outside the damp had started to seep through her thin shoes and into her feet.

She looked round to see Atlanta returning clutching a bulging plastic bag.

'You've done well,' Sarah said.

'I thought I'd stock up. There's never any shops open out here.'

She handed the bag to Sarah. It was filled with cartons of fruit juice, bars of chocolate, even crackers and a packet of cheese.

'What exactly have you got against the country-side?' Sarah asked as they started off again. Atlanta laughed out loud.

'It's so awful. I only came because Ed was going on about it. He'd got it into his head we should go to the seaside. He even said he wanted to go swimming.'

'And did you?'

'Of course not. It was freezing. It always is when you go outside London. Don't you find that? Brighton's OK because there are plenty of buildings. But any-where else it's muddy and everything smells of shit.' Sarah smiled and Atlanta became more insistent. 'No, really. Cow shit or something. They spread it on the fields, someone told me. And there's chicken sheds too. They smell awful. I didn't eat chicken for weeks after going past one of those.'

'What about the fresh air?'

'That's my whole point. It isn't fresh. It smells, it's muddy and it's damp. You can't sit down. If you want to have a drink or have something to eat you have to carry it around yourself because everywhere's shut. The day we went, we wanted to go to a pub, right? More of a restaurant, really. It wasn't even ten o'clock in the evening but they still made a big performance about it. If they hadn't served us then we'd have starved. There wouldn't have been anywhere within twenty miles still open.'

'That's true.'

'Right. But it's the same in the afternoons, too. Nothing to eat until after seven. Tell me I'm wrong.'

'No.' Sarah smiled. 'It's all true.'

'Worse, you have to wear a coat all the time in case it rains. Which it always does, by the way. So you're in a plastic cagoule in a horrible mix of red and yellow and mauve, all clammy too. It's like walking around in a tent.'

They lapsed back into silence. The skies were still filled with low grey clouds, and occasionally a gust of wind or a truck coming the other way would send spray across the windscreen. Sarah was thankful that for once she would be searching from the comfort of a car seat.

'We'll start by finding the pub, shall we?' she said, taking out a map of the coast. 'After you left Hunstanton, how far do you think you went?'

'Maybe a couple of miles. No more than ten minutes, for sure.'

'How fast were you going?'

'I wasn't speeding.'

Sarah wondered about that as Atlanta had driven the whole way at a few miles an hour above the limit, as if speeding were compulsory. But she didn't push the point. The way Atlanta had described the place, she was fairly certain that she and Ed had been to the Smugglers in Martlesham. So they drove straight there, past Compton, and then pulled into the car park.

It was a caterpillar of a pub, a rambling old building in the process of transforming itself into a restaurant. The shell was the same – a row of whitewashed fishing cottages knocked together, with wooden settles and low ceilings for seasoned drinkers – whatever the time of year. But at one end, where the beer garden had been, was a muddy space with newly dug trenches for foundations and piles of bricks and sand. Here the new kitchens, the conservatory dining area and the terrace were being built. The customers had changed long ago, the locals traded in for retired couples, middle-class families and Fulham yachting types staying in their weekend cottages. If there had ever been smugglers here among the boatmen and farm workers, Sarah thought, they were long gone now.

'It could be it,' Atlanta said, wandering towards the back door of the pub. Sarah looked around. Across the main road was a row of charming low cottages, like most of the buildings around built in a mixture of flint and mellow red brick, with the windows picked out in fresh white paint. In the front garden of one of the cottages, an elderly lady was watching them both from the cover of a clump of rose bushes. She looked away hurriedly.

'Yeah, this is it,' Atlanta called over, her voice surprisingly loud in the quiet of the village. 'I remember the menu. I thought it was a joke that all these places have prawn cocktail as a starter, but it's true.'

At Sarah's prompting, Atlanta made some slightly theatrical attempts to remember where they had gone when they left the pub that night.

'I *think* it was left. But I couldn't say for sure. We might have been parked facing the other way. And

JAMES HUMPHREYS

then we'd have turned left to get to the gate and then turned right. D'you see what I mean?'

'Yes,' Sarah said, wondering again if Atlanta was being serious. 'I see exactly what you mean.'

'So I don't know what's the best thing to do. Do you?'

'Let's go left and see what happens.'

They set off, cruising out of the village and down the narrow main road, past the entrance to Martlesham Hall, from where Chris Hannay and Nicola Page had driven the few miles along the coast road to Compton Spit. It had started to rain again, and though it was little more than fine mist falling on the windscreen, the occasional sound of the wiper and the unremitting grey beyond began to tug at Sarah's spirits. It also meant there were few people on the streets, and those there were had themselves wrapped up against the weather. As a way of spotting the man Atlanta had seen, it was fairly futile. Sarah began to think that she was wasting her time and that the action was happening far away.

They stopped in Norton Staithe and sat in the car in silence, except for the rumble of the engine and the flick of the wipers. Someone was waiting for a bus, shivering in the wooden shelter which looked like a garden shed cut down the middle. Apart from that the streets were empty.

'This could take a while,' Atlanta said. Sarah sensed that the other woman was laughing at her or was at least amused by her growing irritation.

As she had said to David, her only guess was that they'd had their share of hassle from the police over the years – of being stopped, questioned, even arrested

126

perhaps – and all just from being black. She knew it happened. Not all the time, not every officer, but enough. So now maybe she was enjoying being a public-spirited witness instead of a potential suspect.

Chapter Fifteen

After an hour or so of rain and boredom, Sarah gave up on their vigil. They returned to the main road and were at the far side of Compton, with the open fields before them, when Atlanta braked sharply, ignoring the blast of horn from a van following behind and the swearing flung at her as it pulled past.

In one of the gardens beside the road was a figure in a green waxed jacket and a flat cap who looked up at them in surprise, a handful of weeds in one hand. She stared at them suspiciously.

'Sorry,' Atlanta said. 'Only it was the right sort of jacket.'

'Half the people around here have coats like that,' Sarah said.

They sat there for a while, as the rain fell and Atlanta stared patiently in front of her.

'Shall we go on?' Sarah said in the end.

'Whatever.'

Sarah directed her into Compton itself and they took up a position in the main street from where they could watch the single village shop and the pub. Atlanta settled back with a sigh. The minutes passed but apart from an old lady with a scraggy dog heading for the shop, the street was empty.

'I saw a picture of the girl you're looking for,' Atlanta said. 'There was a poster up in the police station. She looks very young.'

'In her twenties.'

'How did she die?'

'We don't know, to be honest.' Sarah was surprised by Atlanta's serious tone and added, 'I don't think she'd have known anything about it.'

'Yeah? That's something I suppose,' Atlanta said. 'It always makes me feel awful when you hear on the news about a plane crash. When people know they're going to die. There was one where the whole plane broke apart, miles up, with hundreds of people on board. They reckon they'd have been falling for two or three minutes. And they'd have known what was going on. Can you think of anything worse?'

Sarah couldn't and was glad when Atlanta fell silent again, leaving her with her own thoughts. It must have been something like that for Tom, waiting while the tide came in until he could no longer keep his footing on the sandbank and had to swim for it. There must have been a moment when he realized help wasn't going to come in time as the water chilled him, the tiredness overwhelmed him. But it was hard to imagine; he'd always seemed immune to fear.

One time, they'd gone out in the launch from the boatyard and something had gone wrong with the outboard motor. There was quite a swell and the wind was getting up, so with the engine out the boat had rolled wildly and started to take on water. She'd been frightened, unable to do anything but hold on. But Tom had thought the whole thing funny, coolly pulling the engine inboard, cleaning out some pipe or other, reassembling it, and all the time humming *Heartbreak Hotel*, slightly out of tune. In a few minutes they were on their way again though, thankfully, heading back to harbour.

'I don't know about you,' Atlanta said from the folds of her coat, 'but I'm starving.'

Sarah was sure that Atlanta had eaten at the station but she wasn't going to start arguing.

'We'll go into Hunstanton; there'll be plenty of places open. We'll have a look round and then go and find you something to eat.'

In fact, most of the town was shut except for the amusement arcades and the fish and chip shops around the green. None of them looked inviting; most were empty. One was proudly showing off its only clients, a pasty-faced family chewing their cod and chips and staring morosely out of the windows at the drizzle.

'God, I'd forgotten what this place is like,' Sarah said as they walked back towards the car, sidestepping the puddles.

'Is this where I'm staying?' Atlanta asked. She was huddled into her long black coat and shooting furious glances at the passing townsfolk whenever they looked her way or slowed her down.

'No, Yarwell. That's a lovely place. Nothing like this. I used to live there. I'll show you around later, if you have time.'

'Five star hotel, I hope?'

Sarah couldn't remember the Oak having any stars.

'It's the best hotel in Yarwell,' she said loyally.

'Shit.'

They drove along the promenade towards the older

part of town until they reached a disused lighthouse, standing solidly enough though the cliff had been eaten away almost to its base. Just beyond there was a car park and a low whitewashed building where there was a café and a shop selling postcards, fudge and beach toys. From far away, deep in the surrounding mist, came the sad sound of a fog horn.

The café was a throwback to the fifties with its pale plastics, thin-legged furniture and big picture windows overlooking the sea, or what could be glimpsed of it through the rain. They stood dripping slightly in the doorway, looking around for a quiet table. But as there were only two other groups and a red-haired woman presiding behind the steel counter, this was no problem. Sarah went to the counter and ordered some food while Atlanta gazed at the plastic menu. But the sandwiches turned up with plenty of filling and a crisp salad garnish, and even Atlanta began to thaw towards the place.

'I like it. That coffee machine. The way every-thing's made of Formica. Ed would love this; it's a period piece. If this was in London, right, it'd make a mint.'

'They'd have to put their prices up.'

'I wish we'd known about this place last weekend.'

'So where did you go?'

'Oh, we had a look around for a bit, but there was nothing to do and we didn't want to go into any of the pubs or anything.'

'What's wrong with them?' Sarah asked, but Atlanta only gave her a pitying look.

'What about the beach?' she persisted, slightly hurt

that Atlanta was so dismissive of the place. 'Or the Old Town?'

'You're doing a great sales job, you know.'

'No, really.'

'The thing is, right, we had no idea what it would be like here. It's not our kind of place, and I'd have never come back except for you asking me to.'

'Could I ask you something?' Sarah said.

'Why not? You don't do anything else.'

'No, seriously.' She looked out of the window at the bushes which lined the edge of the cliff, conscious that Atlanta was smiling at her embarrassment. 'What I mean is, I wanted to know whether you had a bad time because of the people here.'

'You mean because we're black?'

'Well, yes. The thing is, this place—'

But she stopped because Atlanta was now laughing.

'That's so sweet. You really want to know, don't you? Well let me tell you,' she said quietly, leaning forward over the table. 'We're walking around the town, right. Well, everywhere we go there's people staring at us. Why? Because we're black. If I went into one of those great pubs you're talking about? There'd be looks, maybe things said. And if I was with Ed we'd be wondering if there'd be real trouble. Maybe someone pushing past or saying he'd spilt their drink, and there'd be a group of them, and just him. Now he used to be in the army, right? So I'm not saying he'd get hurt. But it doesn't make for a relaxing time. I don't let it get to me. If I did, I'd go mad. But I know it's there all the time.'

'I know Hunstanton can be a bit rough,' Sarah said.

'But there's some beautiful villages further along the coast.'

Atlanta was still amused but her voice held an edge where the anger showed through.

'You know what? We were in one of those villages, right, and there was an antique shop and we went in and had a look round. They had a sign up about a holiday cottage and so I asked the woman who ran the place about it. And d'you know what she said? She told me she didn't think it would suit me. Straight up, that's what she said. So what am I supposed to make of that?'

Sarah tried to speak but Atlanta talked her down, her eyes flashing with remembered anger.

'No one wants us here. No one. Not them,' she went on, glancing over at the only other occupants of the café, a retired couple sitting side by side and staring out to sea unaware they were involved. 'Not even you.'

She sat back, taking her turn to stare at the mist outside. Sarah could think of nothing to say that wouldn't risk making things worse.

The woman came over from behind the counter and picked up their plates.

'Was that all right for you?' she asked.

'Yeah,' Atlanta replied.

'Will you want anything else? No point going out in that,' the woman went on, nodding at the weather outside, 'and we've got apple and blackcurrant crumble special. You want something hot in you on a day like this.'

'That would be lovely,' Atlanta said, smiling up at her. 'Two coffees and two crumbles.'

The woman nodded and went back to the counter.

'That's what I need. Sugar and fat.' Atlanta stretched

her arms out above her head, unconsciously relaxing. 'You got her to do that, didn't you? You're in it together.'

'I've never seen her before in my life,' Sarah said truthfully, trying to keep up with Atlanta's changes of mood.

'Like shit,' she replied, grinning. 'Anyway, like I said, I like it here.' She leant back expansively, her feet up on the chair next to her. 'It's got a bit of style. Retro.'

'I think it was always like this.'

'Whatever.' For the first time since they had started out, Atlanta looked positively cheerful. 'These coffees . . . This time I'm paying.'

While Atlanta settled up and then disappeared, presumably to find the toilets, Sarah called her brother Patrick at his surgery. He sounded less than pleased to be interrupted but something in the tone of her voice made him put his irritation aside.

'Don't worry,' he said. 'It's not too bad a moment. What do you want to know?'

'I've been wondering about something since last night. This Diazapam stuff. How much would you need to take to knock you out?'

'To be honest I don't know; I'd have to look it up. But it's quite powerful stuff.'

'And the effects would vary from person to person?'

'That's right.'

'What are the symptoms?'

'It's like any sedative. You start to feel sleepy, perhaps in ten or twenty minutes, or faster if you're tired or have been drinking. You fall into a deep sleep quite rapidly. It lasts several hours, perhaps even more. You wake up pretty groggy, perhaps disoriented.

'Is it like being asleep, or like a coma?'

'It varies. Some people can go into a very deep state. You could shake them, slap them, and get no reaction.'

'And if you were taking something else, like alcohol or another drug, that could have an effect, couldn't it?'

'Yes. Alcohol would be another depressant, in effect, so it could work on top of the effects of the Diazapam.'

'And what if you'd had a kidney infection?'

Patrick didn't say anything straight away and she wondered if he hadn't heard. Or maybe he had a patient in with him who he was having to pacify.

'Pat?'

'I'm here. Look, we'd better have a word about this. I don't want you getting me to criticize another doctor's prescribing unless I know more of the facts.'

'Don't worry about that,' she said bitterly. 'The doctor concerned is dead.'

He paused again and then said, 'All right. If someone had a kidney condition and say their kidneys weren't working properly, then there'd be a real danger in prescribing them any kind of sedative. With the kidneys less effective, it would be much harder for the body to scrub the stuff out of the blood. And if they'd been drinking on top of that and maybe having some other kind of medication, then that would be bad.'

'How bad?'

'You could get a very severe reaction: sickness,

fainting, perhaps a coma. In an extreme case it might even be fatal.'

After she had finished the call that phrase kept going around in her head. If Nicola had been given some of these pills she might have been knocked out completely. Perhaps after doing whatever he did, if he did anything, Hannay left her to sleep it off in the shelter of the groyne, and then something happened to him.

Maybe she was in a coma when Rosemary found her. She might not have been dead at all. The combination of the drugs, the drink and the cold too, lying exposed on a beach all night, might have made her seem dead to the touch. Then Rosemary went off, leaving her there, and then the tide came in and washed her out to sea. I hope to God she didn't wake up, Sarah thought.

Chapter Sixteen

Sarah was silent as they drove back to Compton, her mood so clearly different that she noticed Atlanta glance at her a couple of times, trying to figure it out. They went first past the church, with Sarah keeping her eyes on the road, and then turned into the narrow lane beside it, muddy under the avenue of lime trees. After a few yards they stopped in front of a wooden farm gate. The path went on into the fields beyond, towards the distant pines which marked where Compton Spit began.

'Does this seem familiar at all?' Sarah asked.

'It's difficult to tell. Perhaps if it was dark . . .'

'Ed mentioned about seeing a path to the sea but that there was a gate blocking the way.'

'This could be it,' she said, as if trying to be helpful. 'I don't know, though.'

'Shall we walk down?'

'OK.'

They left the car and followed the path down, avoiding the soggier patches of grass and mud. Sarah was still preoccupied by what Patrick had said and whether she should say anything to Morton or Andy Linehan. Or to Rosemary herself.

'I'm sorry about snapping at you,' Atlanta said unexpectedly. 'Back then. In the café.'

'That's all right,' Sarah said equably, masking her surprise.

'It's just I hate it when white people ask about being black. Like, they want me to say how bad it can be so they can feel better. You know? They can hear about the things some people say, or do, and think "Isn't that awful, I wouldn't do that. I'm better than that." I hate playing that game. I hate it. But I'm sorry I had a go at you, because I know that wasn't what you meant.'

'No, it wasn't. I . . .'

For a moment there was so much Sarah wanted to say and to ask. But she didn't know where to start, or what words to use. In the end she said nothing. They crossed the iron bridge glancing down at the stream, brown and heavy with the first rains of autumn, flowing towards the marshes. Beyond, on Beach Road, the houses looked deserted and the wind pulled at the hedges and the line of poplars.

'See what I mean about the country?' Atlanta said, pointing at one of the bungalows. 'Who'd want to live here?'

'People do.'

They walked on until they were outside Rosemary's house. Sarah stopped, hesitated, reluctant to go in and face up to her suspicions.

'Will you be OK for ten minutes or so? I need to talk to one of the other witnesses.'

'Sure,' Atlanta said, taking out a phone and a small black address book. 'Take as long as you like. I've got some calls to make. And I never did get to see the sea.'

Rosemary seemed much better than the day before, much more what Sarah suspected was her confident almost imperious self. But when she said as much, as Rosemary showed her into the drawing room, the older woman looked a little put out.

'Yesterday was a shock, certainly,' she replied, standing by the fire and leaving Sarah feeling a little uncomfortable in her chair. 'I found it most tiring. But I cannot let it worry me if I want to go on living here and I have no intention of being driven out of my own home.'

'I'm sure that's right,' Sarah replied, dealing with the two dogs yapping and grovelling at her feet. 'There's no reason to think that whoever it was who did this is within fifty miles of here. Or plans to come back. They'd be mad to, for one thing.'

'Perhaps. I won't pretend I slept particularly well last night. I've asked my son Christopher to come and stay for a few days, although that's more for his benefit than mine. He works too hard and the break will do him good. But what's the alternative to staying? Long ago I decided to stay here in this house as long as I can.'

At last she sat, and looked into the flickering flames of the fire. Sarah wondered, as she tickled the ears of first one dog then the other, how much all this had taken out of her.

'I suppose,' Rosemary said at last, in a softer voice, 'I've seen enough of how elderly people are treated in so many of these places, in hospitals and nursing homes, that it frightens me to think that I might end up there.'

After a moment she seemed to snap out of her

reverie, masking her thoughts with the convention of an offer of tea. Sarah's offer of help was politely turned down and she was left to study the sitting room and the surprisingly well-kept garden where there were still a few flowers surviving from the summer. The room itself reminded Sarah of her mother's house, comfortable and shabby, with untidy piles of books, prints and paintings arranged almost at random and solid furniture covered in patterned chintz. Or like her mother's house might be in another ten or twenty years, with more clutter, more dust, the fabric on the chairs worn at the arms and the head and the fire built on the ashes of the previous day's.

At last the tea was brought in. It was so much a social occasion, waiting for the older woman to pour the tea, to offer her an unwanted slice of cake, that Sarah had to stop herself from becoming impatient. She knew that these rituals were reassuring. She felt a little reassured herself. It was hard to believe that anything could threaten this quiet civilized room and its charming spirited owner. Except that she had seen plenty of spirited people broken by a mugging or a road crash and dozens of homes – equally cozy and safe – broken open, their contents stolen or smashed.

'Do you mind if we go over it again? The finding of the bodies themselves.'

Rosemary smiled as she sank back into her chair, her hands moving to take up their usual positions where the thick fabric was most frayed.

'I'm sure you wouldn't ask unless you needed to, my dear.' She put down her cup and looked out of the window for a moment as if gathering herself before beginning. She must have told the tale four or five times already, Sarah thought. Not only the police, but there would be her son, her friends and neighbours, to worry her with questions.

'At first, I thought it was an old sack or a piece of driftwood,' she was saying. 'It was only when I was closer that I could see it was a body. His eyes were open and so was his mouth.' She didn't need to shut her eyes to bring back the scene. It was in front of her as she stared into space.

'I could see he was dead straight away.'

Rosemary paused and looked out of the French windows again. It couldn't be easy, Sarah thought, to stay on in this isolated house, alone, far from help. Even now, with the police still about, it would be eerie. But how much worse it would get in the days and weeks to come, when the days got shorter and the storms blew up and the police were long gone, leaving her completely alone. Then she would start to think of whoever had done this thing returning.

'I looked up and down the beach but there was no one around; there very rarely is at that time. Further along you might find those fishermen there all night with torches and gas stoves and whatnot, but no one ever comes along this part of the coast except when the weather's good, or sometimes for birdwatching. But I suppose they only do that when it's light.'

She leaned forward and took an ashtray from the table, balancing it on one arm of the chair, and then slowly pulled out a cigarette and lit it.

'So I called to the dogs. They were excited, running all over the place, sniffing at things and making fools of themselves, and Daisy wouldn't come. So I went to fetch her. But when I got there she'd found the girl.'

'Nicola?' Sarah said, her voice catching. These were the words that mattered.

Rosemary nodded.

'Was she in the water?' Sarah prompted.

'No, a couple of feet away.'

'Could you describe how she was lying?'

'Of course.' She tapped the ash off her cigarette, her hand shaking a little. 'Well, she was just by the side of the breakwater, facing towards it, with one arm stretched out above her head and her head partly resting on it but also partly rolled forward towards the sand.'

Sarah wondered whether she ought to put the next question at all. But the idea was fixed in her mind and she had to know the answer.

'Yesterday you said something about her looking as if she were asleep.'

'That's right. It was a little like that. She didn't have a mark on her. Except that she was so very pale.'

'And was she curled up like she was asleep, do you think?'

'That's how it seemed. As if she had died in her sleep.'

She crushed out her cigarette and started to take another one from the packet but her hands were shaking too much and instead she clasped the ends of the chair. While Rosemary gathered herself, Sarah looked around the room, at the shelves of old paperbacks, the clutter of photograph frames along the manetelpiece and on the side tables. She noticed the pattern of dirt encroaching along the skirtingboards, the faint patina of grime around the light switch. Rosemary would not be one to tolerate dirt in any form, had she noticed it, which led Sarah to wonder whether the older woman's eyesight might be failing her.

'But was she cold?' she asked after a while.

'Quite cold. And there was a blue tint around the lips.'

'Did you feel for a pulse?'

'Of course.' There was a touch of the hospital matron there. Sarah felt rebuked and wondered if her suspicions were no more than macabre fancies.

'And she was a few feet from the sea?'

'That's right.'

Sarah had one more question she had to ask: 'If she was dead, why did you put your coat over her?'

Rosemary stared at her for a moment as if trying to assess what lay behind the question. But then she shrugged a little, as if on reflection she didn't care too much one way or the other.

'She was so young,' she said softly, staring into the flames of the fire. 'And she looked so cold with her arms and neck bare. It didn't make sense, of course. I knew that at the time. But it felt right. Why do we close the eyes? Why do we draw the sheet up over the face? I've done it so many times but I still can't answer that for certain. For them maybe. For us certainly. A little bit of respect and a certain amount of super-stition. Mostly, in my case, because it has always been done that way. We have always covered the faces of the dead. And I see no reason why I should decide that those before me were wrong.'

Sarah had to blink back a tear, thinking of Nicola Page and her growing certainty about how she had come to die. She didn't want the other woman to see and she stared at her notebook, wrote random letters, as if she was intent on making notes of what Rosemary had said.

'Would you like more tea?'

'No, thanks. I should be going.' Sarah didn't look up. 'I should leave you in peace.' She didn't want to admit to herself that she felt as if she was betraying a confidence. So she stood, shook hands and tried to ignore the lump in her throat.

Sarah climbed to the top of the dunes, from where she could see Atlanta further along the path, almost half-way to the Red House, a dark figure against the grey of the shingle and low clouds. But instead of following or calling out to her, she stepped onto the beach itself to where Rosemary had found Nicola Page, close beside one of the breakwaters. The sea had eaten away at the eastern side of the wooden wall, scouring out the shingle to leave a deep depression with a perfect floor of fine sand. Apart from a pool of water by the groyne itself, it was damp rather than wet, which she found some compensation when she lay down on it.

She moved around as Nicola might have done, trying to get comfortable. She drew up her legs, rested her head on one outstretched arm. The sand yielded a little, moulding itself to her shape, and she found the whole thing surprisingly soporific, listening to the sea, feeling the deep, growling vibration which each wave sent through the mass of the beach itself. On a warm night after something to drink it would be easy enough to slip from tiredness into sleep.

It could have been this way. Not if she'd fallen

asleep, though; she'd have woken long before dawn, stiff and cold. But if she'd been drugged, if Hannay had drugged her, she might have lain here, ill but alive, until the waters claimed her.

Then, above the sound of the sea washing against the shingle, she heard footsteps and opened her eyes to see Atlanta standing above her. Sarah couldn't read her expression.

'Is this where it happened?' Atlanta asked, her voice muffled by the collar of her coat.

'Yeah, just around here.'

Sarah expected the other woman to say something more but she looked away, out to sea. Then, as Sarah scrambled to her feet and brushed the grains of sand from her jeans, Atlanta stepped cautiously down the beach, skirting the pools of water, and walked to the water's edge so that each breaking wave spread a carpet of foam almost to her feet.

'You're still looking for them, aren't you?' she said when Sarah joined her.

'Yeah.'

'That's so horrible. To think of them out there.' Atlanta looked away from the horizon, down at the dead seaweed and the other rubbish strewn along the beach, turning over an empty plastic bottle delicately with the toe of her boot. A trickle of deep brown water spilled onto the sand.

'Will you find them?'

'Probably.'

Atlanta stared at her for a moment with a look Sarah could not fathom, and then without saying anything else she started back up the dunes, walking so quickly that Sarah had to half jog to catch her up.

Back at the car, there was a message to call Andy Lineham. A yacht had reported finding a body and the Yarwell lifeboat was going out to investigate. As Sarah started the engine and turned up the heating, she noticed that Atlanta was shivering despite her coat.

'I'm sorry,' Atlanta said. 'I know it's much worse for you.' She looked away, towards the village and the trees and the tower of the church. 'I don't envy you your job.'

'No,' Sarah agreed.

Chapter Seventeen

The lifeboat station was at Yarwell Point, only a few minutes' drive away. They parked by the holiday camp, on the other side of the sea wall to the lifeboat station. Sarah suggested to Atlanta that she might prefer to go on to the hotel, that it could take an hour or more, but she was happy to stay.

'Take as long as you like. I might do some sketches,' she said, seemingly back to her usual self-possessed, amused state.

'Sketches? What of?' Sarah asked in surprise.

'I don't know yet, do I?'

She leant into the back of the Jeep and opened her bag, pulling out first a sketch pad and then a bright orange furry pencil case.

'I had one of those,' Sarah said. 'At school.'

'Yeah?' Atlanta replied as if she couldn't care less, continuing to dig around in her bag, looking for a sweater. Clothes spilled onto the back seat.

'Don't you have anything but black clothes?' Sarah asked, nettled.

'What's wrong with black?'

'It's depressing. Like funerals.'

'Maybe you go to the wrong kind of funerals.' Atlanta pulled out a sweater and held it up to the

147

light, considering. 'That's where me and Ed first got it together, you know. At a funeral. I was a bit down and so we headed off for a drink, and things sort of went from there.'

Sarah didn't say anything. She was thinking of Tom's funeral, of them all standing around outside in the churchyard, sweltering in black under a cloudless sky, grateful when the time came to file into the cool of the church.

Sarah watched Atlanta as she followed the path past the café and towards the beach, sketchbook in one hand, the hem of her coat flapping around her calves, stepping carefully around the puddles.

The holiday camp was set back a little from the point itself, sheltered by some trees, but the lifeboat station was right on the end, open to the battering of the wind and even, if the wind and the tide were both high, of the sea as well. It was made of steel panels on a steel frame, painted white all over except for the bright red roof, and stood on a vast block of concrete with a ramp at the front to launch the boat and drag it back in afterwards. But it wasn't the main lifeboat Sarah was interested in but the smaller inflatable which was much more suitable for inshore work, for nosing around the sandbars and creeks. Two of the crew, dressed in their orange drysuits, red helmets and life vests, were fussing over the boat, readying it for launch. She wondered if they were the same crew who had gone out the day Tom was lost; if they had helped search for his body afterwards. She remembered standing at this very spot, looking out to sea, waiting for news, turning over and over again in her mind the one question that she had to have an answer to. Not was Tom alive. She had known at once he was dead, somehow. It was the question of what he was doing on the boat with Kelly Newsom.

Kelly, who had finally managed to swim ashore. Who had raised the alarm. Who had been at school with Tom. An old friend, he had said, as if she might once have meant more. Kelly, who flirted with him even when Sarah was there, so that Tom was left a little embarrassed, not sure whether to ignore it, pretend it wasn't happening or laugh it off and risk upsetting one or both of them.

Sarah had wanted to tell him that it didn't matter. That she knew he would never betray her, that a thousand Kellys could surround him at parties, looking up at him with that special brightness in her eyes, striking poses, and smoothing down her gauzy dress, asking him as a special favour to fetch her another drink. Or sit draped alongside him on a sofa, laughing at his jokes, touching him more than she needed to, pretending to be a little more drunk, more flirty, than she was. None of it mattered, because she had known he would never betray her.

But they had all been so evasive, so cautious about why Kelly was on the boat. She wondered why Tom hadn't told her he was taking Kelly out for a sailing lesson. And why would Kelly want to learn to sail, anyway? It was so out of character. Somebody – she had no idea who, the whole day had blurred so much – had mentioned that they had been out several times. Someone else, not meeting her eye, had muttered something about them always being close.

And so she had spent the afternoon feeling her whole life slowly fall apart. She had tried to convince herself that he was too good a sailor to come to harm, that the seas were calm, warm too, that they knew where he was and there were plenty of searchers, that he would soon be brought ashore, grinning sheepishly, wrapped in a blanket, feeling embarrassed at having put the authorities to such trouble.

She had pictured that public reunion and tried to do the same for the private one: they would lie in bed and she would touch him, rediscover him, and hold him so he would never leave her again. But neither had happened. As the day wore on and night fell, she had seen the hope that others had spoken of so casually, so certainly, fade away. Some of the waiting crowd looked grim, others drifted away and new figures, hanging back as if ashamed of their ghoulish curiosity, had gathered on the sea wall behind her, so that she sometimes caught sight of them out of the corner of her eye and quickly looked away.

Even later, when she had found out the truth, she still couldn't square it with her memories of him. How much of the time they had been together had been a lie? It was impossible to know. Maybe from the start. He had known Kelly longer than he had known her.

Sarah jumped down from the sea wall, suddenly anxious to be moving rather than thinking, and walked hurriedly over to the station itself. The doors to a smaller shed at one side were standing open and as she approached a man came out. She recognized the weathered face, the hard brown eyes and the reassuring smile and remembered him as the owner of a record shop in the upper part of town where Tom used to go browsing from time to time. The passing years hadn't changed him much, though the beard was a little more grizzled. He certainly seemed to know her and shook her hand firmly.

'Jim Stewart,' he said. 'It's very good of you to come,' he added, leading her through the boathouse into a cramped office. 'I suspect it's not your body, if it's one at all. The report's come from a yacht called the *Salamander*, three miles off the coast. About due north of here.'

Sarah could picture the chart clearly, and knew where this must be.

'On Sheep Sand?'

'Yes,' he replied, a little surprised. 'Or just off them. A bank called the Knock.'

'I've heard of it.'

'Yeah?'

'Constable Delaney used to do a lot of dinghy sailing,' Nick said, appearing unexpectedly behind them. He was wearing an orange drysuit and helmet and carrying a life jacket casually over one arm. She'd forgotten he might be on duty with the inshore boat.

'I've never been out there,' she said.

'Good thing too,' Jim said firmly. 'It's pretty wicked, whatever the weather. A flat calm like today's best but that means you can't see a damned thing, likely as not.'

'As I'm about to find out,' Nick said, stuffing some equipment into a bag. He looked up at Sarah, struck by a thought. 'You'd be very welcome to come with us.'

She didn't want to go. She hadn't been out in a boat since Tom had died. She told herself there was little point in going. They knew everything there was to know about the tides and currents, or about finding a sandbank which would be hardly higher than the sea around it. There was plenty to be going on with back at the office.

But she sensed there was something of a challenge in Nick's voice and in the end that decided her.

'If you're sure I wouldn't be in the way.'

'Not at all,' he said easily.

'You know it won't be pretty, if we find anything,' Jim said hesitantly. 'Though I expect you're used to that in your line of work.'

'That's right,' she said with more confidence than she felt.

They found her a drysuit, life jacket and helmet and went back to the beach, where the boat was sitting in its cradle, the water lapping around. They helped her climb along the frame of the trailer and into the unfamiliar boat. Nick came out with occasional orders which were more like comments on what Ray Hall, the other crewman, was already doing. Jim sat in the bows, watching them but taking no part. Sarah realized he was a passenger too, and that usually Nick and Ray alone would take the boat out. She stashed herself out of the way and watched as they cast off, let the current carry the boat away from the sand and then gunned the engine. The boat turned in its own length and headed out to sea.

They were past the point and into the main channel before Nick broke the silence. 'Any more news about the inquiry?'

She would have told him but not in front of the others. She muttered something about there being nothing significant.

'I heard they'd been stabbed,' Ray said with a hint of relish which Sarah didn't find surprising. Ray was the kind of short, cocky man she and her colleagues so often encountered when called to a domestic dispute or a fight in a pub. He would enjoy starting something violent, or joining in, as much as hearing about it. Yet here he was in a lifeboat crew, giving his time, perhaps even risking his life on occasions, to help people he didn't even know.

'The man had,' she said, turning slightly to bring him into the conversation. 'The woman we don't know about. That's why we're so keen to find the bodies.'

'Local, were they?'

'From Norwich.'

'Ah. Right.' Norwich wasn't exactly foreign but it could explain quite a lot of strange behaviour. Like being killed.

'Was it the boyfriend, d'you think?' Ray asked.

'There was that love triangle in Frampton last year,' Jim said unexpectedly. 'The man killed his wife, then himself, when he found out she was seeing someone else. Could be something like that, couldn't it?'

'Horrible thought,' Nick said. 'But I reckon it's got to be a stalker. Some kind of nutcase.'

Listening to their thoughts, she wondered if she or anyone in the police knew any more than that. The obvious possibilities but still no idea who, or why.

'We'll be about fifteen minutes going out to Sheep Sand,' Nick said. 'Can't go much faster with visibility the way it is. Beats me how the yacht saw anything in this.'

'Maybe it's a bit clearer further out,' Jim suggested. 'Sometimes that's the way it is.'

They ran on, saying little except for Ray asking Jim's advice about a van he was considering buying. There was some question about the MOT certificate and Sarah tried not to think about the legality of what Ray was planning to do.

They fell silent and Sarah began to find the way the billowing grey curtain parted in front of them hypnotic. It seemed to have its own substance and occasionally, when it swirled a little thicker, she almost flinched as they passed through it. But they eventually came out into daylight and Nick, who never seemed to doubt where they were, grunted in satisfaction and turned up the throttle.

'Where are we now?' she shouted above the increased roar of the outboard motor.

'Two miles north of Yarwell, more or less. In a minute we'll head east again.'

Though the sea was calm and they were still going fairly slowly, she began to realize why these launches needed the foam mats in the bottom of the boat. Each time it hit a wave the shock went right through her. An hour of this would be tiring and much more than that an agony.

'These boats can stay out for hours, if we need to,' Jim replied, when she said as much. 'Three hours easy.'

'A bloke I know's got one fitted with long-distance tanks,' Ray said. 'Says he could sail across to Holland from here.'

'Says, maybe,' Jim said sourly. 'Like to see him do it.' He turned to Sarah. 'They're all right inshore, these inflatables; great for getting damn fools off sandbanks but in a big sea they'd be over in no time.'

'We never go out in anything above a force six,'

Nick said with a smile. 'Anything more than that and we leave it to Jim's all-weather boat. Or the helicopters.'

He broke off, slowed the boat down and took a last bearing on a distant buoy.

'This yacht was going down the middle channel when this lot clamped down on them,' he went on. 'Can't be from around here or they'd've known better.'

The engine was pushing them along so slowly that the main motion was up and down, each wave lifting the boat and sliding it down into the following trough. The mist drifted past in thin cobwebs, and from time to time it fell back to show a wider expanse of flat grey water.

She found herself staring at Nick's hand, the fingers spread out where he was leaning against the smooth side of the boat. It was odd that he bit his nails, she thought. He was otherwise such a relaxed, outgoing man. A brave man, too. It must have taken some courage to be the one to come and tell her that Tom was missing.

She wondered if he was thinking of that time, that search. The lifeboat must have done exactly this, nosing through the mist, listening out for a cry, scanning the baffling curtains of fog for a glimpse of a darker shape or a gleam of orange or yellow. That time, though, they had still had some hope.

She thought of taking his hand. It would be a comfort. But she knew he would take it the wrong way. He would think it meant both less and more.

The quiet was broken by the slap of water against the rubber sides of the boat and further away the cries of gulls. No one spoke. Jim had his eyes trained forward, ready to respond if anything loomed through the fog, while Nick peered away to his right. But most of all they listened, either for a hail from the yacht or the breaking of waves on the sandbar.

It will be Hannay, Sarah thought. The two bodies had come to fill her thoughts, and she pictured Nicola Page lying peacefully on the sand, seemingly asleep, as if at any moment she would stretch and sit up, looking around her in surprise. Hannay though was a rotting corpse, waterlogged, bloated, staring eyes, wrapped in slime. The idea of his rising from the waves was abominable.

After a while Nick turned the nose of the boat round a few degrees. Soon she could hear another metallic sound above the thud of the diesel: a mournful clanging as if a cow, lost on a bank and cut off by the rising tide, was slowly turning its head and jangling the bell beneath its neck.

'Sheep Buoy,' Jim said by way of explanation. 'It's an old one. Most of 'em have fog horns now 'stead of bells.'

They reached the buoy a few minutes later and watched it sway to and fro. It had originally been painted bright green with a huge letter H in white, but the paint was flaking and it was stained brown around the water level. A seagull flew by. And then they heard voices, seemingly close by.

'Ahoy,' Jim called in an immense voice. 'Ahoy, *Salamander.*'

The cry was returned, and though Sarah had no idea which direction it had come from Nick had no hesitation in shearing off to the left. In a few moments they were pulling alongside a long white-hulled yacht, drifting in the current, its sails flapping limply in the still air.

The skipper of the yacht leant over the rail to tell him that they had lost sight of the body – if that's what it was – before they had a chance to bring it on board. The man looked like a City broker, well fed and with soft skin. His sailing gear was expensive and still immaculate, the boat the latest model. He was trying to sound professional and in command but his voice betrayed his excitement.

Sarah felt a little sick now the body was near. In a way she hoped it was Nicola. It would be better for her family, her friends, and she felt more sympathy for them. But she hated the thought of seeing what was left of that sharp young face.

They began to circle the yacht slowly, looking out keenly, widening the circle slightly each time. Within a few minutes the yacht had vanished into the mist and they were left with the noise of the engine and the oppressive blanket of fog.

'Is there much chance of finding the body?' she asked.

'If it is a body. Could be anything.' Nick thought about it. 'Remember when we found that cow?'

'Fuck, that was nasty.' Ray's laugh was like a bark.

'I stood under a shower for half an hour and I could still smell it.'

'That's just you, Nick.'

'Very funny.'

They ploughed on through the mist.

'The worst of it,' Jim said, 'is that if it is for real, they could have got it on board themselves. Saved us the journey. I bet they didn't fancy the look of it. Or the smell.'

'They'd leave it in the water?' Sarah asked.

'Oh yes. I've known that before. A real seaman wouldn't do it but some of these weekend types . . . Thinking too much of their paintwork. It's a hell of a business, cleaning up afterwards.'

She thought about this. The waves were the same, the note of the engine and the ever-tearing curtain of mist. But the seagulls were flocking more thickly, a few sitting on the water, jaunty, watching them with hard eyes. Others were calling and flying around, their legs fanned out to slow them down as they fluttered past their heads and onto the surface of the sea.

And soon afterwards they came upon a dark bundle in the water, shining, awash. Ray produced a boathook and prodded at the shape, which rolled half over and then back again. As it broke the surface, a vile stench rose up, of stagnant water and rotting flesh, hitting them with the same force as a blow.

'Jesus.'

For a moment, Sarah thought that the skin had turned blue-black, rotting into a shiny, leather-like case. She thought, *I mustn't scream, or be sick*.

Then it rolled over again, a horribly stumpy arm rose up and she saw it for what it was – the flipper of a dead seal. The tail rose to the surface and then she caught sight of the dog-like head, partly eaten away by sea creatures.

It only took them twenty minutes to reach the bar which lay outside Yarwell Harbour and the breeze coming over the front of the boat as they sped along was welcome. It wafted away the lingering traces of the smell of the seal and it gave them a sense of purpose, of direction, after a wasted trip.

The lifeboat crossed the bar, bucketing a little where the waves broke up in disorder as they passed over the sandbank below, into the main channel. Here the outgoing tide was now running in the same direction as the outflow from the river and even with the outboard motor at full throttle the boat hardly made any headway against the current. Nick was used to this and steered almost to one side of the channel, following a line of red plastic markers.

'You have to take it wide unless you want to spend all day out here,' Jim said, forgetting she knew the harbour well. 'If you're out in the middle of the run you're being pushed back almost as much as you're making.'

The boat then turned to cut across the stream as quickly as possible but even so was carried a hundred yards further out by the combined weight of the river and the ebbing tide. Sarah thought of the signs all around the harbour, warning against bathing. The current from the river Ash meant that anyone going in, especially in the outer harbour when the tide was heading out, would have little chance of swimming back to land. Someone had been swept out and drowned only last year. That was the main reason for the inshore lifeboat. During the summer, hardly a weekend went by without someone needing to be rescued after falling into the harbour, or being caught by the tide on the flat expanses of sand beyond the point, or being blown out to sea clinging to a lilo.

Ray took out a mobile phone and dialled a number.

'I'm on the boat,' he said when he finally got through. 'Any messages?'

They touched gently on the sand just below the lifeboat house. Almost without thinking, Sarah slid overboard into the water to help brace the boat against the rush of the current. It was just what she would have done in the old days, out sailing with Tom. Thinking of this brought back the memory of the seal they had found and she fought to keep down the bile that rose in her throat. It had taken them ten days to find Tom's body. She hadn't seen it, but she knew it would have been much the same.

Atlanta was sitting in the passenger seat of her car, the seat back as far as it would go, her feet up on the dashboard. She was reading her book so intently that she jumped when Sarah opened the door.

'Jeez,' she said, and then relaxed. 'Any luck?'

'Nothing,' Sarah replied shortly.

They set off with Atlanta at first explaining how absorbed she was by the story but then falling silent as Sarah continued to stare mutely out of the window. She was thinking about the time after the funeral when it had seemed the easiest thing in the world to drop everything that linked her to Tom. She had left the flat, moving back to stay with her mother. She had taken a job in Diss, working in an electronics factory, soldering together circuit boards without even knowing what they were for and listening to Radio One or to the chat of the other women on the line, her mind deadened by the hours and by her sleepless nights.

She could still smell the sudden whiff of solder, the sharp sweet solvents they used to clean the boards, the shouts carrying on the winter air as the evening shift left, calling to each other about which pub or bar they would meet in; as if the hours at work hadn't been enough.

Then she had joined the police. Three years of training, of dull routine and occasional moments of excitement and fear. The growing realization she was in the wrong job. But now, before she could leave, a final twist. She was back at Yarwell, back searching for a man's body. And so, despite Tom's betrayal in screwing the other girl, his betrayal in dying, she remained tied to him.

Chapter Eighteen

Back at the station, Morton wasn't in his office or the incident room. Sarah was conscious at once of the conversations broken off as her colleagues glanced over at them. Atlanta, with her hands clenched deep in her coat pockets and her face set in what could have been any expression but was probably resentment, followed her, not catching anyone's eye. Sarah thought again of the pubs of Hunstanton.

'He's in the canteen,' Linehan said as he passed by. 'Why not join us?' But Sarah had no intention of seeking him out there and said they'd wait for him in his office.

'Sure,' he said, a little surprised, and wandered off.

While they waited Atlanta phoned Ed and Sarah wrote up her notes, still wondering how much to tell Morton of her suspicions about how Nicola died. She could imagine Rosemary's appalled reaction if she discovered they suspected she might have left Nicola to drown. Sarah didn't want anyone saying anything to her unless they were absolutely sure. And even then would it help? Perhaps it was better to leave it be.

She found herself listening to Atlanta's conversation. It wasn't so much the detail as the sense of amusement as she described the journey to Ed. She could hear a couple of bursts of laughter too from the phone.

'Yeah, she's been very good.' Sarah looked up to see Atlanta smiling over at her. 'She's put up with me going on at her all day. She even bought me lunch.'

'. . .'

'No, but she tells me it's very, very comfortable. A minibar and everything. So I'm OK, star.'

'. . .'

'No, I saw the place,' Atlanta said in a different tone. 'It's really horrible to think of what happened.'

'. . .'

'You do that,' she said, smiling again. 'Tomorrow night, or the night after for sure.'

Morton came in then, clearly surprised to find Atlanta with her feet up on his desk. But he greeted her politely once she had hurriedly sat up and finished her call. Surprisingly he didn't suggest that Sarah stay but only asked her to arrange for some tea to be sent in.

This done, Sarah went back to the incident room, only to face a series of more or less subtle questions about her witness: who was she, what had she seen and what had she been doing in Norfolk in the first place? She soon tired of this, went back upstairs to her own office and sat disconsolately at her desk. There were a couple of fresh envelopes in her in tray and she opened them more to take her mind off her work than with the idea of doing anything constructive. The first was an expenses claim, returned unpaid with a query over one of the receipts.

'Shit,' she said, as she'd been counting on the claim being paid to avoid going overdrawn at the bank.

'Swearing to yourself?' David said, pushing open the door with one foot and juggling a mug of tea and a pile of reports. 'First sign of madness.'

'They've sent this poxy form back and there's nothing wrong with it.'

'Give them a call.'

'At ten past five? They'll be long gone.' But she picked up the phone and waited while it rang.

'How's the case?' he asked.

'I'll tell you all about it later. First I need to find a camcorder. You haven't got one, have you?'

'Me? No. But Alice has one. You know, Alice in the press office.'

'Brilliant.'

'Oh, I've taken a couple of messages. That seems to be my role in life these days. One from your friend Nick Walton, one from some bloke called Alban. Are there really people called Alban? He left a number.'

Sarah nodded, still waiting for someone to answer the phone.

'I'm surprised you've got time for all this,' David said, leaning back in his chair and watching her with amusement. 'Now you're working for CID.'

'They've got me as a tour guide. That and searching for dead bodies. Not exactly what I'd imagined CID being about.' She slammed down the phone.

'How do you find it, working for Morton?'

'I don't see much of him. He seems all right.' She looked at him more closely. 'Why do you ask?'

'No reason.'

'No, really. What's up?'

'Oh, just gossip.'

'What gossip's that?' she insisted, and he looked a little uneasy.

'Ructions at the top, mainly. Some doubt about whether Morton's handling it right. That sort of thing.'

'He seems to be doing fine to me.'

'Well,' David said, smiling. 'you're on the inside now.'

'What things are they saying?'

David turned back to his computer, now clearly discomfited at having told tales. 'Nothing much. Only that Morton is sure it's a domestic which most people don't buy. Plus this evidence going missing.'

'What evidence?'

'Hadn't you heard? Some scene of crime stuff was sent over to the labs in Huntingdon but never got there. A holdall someone had left on the beach and a few other things. They're turning the place over. Same here, too. But no trace.'

'Was it important?'

'No one knows. I don't suppose there's any way of telling now that it's gone,' he said gloomily. 'But if we don't make an arrest, the knives'll be out over it.'

'They can't blame Morton for that,' she protested, but David only shrugged.

'They can and they will. Anyway, the other thing is the defence will make hay about it, if it ever gets to trial.'

Alice Perryman was pecking at the keyboard of her computer, a coffee and half a sandwich at her side. She pushed a pile of papers aside so that Sarah could perch on the edge of her desk.

'I hear you're working on the Compton case,' she said, brushing a few breadcrumbs from her lap.

'Sort of.'

'Well, it's come as a relief to me, that's for sure. It's saved me from doing yet another bloody crime prevention launch. Can you think of anything more boring? Fortunately no one's going to run a story like that when the seas are filled with murdered doctors and nurses. The *EDP* are going to splash on it in the morning, the BBC are still thinking about pulling their crew off the bypass story for tonight's bulletin and now the nationals are sniffing around. After all, it's got everything they want:.sex, mystery, not too far from London and some decent hotels to stay in.'

She drew breath and Sarah took the chance to ask her favour.

'I've got a videotape which the nurse had. Can you play it back?'

Sarah handed over the tape, still in the thick plastic evidence bag. Alice peered at it then nodded.

'No problem.'

She went over to a video at the far side of the room and switched on the TV, then dropped the tape into a larger cartridge and shoved it into the player. After a few seconds of black, the tape showed a group of six or seven people in their twenties, casually dressed, walking across a beach holding a collection of bags, blankets, folding chairs and sports gear. A dark-haired man at the front was holding a cricket bat, sometimes striking at the sand and sometimes waving it high above his head like a standard to lead the others. A woman was taking off her shoes and then began to splash through the pools on the sand. Another man, who might have been Alban but was too near the back for her to be sure, had a case of lager which he kept swapping from shoulder to shoulder.

'Which one is the victim?' Alice asked.

'The one at the back, talking to the girl in the white sweater. I think that's her.'

'And the man?'

'I can't see him. I don't think he's there.'

Sarah recognized Amina from the ward and Suzy who had come in while she was searching Nicola's room. The group walked on while a man with a neatly-trimmed black beard and a manic grin picked up a piece of seaweed and began to wave it at one of the women and then chase her across the beach, her screams and laughter oddly muffled by the tape.

'You can't see her very clearly,' Alison said as the scene changed to show them all sitting around in a circle, having a picnic. One of the women was leaning back-to-back against the man with the cricket bat but otherwise it was impossible to be sure who were in couples and who were single. Nicola was sitting with her arms wrapped around her knees, facing away from the camera out to sea.

'The quality's not as good as I'd hoped,' Sarah said.

They kept watching though. There was a horrible fascination, Sarah thought to herself, about seeing someone you knew was dead. As if there should be something to mark them out, some sign of foreknow-ledge. It was eerie, too, that she was on a beach. And one of the people there, so innocently mucking about or lazing in the sunshine, with cheese and bread and salad and cans of lager around them, may have killed her.

The scene changed again. They were still on a beach, but now it showed just Nicola and a thin, fair-haired man in his early twenties. The sunshine was gone and there was no way of knowing if it was later on the same day or a different day, though Nicola was now wearing a silk top. It was certainly colder because she looked chilled. Her trousers were flapping in the breeze like flags and she held her hands in front of her with the sleeves of her top pulled down over them. The man had his arm rather clumsily around her and the two of them were drawing patterns in the sand with a stick.

There was something about the way that they stood and then crouched down, he explaining to her what-ever it was that he was drawing, she always on the point of laughing despite the cold, that Sarah found deeply saddening. They were so clearly absorbed in each other. Very much in love, her mother would have said. And now Nicola was dead.

'Who's that, then?'

'It's Nicola Page,' Sarah replied. 'And her boyfriend, I think.'

'Not the guy who was killed?'

'No.'

The camera moved around behind them, looking over their shoulders to show the pattern of lines on the sand, a pattern that meant nothing to Sarah.

'And who's holding the camera?'

'That,' Sarah said, 'is a very good question.'

She hung around, waiting until Morton called to say he had finished with Atlanta, filling in by scanning the reports from the search parties and from the coast-guard. None of them had turned up anything substantial though there was a growing pile of bagged and tagged items in one corner of the incident room: old shoes, scraps of cloth, combs, a smashed pair of glasses and a hundred other pieces of rubbish. It would be astonishing if any one of them had the slightest bearing on the case.

As she started to pack up Andy Linehan came over.

Anything?' he asked briefly.

She shook her head. 'You?'

'Nothing. We've made contact with Hannay's family; they're coming up from Surrey tomorrow morning. Page's parents are away abroad – Canada, would you believe it – and they didn't leave their address with the neighbours. There's a brother or sister, apparently, so we're trying to trace him, or her. Apart from that, nothing.'

He took a swig of coffee and yawned.

'You know,' he said, 'I think our big hope's gone.'

'What was that?'

'A third body. Someone kills the two of them then goes off and does himself in as well.'

'Him?'

'It's always a him. He'd have followed the two of them, killed them in a rage then realized what he'd done. Can't face the music. Wants out. So he tops himself. If he's a bit squeamish, he'll fix up the exhaust of his car and do it that way.'

'But nothing yet?'

'No. Unless he's in a garage somewhere or maybe deep in woodlands – funny how they choose these places, isn't it? Anyway, it means it's over to you.'

'How do you mean?'

'We'll have to crack this case the hard way. That means a body or two. And I rather think that's your job.'

Chapter Nineteen

They had booked Atlanta in to the Royal Oak, in the upper part of Yarwell. It was an old coaching inn facing onto the square, with a plain but handsome Georgian front and a warren of rooms and corridors to the rear.

'It's clean and warm,' Sarah said as they walked into the lobby, 'but it's not very lively.'

'I see what you mean,' Atlanta said, looking around at the faded carpets, the sporting prints and the racks of leaflets offering exciting days out in North Norfolk. The place was silent, the reception desk deserted though the computer sitting incongruously on the counter was switched on. Sarah called out, while Atlanta dumped her bag and sat on a chair looking unimpressed. Eventually a brightly incompetent girl turned up, all smiles, and tapped away on the computer for a while without success. In the end she found what she was looking for in an old-fashioned ledger kept beneath the counter.

'There we are, Miss Mabbott,' she said. 'You're in Room 314.'

'Thank you,' Sarah replied, taking the key. 'That's Miss Mabbott.' She pointed behind her. The girl looked startled and when Atlanta smirked at her she looked even more worried, before smiling back uncertainly.

'Third floor, fourth on the right. Let me know if there's anything you need,' she called after them as they trudged up the stairs.

The room was a pleasant surprise; not only clean and warm, as promised, but spacious and with a fine view over the town to the sea. Atlanta fell back onto one of the beds and lay sprawled out, hands behind her head.

'Too much driving,' she said, flexing her shoulders. 'I'm not used to it.'

'Could you face going out again tonight?'

'Yeah, but I need a bath first. And maybe a sleep. And something to eat.'

'There's a restaurant in the hotel.'

'Yeah, and I know what that'll be like. Lots of atmosphere and amazing food, right?'

'There's a few other places around town. D'you want me to show you around?'

'Yeah.' She sat up, suddenly enthusiastic. 'Maybe somewhere down by your very fine harbour I've heard so much about.'

They left the hotel, leaving the key at the empty reception desk, and walked towards the sea, past the bus shelter and Costcutters and the rest of the familiar fabric of the town. Without thinking, Sarah turned into Quay Street, a steep narrow lane with shopfronts and doorways that gave straight onto the street. It ran straight down to the harbour and an expanse of golden sand could be glimpsed beyond its far end, framed by the whitewashed cottages. Here too everything was much the same as Sarah remembered, except that the bakery had been extended and the old-fashioned ladies boutique had gone, to be replaced by a shop selling sports gear.

Atlanta, who had stopped to study the window display of an art shop, caught up with her.

'Did you really use to live here?'

'Yeah. Further down this street. The one on the left by that gallery.'

It hadn't changed, and certainly hadn't been touched by paint or plaster since she had moved out. If anything, the windows were dustier, the paint peeling off the woodwork in larger flakes. Sarah wondered how long it had been standing empty.

'So why did you move?'

'I wanted a change,' she replied, walking away towards the quay and ending up leaning against the rail which ran along its length. She remembered the moment she had first stood here, feeling the sun on her face, the roughly painted steel of the rail warm under her hands, hearing the chug of a boat leaving its berth, the mumble of holidaymakers strolling along behind her, the screams of the gulls. Sniffing salt and fish and warm wood. And then opening her eyes to look out over the boats crammed in beneath, and over the sandbanks and dunes to the sea beyond.

She remembered one time when she and Tom had got up at six and taken the boat out at the turn of the tide, using the ebb and the flow of the river to carry them further out than they had ever gone before, to Coldharbour Sand where the coast was only a thicker line on the horizon and they had to steer by the buoys which marked the safe channels for larger boats. The breeze had stayed steady all morning until the tide had fallen far enough to turn the sea into a maze

of sandbanks and channels, and they had threaded
amongst them until they had found a patch of sand,
free from weed and mud. Here they had drawn the
boat up, dropped the sail and chased about on the sand
like kids until they had each wrestled the other into
one of the pools of cold salt water left behind by the
retreating sea.

There had been something magical about lying on
the sea bed, knowing that in a few hours' time it would
be drowned twenty feet below the surface of the North
Sea. But in the sun the sand was soon dry enough
to spread out a rug, fetch the picnic basket, eat the
sandwiches, fruit and chocolate, and drink great gulps
of the precious water. They had made love, lying in
the shadow of the boat, alone except for a distant
coaster feeling its way down the narrow winding
channel towards the Wash. They had dozed in the sun,
only staying awake to keep an eye on the weather, and
had lingered until the incoming tide had cut the acres
of sand down to a narrow bank besieged by the sea,
then jumping aboard. The wind had stayed fair and
they had run back to Yarwell in only two hours, hardly
needing to change course or trim the sails all the way.
A fantastic day's sailing, the kind to come only once
or twice a year, the kind to savour during the long cold
winter.

The day was fading behind the lights on the quay.
Sarah could make out the green and red lights marking
the channel to the distant sea. It was cold too, though
there was no breath of wind.

For years, she had refused to think of Tom. At
first it had been a defence. The reminders had been
constant – passing the boatyard, hearing the cry of a

gull or smelling the salt on the air – but over time
these had become less pressing. Now she didn't think
of him because there was no reason to. She had her
new life. New friends too. But there were still times
when she missed him so much. After such a day, the
fear she had felt the morning before, the grim work of
searching through the remains of the girl's life and
then the search for the two bodies, she needed him –
or someone like him, or someone – to hold her.

'Are you OK?' Atlanta said, leaning on the rail
beside her.

'I'm fine,' Sarah said, standing upright abruptly.
'Come on.'

The boats which lined the quay were almost
touching the bottom as the tide ebbed away and there
was a strong smell of fish. One of the amusement
arcades was open, an oasis of flashing lights, but there
was no one inside except a couple of faintly menacing
staff. A couple of kids were sitting on a bench further
along the quay, eating chips. Apart from that, the place
was deserted; but Sarah still felt self-conscious with
Atlanta beside her. She was pleased that the mist and
the cold meant there were so few people around. The
feeling reminded her of the first time she'd come on
patrol in Yarwell soon after she joined the police. Then,
being in uniform had marked her out, had made people
treat her differently, even people she knew or recognized. It was the same now, making her think of the
times when as a child she had hated to stand out, to
be conspicuous or different in any way. And she felt
ashamed, too, that she felt that way.

They reached the end of the quay and both turned
to look back along its length, to where the setting sun

was trying to cut through the banks of cloud. To Sarah, the way the light was reflecting off the wet tarmac made the scene unexpectedly beautiful. But Atlanta, trudging along morosely, saw it differently.

'It's really, really lovely,' Atlanta said after a while, her voice heavy with irony.

'You should see it in the spring.'

'No, really. It's so beautiful. Like the south of France. San Tropez, somewhere like that.'

Sarah turned away. The gates of the boatyard were standing open and beyond was the marina and the sluices at the mouth of the river. There was no one in sight in the yard though there were lights on and a couple of cars parked by the further sheds. Nick used to have a flat above one of the sheds, partly extending over the water itself. Sarah remembered the times she had spent there after Tom's death, lying on the sofa, listening to the records Tom had liked, talking about him.

They climbed onto the wooden jetty that ran into the middle of the harbour. The piers of the jetty were made of massive baulks of timber encrusted with barnacles and weed, a little like the breakwaters on Compton Spit. Beneath their feet they could see the flow of the sea. It was unnaturally calm even for such a sheltered harbour and was hardly moving at all. A slick of weeds and leaves floated slowly by, a bright red Coke can embedded in its midst.

As a child, Sarah had always loved to swim in the sea, a living moving thing, but swimming pools had frightened her; even now she found the way the water slapped lazily against the hard smooth sides disturbing. That was how the sea was today, with the faintest of swells pulsing against the furred and slimy wood of the groynes, making a slight sucking noise. She shivered.

They walked on, falling into step, with Atlanta shrugging herself deeper into her coat and Sarah almost enjoying the fresh misty rain on her face. The marina had a few dozen boats in, mainly small yachts. The bigger boats were moored further downstream, in the estuary. The far end of the pier was closed off where the river ran beneath it in a series of sluice gates and the currents were dangerously strong. All around the quay there were life belts and warning signs. Atlanta stopped to look at one of these: DANGER. STRONG CURRENTS. NO SWIMMING AT ANY TIME.

'Not much of a holiday place, is it? You're not allowed to go swimming, even.'

Sarah felt a flash of anger at Atlanta, standing there safely laughing at the warnings while a few miles out to sea the search went on for two bodies.

'Someone drowned here last year,' she said coldly. 'They thought they knew better than the signs. They went swimming at night, after a few drinks, and three days later they washed up ten miles down the coast.'

'Don't worry about me.' Atlanta laughed. 'I'm not going in there no matter how much I drink.'

She stepped back from the edge of the harbour and walked off towards the centre of town.

'I've got to go back,' Sarah said. 'Will you be all right?'

'Yeah, no problem. I'll go back to the hotel. I could do with a sleep.'

'I'll see you there at eight, then.'

*

Back home, Sarah found her flatmate Rachel lying on the sofa, nursing a mug of tea and watching the local news on TV.

'Your case was just on,' she said, switching it off and making room on the sofa. 'Not that they said much. What have they got you doing?'

'Don't remind me,' Sarah replied, lying back and stretching out her legs. 'I've spent the whole day stuck in a car with this supposed key witness, seeing if she can spot the killer wandering about on the streets. It's a complete waste of time, of course.'

'How come?'

'We spent two hours parked in Compton, and only half a dozen people went past. I don't thing Haydon had thought it through, but I can't exactly go back and tell him. Plus we're not exactly inconspicuous. We're going around in the car, which is a huge Jeep thing, because there isn't a spare unmarked car. She's six foot tall and the only back woman for a hundred miles. Plus she only wears black clothes.'

'What's wrong with that?' Rachel asked mildly, heading for the kitchen.

'I reckon she's making some kind of point. She was wearing a black sweater and skirt, black tights and boots. Even her hat's black.'

'Do you want a glass of wine?' Rachel called out.

'No thanks. I've got to go out again in a bit.'

'So no supper, then?'

No. I'll . . . er, I'll get something while I'm out.'

Sarah went to get changed, but ended up lying on her bed in the dark, listening to the muted sound of the TV. She knew she shouldn't have become so annoyed at Atlanta, or even at Morton. The truth was she was tired, and anxious about how well she was doing her job, and worrying about seeing Nick that evening, and sick of being pursued by memories of Tom.

She thought about forgetting about them all, staying there on her bed, or spending the evening on her own sofa, watching some rubbish on the TV. But she was still intrigued by Nick's invitation, and what it might mean.

She spent a little longer than usual deciding what to wear, in the end choosing a white long-sleeved top and a navy pinafore dress she hadn't worn for years. She wanted to look her best for Nick without being obvious and without sending out the wrong signals. If she knew what they were.

'You off, then?' Rachel asked from the sofa. She taught at Frampton junior school and like most term-time evenings, she had a pile of marking to one side and a bottle of wine to the other.

'Yeah. I'll probably be late.'

'And I'm supposed to believe you're working, am I?'

Sarah glanced down at her clothes.

'I'm, er . . . I don't have to wear uniform while I'm doing this witness liaison. It's supposed to be less intimidating.'

'Anything you say, Sarah. I won't wait up for you. You have a nice time.'

Chapter Twenty

As they set off into the gathering dark, Sarah tried to remember a time when the mist had hung on so persistently. It meant that Atlanta wasn't driving too fast, so that a car caught them up and followed close behind, making Atlanta snort with annoyance. She began to fiddle with the rear view mirror.

'Isn't there something you can do with this to stop it shining in your eyes?'

'Do you want me to do it?' Sarah asked, as they drifted towards the hedge to her left.

'Yeah, thanks. I'm not used to driving without street lights.'

Sarah glanced behind.

'Pull over and let him past if he's annoying you.'

At the next stretch of straight road Atlanta did as Sarah had suggested and the other car drove past and away.

'Probably just some boy racer,' Sarah said. 'Round here driving's the most exciting thing you can do if you're seventeen.'

'Yeah? Is that what you used to do at seventeen?'

They drove through Compton and turned down the lane to the beach. It was if anything even darker among the low trees. The road was laid with rough chippings, and the sound of the tyres rolling over these drowned out any whisper from the engine. Atlanta slowed down as they passed the church, the Jeep seeming to fill the road. They parked by the gate, half in the shelter of overhanging trees. The headlights made the scene look strange, like a photographic negative, until Atlanta switched them off, leaving them in darkness except for the faint light from the dashboard.

'This is where we parked,' she said. 'I remember the gate now.'

Sarah listened to the distant sound of the sea and the faint night sounds around the car. She could imagine being here alone and finding it far too isolated, too dark.

'Did you get out at all?'

'Just for a minute.'

'Do you want to have a look around, then?'

They walked to the gate, with Atlanta looking around and Sarah watching her.

'Which way did Ed go?' she asked.

'Towards the beach. But only a little way.'

She climbed over the gate and turned to Atlanta, who followed reluctantly. They followed the path in step, as they had done earlier that day, Sarah looking up at the night sky to see a handful of stars through a gap in the clouds and Atlanta staring at the earth, picking her way around the darker patches where the path was muddy.

After a while they reached the iron bridge and crossed onto Beach Road. It was very quiet, with the buildings and trees and the dunes themselves muting the sound of the sea almost to a whisper. No noise came from any of the houses, though it was still early.

Sarah wondered how many of the residents had decided to move away for a while, perhaps until the murderer was caught. It couldn't be much fun living out here with the idea there might be a psychopath lurking or even living nearby, which made her wonder how wise it was for them to be out here at night. She wasn't sure if any of her colleagues were around and she had left her radio on the back seat of the Jeep.

They passed Rosemary Aylmer's house, dark except for a single lit window downstairs. Sarah looked back from the end of the lane, wondering what Rosemary was doing now, whether her son had arrived. If not, would she have the television or the radio on to provide the illusion of company, or forgo such false reassurance for the bare sound of the distant sea? She imagined her reading a book, a glass of red wine to hand, enjoying the wood fire and perhaps also finding comfort in the iron poker she used to stir it into a blaze.

Sarah turned to ask Atlanta if she would mind if they called on Rosemary to see if she was all right, only to find she had gone on ahead. She ran after her, as fast as she could with the dress catching at each stride, and found her standing at the top of the dunes, silhouetted against the faint starlight. It was surprising just how conspicuous Atlanta was, in the instant before she stepped out of sight. In the end Sarah caught up with her at the water's edge where she was watching the waves breaking along the shore and scurrying along the line of the nearest breakwater in jets of phosphorescent foam.

'It's beautiful, isn't it?'

But Sarah was in no mood for appreciating the

wonders of nature. She had a sudden thought that there was every reason for the killer to return. What if, somehow, he had heard about there being a witness? Rumours got around; some of her colleagues were hardly discreet. He might know the witness was back in Norfolk. It wouldn't be hard to find her if he'd heard some incautious talk in the pub, say. Or even if he only knew she was black.

Sarah looked back at the dunes. There was nothing to be seen but that meant nothing. He could have followed them. Perhaps in the car that had sped past them? It could have waited further on, lights off. Or guessed where they would go.

Atlanta picked up a stone and threw it into the dark, listening for the splash.

'We'd better get back,' Sarah called to her in a half-whisper.

Atlanta nodded, threw another stone and then dropped a couple more onto the beach. She climbed back up, smiling.

'It's amazing. So quiet.'

'It's later than I thought.'

'Sure. Whatever you want. Just seems a pity to leave.'

It was a lovely night, with the sky clearing but only the faintest of breezes and that with a hint of summer still in it. It must have been like this on the night they died. Sarah could understand why they might have come out here to sit on the beach, look at the stars, throw stones into the calm waters. But she couldn't understand how Atlanta could be so relaxed; she, after all, was the one who had actually seen the man and had managed to capture something of his menace in that drawing. But here she was, strolling along, without a single care. It needled Sarah into trying to puncture her unconcern.

'Some people would be worried about the man coming back.'

'What man?'

'The one you saw.'

'Him? He wouldn't come back, would he?' Atlanta laughed. 'Good for you if he did, though. You could capture him single-handed. Or maybe not, in that dress,' she added.

They reached the gate.

'You're not scared, are you?' Atlanta asked as she climbed over it. Looking up at her, seeing her strength and poise, Sarah wanted to believe nothing could happen to them, to either of them; that there were people who were immune from the nightmares of disease and decay and death.

But she wanted more than anything to be away from this place.

Atlanta jumped down from the top of the gate, landing lightly, and then watched Sarah hitch up her dress and climb over more carefully.

'Come on. Time to eat.'

But as they reached the car the incident room called Sarah to tell her there was another briefing she had to attend. She cursed, working out that by the time she had gone to Frampton and back, Nick would be long gone. She had been in two minds about the evening, but now it was being taken from her, she wanted it more.

'I was supposed to be meeting a friend,' she

explained when Atlanta smiled at her obvious disappointment.

'How could I guess?' was all she said in reply.

They reached the outskirts of Yarwell before Sarah spoke again. 'Would you mind if we went to meet my friend first? I haven't got his number.'

'Sure, honey. You just tell me where to go.'

They reached the pub a moment later and both went inside. Nick was by the bar, chatting to some people.

'Nice to meet you,' he said to Atlanta, and lead them both over to a quiet corner. 'You've got time for a drink, at least?' he said to them both, in spite of Sarah's explanations. And she did have time, she guessed, if she cut it fine.

He returned from the bar and immediately demanded to know what they had both been doing all day.

'I saw you, you know. Speeding through Martlesham, just before lunch. I wouldn't have believed it of you, Sarah, being police and all that.'

'I didn't have much say in the matter,' she said absently, her mind on what development might have made Morton ask the whole team to return. Meanwhile Nick and Atlanta were chatting animatedly about what Atlanta thought about the area and places Nick wanted to show her to prove it wasn't as bad as she was saying.

'Until you've eaten oysters pulled out of the sea right that minute,' he said confidently, leaning back in his chair, hands behind his head, 'you can't tell me anything about good food.'

'Well I'll try it,' Atlanta said, laughing and shaking her head. 'But I won't be happy if they're full of grit.'

'I'll risk it.'

Sarah had to go and it was inevitable that the other two would stay. After all, Atlanta knew no one in the town and Nick had been stood up and was at a loose end. But Sarah still felt upset and anxious. It seemed so unfair that yet another evening should be ruined. It seemed worse that Nick should be getting on so well with Atlanta so that when he said how sad it was that Sarah had to go and how she had to promise to make it up to him, it grated a little with her.

Putting her coat back on and downing the rest of her drink, Sarah had to try to recognize her own jealousy; it was nothing more than that. Atlanta was a good-looking woman and she and Nick were getting on well. It didn't mean anything beyond the fact that they wanted to be entertained by each other. And in any case what was Nick to her? An old friend. Nothing more.

Chapter Twenty-One

By the time Sarah arrived, Morton was already running through the developments and she slipped into a vacant seat at the back, hoping to escape notice. She soon realized he was passing on what the team had learnt about Chris Hannay.

'It could all be professional jealousy, but two different people have hinted – no more than that – he might have been fiddling some prescriptions. This may be why he moved on from St Mary's two years ago. One suggestion is he'd write prescriptions for patients that didn't exist and then pick them up on their behalf. But it may be he was nicking stuff from the hospital itself and needed Page's help. So we'll need to look tomorrow at what access Page had to controlled drugs. And that means what really happens, not what anyone tells you the system is. I hope you know well enough that no one ever works exactly by the rules. If not, just think of some of the overtime claims you lot put in.'

There were a few sniggers and one or two people shifted uneasily in their seats.

'I'd like Dines, Peterson and Ross working on that. Spend the whole day at the hospital if you need to. You might also try talking to some of Page's colleagues while they're off duty. They might open up a bit more if they aren't at work.'

Finally Morton mentioned that they had a reported sighting of a suspicious figure and that an artist's impression was being circulated. But he seemed intent on playing down the significance of the information. Sarah wondered if he had begun to think Atlanta's evidence was irrelevant, a coincidence or a distraction from the real criminal. Or perhaps he couldn't trust his own officers to keep the story to themselves.

Afterwards he asked her to stay, then led her back to his office asking how the day had gone, but as if he wanted to avoid an awkward silence and keep his real question until his door was firmly shut behind them.

'Your witnesses,' he said, waving her to a seat. 'Do you believe them?'

'How do you mean?'

'We can't ignore the fact that they were there that night. Right on the scene. The thing is, Ed Denton is known to the Met. Not a criminal record, but as the known associate of some seriously dodgy people, including a couple of big-time criminals into drugs, guns, armed robbery and the rest of it.'

'I didn't know,' she replied.

'There's no reason why you should have done. And to be fair, being a known associate doesn't mean that much. But they were there at the time.'

'But we can't start accusing then of anything. Not if we want their help.'

'I appreciate that. I only want you to keep an open mind. OK?'

'Sure. But what is it you think they were up to?'
She knew, but she wanted to hear him say it.

'Drugs. That could be the link between Hannay
and either or both of them. The stuff in the glove box
might have been samples. Or maybe there was a bigger
batch which the two of them made off with.'

'It's not very likely, is it? It would mean Page was
in it too; otherwise why drag her along? And the same
for Mabbott, too.'

'That's probably right.' Morton sounded tired and
on the edge of becoming irritated. 'I'm not saying anything; it's only an idea. But go and talk to Ross. She's
dug up some stuff and it'd be worth you two comparing
notes.'

'But do you really think Mabbott's involved as well?'

'She's the most interesting one, to be honest.
Denton is clean, as I said. But Mabbott's got a record,
apparently.'

'What?'

'The charges were dropped. But she had a formal
caution.'

'What charges?'

'Possession, with intent to supply.'

Lisa Ross was at one of the desks in the main room,
typing in some notes on the investigation database.
She was about the same age as Sarah, dark, slight
and a little intense – a great one for networking, and
cultivating her seniors and sticking the blame for
anything that went wrong onto someone else. Yet
somehow she managed to be one of the most popular
members of the team. Sarah had never been on the

receiving end of her less attractive traits but she had no intention of starting to trust her now, however cheerful her greeting.

'Morton said I should have a word,' Sarah said, regretting how abrupt it sounded. After all, they were supposed to be colleagues and she could see another officer look up in mild surprise.

'Er, yeah, that's right.' Lisa said, swinging round in her chair. 'It's nothing much. Only some background on your witnesses. Why don't you pull up a chair and I'll show you what I've found?' Lisa began to print out several pages and handed them to her, one by one. 'I ran them both through the system and got leads on them both. Then—'

'Yeah, Jeremy said all that,' Sarah cut in. 'But what I don't understand is why.'

'How do you mean?'

'Well, if you had suspicions, why didn't you tell me?'

'I was only doing a routine check.'

'But you must have had some suspicions or you wouldn't have bothered checking.'

'But I was right to check, wasn't I? After all, I've found out that they both have form.'

'But you wouldn't have checked on, I don't know, on Mrs Aylmer, would you?'

'Of course not. But what's your point?'

Sarah, surprised by the blank look the other woman gave her, wondered if she had acting skills quite out of the ordinary or whether perhaps she was in fact rather stupid.

'It doesn't matter. What's she supposed to have done?'

'Possession of drugs. Almost exactly two years ago, in London. It wasn't a conviction, only a formal caution, so there's no details on file. I haven't spoken to the arresting officer yet to find out more.'

'So what do you think this means?' Sarah asked in the end.

'Well, it means there could be a link between Mabbott and her boyfriend on the one hand, and Hannay and possibly Page on the other.'

'And what do you want me to do?'

'What do you mean?'

'Do you want me to ask them? Only if it turns out they've got nothing to do with it and then we say can they carry on helping us to find who really did it, they'll tell us to piss off, won't they?'

'I'm not telling you what to do.'

'Well it certainly sounds like it.'

She knew she should leave it there. The nearest officer had given up any pretence of typing. He'd kept his head down behind his computer screen but Sarah could almost hear his ears flapping.

'I'm only doing what you should have done,' Lisa said defensively.

'They're not suspects.'

'Do you really think they had nothing to do with it?'

Sarah stopped, surprised. Had any of the rest of the team come to the same conclusion?

'I don't believe it.'

'Well, you're making a big mistake,' Lisa replied, her confidence growing. 'Think about it. What were they doing there?'

'They were on a day trip.'

'It doesn't make any sense. How many people like that come up here for the day?'

'D'you mean, how many black people?' Sarah could hear her own voice thicken with anger.

'If you like, yes. How many black people?'

Sarah stared at her colleague, saw her set face and hard glittering eyes, and wondered what she could say.

'There's no point being PC about this,' Lisa went on remorselessly. 'You only have to ask yourself what seems most likely. That you have a lone maniac roaming the beaches stabbing people? Someone who comes from nowhere, goes back to nowhere, leaves no trace, no motive, nothing? Or that it's a drugs deal gone wrong?'

'There's no evidence for any of it.'

'That's where you're wrong. Hannay had drugs with him. The nurse could have had access to drugs. Denton associates with at least one convicted drug dealer. And Mabbott has a record for possession and supply. It can't just be coincidence.'

'You're just guessing.'

'What were they doing there?'

It always came back to this and Sarah had no answer. Even if she couldn't say it aloud, she wasn't really convinced by their story of a day trip to the seaside. It was out of character. It made no sense to go all that way for a day, and not stay overnight. They weren't short of money and there were plenty of places to stay. Most of all, the only part of the story that had the absolute ring of truth was how out of place they had felt.

'I don't have to listen to this,' Sarah said, walking off. But Lisa caught up with her in the corridor.

'What do you mean by that?' she said in a low voice which contrasted with her furious stare. Sarah wondered how on earth she could escape from the argument. She couldn't think of anything that wouldn't make things worse but she sensed that saying nothing was just as provoking.

'I know what you're thinking,' Lisa said, nodding. 'Well let me tell you something. Who the fuck are you to stand in judgement? You think you're so cool and clever but you've got this completely wrong. You're the racist. You think we should treat them differently because they're black. Well, in my book, that's being racist.'

Sarah sat at her desk for a while, sick with anger, still rehearsing everything she should have said. So Ed knew some dodgy people, perhaps people he'd been to school with or grown up with. He might not drop them, disown them, just because they were living on the other side of the law. But that didn't mean that he too was a criminal. And the same with Atlanta. She could have been done for possession, sure, but being unlucky enough to be caught carrying a spliff or two was different from dealing. And murder was another thing altogether.

In a way, she found Lisa's accusation that she hadn't bothered checking up on them the most wounding. Perhaps because it was right. She hadn't bothered, first because she had other things on her mind and then because she was too caught up in her fantasy of being the one to break open the case.

The one to produce the star witness and to use her to track down the murderer.

'I heard about your frank exchange with Lisa,' Andy Linehan said, coming in, a smirk planted firmly on his face. 'Most entertaining, from the sound of it. Wish I'd been there myself.'

'Not now, Andy.'

'I'm only passing,' he said, taking the seat opposite. 'But you've got to admit she's got a point.'

'Don't you start.'

'No, come on, hear me out. This isn't about race, it's about method.'

'I thought it was about convenience; finding someone from outside to pin it on.'

'Come off it, Sarah,' Andy said. 'It's not like that. If you've got people on the scene and their reasons for being there don't really stack up, then you check them out. That's all we're doing.'

'Right.'

'Like Morton always says, keeping an open mind cuts both ways. It means not ruling anyone out as well. So if you're asked to do a bit of digging around tomorrow about the two of them, then I hope you won't have a problem with it.'

'No,' she said sullenly.

'That's good. It's not easy sometimes, this kind of thing. But I know you can handle it.'

He smiled reassuringly and headed for the door.

Outside, under the clear skies, the town was washed in moonlight. Her footsteps sounded unnaturally loud as she walked through the market place. The streets were quiet, though each pub and restaurant she passed was filled with warm light and chatter and music. She wondered how Nick and Atlanta were getting on. It was too late to return to Yarwell and try and find them, and in any case in her present mood she wouldn't be much company.

Sarah decided on a bath, as hot as she could bear, but by the time she got home she was too tired. Instead she collapsed on the sofa and stared at the ceiling, listening to the noise from the café below. Usually these sounds – the hum of conversation, the clink of plates and glasses and the occasional burst of laughter – were a comfort. But tonight they served only to make her feel more alone. She wished Rachel hadn't gone out.

The ceiling needed painting, she decided. The original white had faded and there was a nasty ring of grey around the light which she had never noticed before. The walls too were dingy, with what had once seemed a pleasant neutral magnolia now clearly an unpleasant shade of putty. And she wondered why she had never realized how vile the light itself was, with its dusty paper shade speckled with brown spots she guessed were something to do with flies. She considered taking the shade down straight away – even a bare light bulb would be better than the horrible thing hanging there above her – but it was too much effort.

That night she dreamt that she awoke in the middle of the sea, far from shore, hardly able to see any distance because of the height of the waves. She was waking up just so she could drown. She was far out to sea without the strength to keep herself afloat. Without a life jacket. Surrounded by the roaring of waves breaking on a sandbank somewhere nearby. The weight of the water pressed down on her, driving her under, and she struggled for breath and woke up shouting.

And even when she was awake she was sure she could smell the sea, and thought she was back in the attic bedroom in the flat in Yarwell. She even reached out for Tom beside her. But the bed was empty.

Chapter Twenty-Two

The following morning brought a sharp wind blowing from the south to go with the scudding clouds and the patches of bright blue sky. Maybe, if the rain held off, they would have a fine day. Sarah's gloom had gone along with the mist, and she found herself humming a tune as she dressed, and brought Rachel a mug of tea with a cheerfulness that wasn't returned.

'Remember the boxes?' Sarah said. 'I'll leave them in the hall, if that's all right.'

'Whatever you want,' Rachel grunted, surfacing from her duvet. 'How did last night go?'

'Complete washout,' Sarah said brightly. 'I had to go back to work so he ended up going out with my witness.'

She remembered her suspicions about Nick and Atlanta with a smile. It wasn't at all that she could trust Nick – quite the opposite, and in a way that made him all the more attractive – but she had seen Atlanta and Ed together and they had the kind of relationship that meant a fling, a one-night stand, was out of the question. All it showed was that she was letting the case get to her.

'That's a bit rough.' Rachel yawned.

'Not really. If I really wanted to see Nick again, I

could do so any time. And it'll be interesting to see what Atlanta makes of him. She's pretty sharp. And funny.'

'So you two are going to spend the day sitting around gossiping?'

'Yeah.' She glanced at her watch, anxious not to lose time collecting the boxes and suspecting Atlanta wasn't one for early rising. 'I should be on my way.'

There were very few people around as she drove into Yarwell and parked by the green. She dropped into Costcutters to buy the morning paper and a sandwich for later. The killings were still running on the front page though in a side bar; not the main story. And there was no sign of Atlanta's drawing. Morton must have decided to hold it back.

There was no one at reception in the hotel and no sign of any human presence except for the sound of a vacuum cleaner coming from the back of the building, so she went straight upstairs. At the top of the staircase she was about to push open the fire door which led to the corridor when she caught sight of Nick Walton. Coming out of Atlanta's room.

He shut the door quietly and looked carefully around him before walking briskly the other way down the corridor towards the back stairs.

Sarah burned with anger and embarrassment, trying to think of some other explanation than the one that had slapped her in the face. She went back downstairs to the toilets on the ground floor and splashed water on her face until she felt a little better. There was nothing between her and Nick, she told herself. That was over years ago or, if not, it was certainly over now.

She wasn't that surprised about Nick. It was part of his attractiveness, that mix of slightly childlike egotism, a thirst for life, and irresponsibility. It was as much a part of his nature as his infuriating habit of borrowing something and not returning it, or breaking it, or lending it on to someone else altogether. But she would never have thought that Atlanta would go off with a man she didn't know, who she'd met little more than an hour before. Sarah would have said it was so out of character. But maybe that only showed how bad her own judgement was.

Atlanta seemed genuinely pleased to see her, though she apologized for running late and for being only half dressed. Sarah noticed that the other bed hadn't been slept in.

'Did you sleep all right?' Sarah asked, and then instantly regretted doing so; she could hear the bitterness in her voice. But Atlanta took her question at face value, saying she'd slept badly. And she did indeed look tired, not the unmistakable sated tiredness of the morning after but drained and anxious, even ill.

'It was a bit creepy. It's so quiet here.'

Sarah couldn't think of anything to say in reply and some of her mood must have transferred itself to Atlanta who apologized again, this time with more feeling.

'I'll be ready really soon,' she said, fetching her boots from the wardrobe.

'Have you eaten?' Sarah asked, looking around for evidence of breakfast in bed for two. Something hearty, she thought sourly, to restore them both after a tiring night.

'I made myself some tea. Do you want a cup? There were some biscuits but I ate them.'

She started to pull her boots on. Watching her, Sarah thought of the night before. The two of them coming back, Atlanta sitting there with Nick kneeling in front of her helping to take off her boots, fumbling with impatience, then pushing her back onto the bed.

Sarah went to the window and pulled back the net curtains to look at the view of a blank wall opposite. She knew Atlanta must guess there was something wrong; there was nothing for her to look at. She would realize that Sarah knew about her and Nick.

Perhaps they'd done it on the floor. Sarah looked at the carpet, tracing the patterns of red and yellow and brown designed to cover up the dirt. There were any number of faint marks, stains and spills, acquired over the years in all kinds of ways she preferred not to think about.

'I guess you want to get going as quickly as possible,' Atlanta said, fiddling with the laces of her other boot.

'Whatever.'

'I'm just going to clean my teeth.'

While Atlanta was in the bathroom, Sarah looked over the room with a professional eye. She took in the furniture in its normal place, the crumpled towel on the floor, the bag Atlanta had brought – open on the other bed – filled with yet more black clothes. There was a cup of tea by the bed, next to her car keys and a copy of *Bleak House*. She picked it up, noting the bookmark over halfway through. But why should she be surprised? What did she really know about Atlanta Mabbott? Nothing.

'Help yourself to tea, if you like,' Atlanta called out.

There was a tray on the window ledge with a kettle, a bowl stuffed with individually wrapped packages of tea, coffee and sugar, and one remaining cup. It was wet to the touch where Nick must have rinsed it out and replaced it. This seemed needlessly discreet. Surely the Oak was used to a bit of infidelity?

She gave up on the tea and walked around the room again, noticing for the first time the tiny silver photo frame sitting by the bed. It opened out into three parts, a picture of an older woman in one and two little girls in another. But the third one surprised Sarah the most. It was of Ed, smiling warmly, in an army uniform.

She wondered how Atlanta could have slept with Nick with the photo there at the bedside. But then, how could any of the things happen that did? How could Tom have taken Kelly out onto the sands to screw her as if what he and Sarah had shared meant nothing?

Atlanta came out of the bathroom, smoothing down her white polo neck and smiling.

'Shall we go?'

They drove into town and along the harbour front towards the main road. One of Sarah's colleagues had told her that the travellers they had evicted on Sunday had set up camp in the car park on the quay, but she wasn't prepared for the sight of the cars and caravans parked in a circle as if to fend off a sudden attack.

'I bet they reckon they're really clever, parking there,' Sarah said.

'Why shouldn't they?' Atlanta asked innocently.

'Firstly, they're not allowed to. That's for visitors, and there won't be many of those once the word gets around travellers have moved in. But the main reason is that at high tide tomorrow night they'll find themselves under several feet of water.'

'How come?'

'The whole of the sea front here floods if there's a spring tide. They'll be . . . Why are you stopping?'

'Don't you want to tell them?'

'Me? No. They'll have been told but they won't believe it. They'll think they know better, that people are just saying it to try and get them to move.'

'But that's awful. You should do something.'

'There's nothing I can do,' Sarah said, starting to feel a bit defensive. 'They're certainly not going to believe the police.'

'You could try. You can't let that happen to them. And finding it funny, too. That's horrible.'

'There's nothing I can do about it. Like I say, they won't believe—'

'You could get Nick to talk to them. He goes out in that lifeboat. They'd believe him.'

'Don't be stupid,' Sarah snapped, wincing at the bitterness in her voice but unable to stop herself. 'You don't know him very well, do you? He'll find it as funny as anyone when the tide comes in.' Unless, she thought to herself, he wanted to impress Atlanta enough to be bothered to pretend otherwise. 'He might turn out to help rescue them but he'd laugh louder than any of the others in the pub afterwards.'

She expected Atlanta to argue, but she only looked at Sarah in amazement, surprised and hurt. Then she started off again without another word.

Despite the warmth and the sunshine, the atmosphere in the car remained brittle and cold. Sarah found bitter amusement in the way Atlanta was puzzled by the change. She considered talking about Nick, making it clear that he had asked her out for a drink and that they'd once gone out together, and trying to get some reaction from Atlanta. But she couldn't face even the thought of the embarrassment. She had to keep her mind on the job in hand as well. Atlanta was still a key witness, and one who was strong-minded enough not to cooperate if she didn't feel like it.

'Ed's planning to come up tomorrow,' Atlanta said cheerily, after a while. 'Unless you think I'll be finished here before then?'

Sarah stared at her in surprise, but Atlanta still had her eyes on the road and didn't seem to notice.

'He can stay at the hotel, right?'

'Yes, of course,' Sarah heard herself say.

They drove on, and Sarah began to wonder if maybe she'd made a horrible mistake. What if Nick had been there for some entirely innocent reason? Say Atlanta had left her bag in the pub, and he'd found it and taken it around to her that morning. Something so ordinary that she wouldn't even think of mentioning it to Sarah.

For a moment, she convinced herself that this must

be the way it was. Except that Atlanta hadn't said any-thing about the night before. And if she had spent an entirely innocent evening she would surely mention it, even if only to commiserate with Sarah for having her evening ruined.

And, Sarah thought with a hollow feeling, if she could lie so well and deceive her boyfriend like that, and sit there so calm and cool after what she had done, what else might she be capable of?

They went first to the flat, where Sarah had trouble persuading Atlanta to park legally in the market place rather than directly outside on double yellow lines. She had no intention of having to explain to one of her colleagues what she was doing there with the witness she was supposed to be looking after.

Oddly, given she had been so helpful, Atlanta refused to carry any of the boxes and trailed along behind with nothing more than a few bags. Once in the flat she excused herself from any more removals work, saying she would make tea instead. Sarah found it hard to match Atlanta the athlete with Atlanta the layabout.

Sarah returned with a second box, full of books and with the bottom threatening to give way, to find Atlanta scanning through her CD collection.

'Looking for anything in particular?'

'No,' she said with a shrug. 'Just looking. Seeing what you got.'

'Found anything you like?'

'No,' Atlanta said in the same matter-of-fact tone. 'But I'll keep looking, if you like.'

Sarah dumped the box and by the time she returned with the next one Atlanta had made the tea and was lying on the sofa reading one of her *Lonely Planet* guides.

'You been to India?' Atlanta asked.

'Yeah. A couple of years ago.'

'And all these other places?' She nodded towards the shelf.

'Most of them.'

'That's amazing.'

She sounded genuinely impressed, though Sarah herself found the books and the trips themselves something of an embarrassment. She had gone around the world, spending several months in India and then a few weeks covering Thailand, Australia and then back via San Francisco. She had hardly met anyone who wasn't a traveller or a tourist, or working for a tourism business. By the time she returned, she felt depressed both by the experience and by the realization that she had gone for all the wrong reasons.

'How come you don't still listen to these?'

Atlanta had found a handful of old cassettes. With a pang, Sarah recognized Tom's handwriting: compilation tapes he had made for her, each one supposed to capture a mood or a time. Each had come to hold its own clutch of memories and so all of them had been pushed aside. She had tried listening to them, trying to recapture something of the man behind them. But she had wondered if Kelly had listened to them too, if he had made a second copy for her.

'Mind if I bring them along? They've got some fantastic stuff on.'

Sarah shrugged; telling herself they meant nothing to her any more.

'Keep them,' she said.

Sarah had arranged to meet up with one of the search teams at Blundell Beach, but they were packing up to head back to Frampton by the time she and Atlanta arrived. She knew the sergeant in charge, Kevin Sands, from a training course they'd both been on at Ashford. He'd put on some weight, but the brushed-back hair and the smile were the same as ever.

'They're putting up a helicopter,' he explained. 'Pity. Looks like a lovely day for a walk on the beach.'

The rest of his squad had finished climbing into the van but he stood with one hand on the front passenger door, happy to chat for a moment.

'So where have they been keeping you, anyway?' he asked.

'Same as you,' she replied. 'In a Transit van, mainly. Tactical support.'

'Ah yes,' he said absently. 'We all have to do it.'

Kevin was looking over her shoulder and she caught a fleeting, hungry look, like a terrier spotting a rabbit. She turned to see Atlanta walking towards them, clutching her coat, art pad and pencil case.

'This is your witness, then?' Kevin said casually. 'Got an ID yet?'

'Nothing yet.' Sarah was surprised that he should know what they were doing. It showed how much time they all spent gossiping.

'That's the story of this whole investigation,' he said heavily. 'A whole lot of nothing.'

'It's still early days, isn't it?' she replied, conscious of the police in the van watching Atlanta. She saw one of them through the rear window say something – she could imagine all too well the kind of thing it would be – and the others laughed.

'I saw Blake this morning, at the station,' Kevin said. 'He was saying they've got a strong lead. Information received. So things might start to move now. Not before time.'

Atlanta joined them and took out her phone, only for her pencil case to slip from under her arm. She groaned, bent down and picked up the case, dusting it off on her sleeve while Kevin watched, making no effort to help.

'You're not much of a gentleman,' Sarah said to him and he blushed.

'I could drop it again if you like,' Atlanta said.

There was more laughing from the van and someone started hooting the horn. Kevin smiled, nodded to them both and climbed into the van. It turned around quickly, the engine racing, and sent gravel skittering around their feet. They watched it disappear down the lane.

'Aren't they going to search the beach?'

'There's no point,' Sarah said. 'The helicopter will do it much faster. Come on,' she added briskly, heading back to the car.

'Where are we going?' Atlanta asked in surprise, though still starting to follow her.

'Back to the station.'

'Are you joking?' Sarah stared at her. 'This is the first sunshine all week, right? We're at the beach. And you want to go rushing off?'

'We have to go back.'

'No. Wait,' Atlanta said, walking off and holding the side of her head like a stage medium. 'I think I remember something about that night. Yes, it's all starting to come back. This place is important in some way.'

Sarah sighed and followed her. After all, she told herself, she was supposed to be on leave today, and no one at the station would be that bothered about what she was up to. They passed through the gate and joined a sandy path beneath the trees that threaded its way between gorse and bracken. Underfoot, the thick carpet of sand and pine needles gave slightly at each pace, but even this faint sound was lost in the desolate sound of the wind in the trees. Apart from that, the place was silent. No birds in the trees, no other people.

'I can't get over how quiet it is,' Atlanta said as Sarah caught her up.

There were two or three banks of dunes, and after the last one Atlanta stood amazed. She could now see the whole expanse of the beach, the vast flat plain stretching away to the horizon. Apart from the line of trees curving gently away to each side, there was nothing to see but sand.

'Where's the sea, then?'

'About a mile that way,' Sarah replied, pointing to a distant line of dark grey.

'Crazy,' Atlanta said, a touch of admiration in her voice.

'They use this beach as a film location sometimes. As a Caribbean island.'

'Really?'

Atlanta led them down onto the beach itself and

started walking towards a line of distant dunes. Sarah glanced at her watch.

'I'll catch you up. I've got a call to make.'

Nick was in the boatyard and it took a while for one of his colleagues to track him down. Sarah was left with the background noise of thumps, high-pitched drilling and Radio One she remembered so well.

'Hiya,' Nick said unexpectedly. 'Pity about yesterday, eh? Still, maybe another time? Maybe tonight?'

His assurance shook her. Again, she wondered if she had got it wrong about him and Atlanta. Not that she cared, of course.

'Maybe. I'll, er . . . I'll see how it goes.'

'Well, don't sound so keen. Anyway, what can I do for you?'

'I wondered if you were going to be about later on.'

''Fraid not; I'm about to take a party out diving. I was sorting out the gear just now. Why do you ask?'

'Atlanta has to stay up here for an identity parade later this afternoon, but I don't think she'll want to spend the day following me around and I don't want to leave her on her own. So I wondered whether, if you were free . . .'

'She's welcome to come diving,' he laughed, 'but I don't think that's really her scene, do you?'

'I suppose not.'

He began quizzing her about the investigation and she answered absently, wondering how best to ask him the other favour. But in the end he asked first.

'Something else I can do?' he said.

'It's about the travellers,' she said. 'On the quay. Have you seen them?'

'The gypsies? Oh yeah, I've seen them. What about them?'

'Could you go and tell them that they're going to get flooded at the next spring tide?' she said in a rush. 'I know they shouldn't be there and honestly I can understand if you'd rather not. I mean, they could have parked in your yard or anything. But if you had your RNLI jacket on then maybe they'd believe you and—'

'Sarah, it's fine. You're right. I'll have a word with them later on.'

'That's great. I really appreciate it.'

'You owe me a drink now of course. Maybe the day after tomorrow, if you're busy tonight. Then you can tell me what this is all about.'

Chapter Twenty-Three

She found Atlanta lying on her coat, well hidden amongst the dunes, her face towards the sun, arms at her sides with the palms facing up. Her eyes were closed but she must have heard Sarah's footsteps.

'Great, isn't it?' she said without opening her eyes.

Like the night before Sarah was surprised at Atlanta's composure. It could have been anyone standing above her. It could have been the murderer. And yet she lay stretched out like a contented cat.

'Any news?' Atlanta asked, still without looking at her.

'Nothing,' Sarah replied, sitting beside her. She had to admit it felt very secure there; no noise except for the occasional sea bird flying past and the ever-present breeze rustling over the sand, hidden in the natural sandy hollow and shielded by the spikes of marram grass all around. She lay back in silence, enjoying the way the trees above broke up the sunlight into patterns, the sound of the wind and the smell of the pines. But she couldn't completely relax. She was still thinking about what Lisa and Andy had said the night before.

'Atlanta,' she said carefully. 'This man you saw that night. Are you sure you saw anyone?'

'Course I did.'

'Only say you and Ed had gone to the beach for some other reason, not connected to the murder but still . . . well, illegal. Or something you wouldn't want us to know about.'

Atlanta didn't reply, leaving Sarah less and less sure she was doing the right thing. But she went on.

'If you did then it's still best to tell us now. To tell me. It would be worse if it all came out later.'

'So you're saying I'm lying?' Atlanta said, ominously calm.

'No, because I don't know that. But you haven't told me the truth, have you? At least not the whole truth.'

Atlanta looked at her for a moment, and then consciously relaxed back onto the sand and faced the sun again.

'What else have you found out?'

'About Ed. And some of his friends. Previous convictions, that kind of thing.'

'Yeah, well that's all shit,' she said fiercely. 'Ed's never done nothing wrong in his life. He's not like that. He may know a few people who don't see things the same way but they're people he's known for years. Since from school. He's not going to never see them again, is he?'

'Even if that's so, you can't blame us for starting to wonder.'

'Who's this "us"?' Atlanta said scornfully. 'It's you talking, you know. Saying these things. It's you that's calling me a liar and telling me Ed's some kind of gangster and that I made the whole thing up. And what gives you the fucking right to do that? How can you do that?'

'You didn't—'

'Fuck what I did or didn't.' She sat up, really angry. 'Fuck it. You and I've been driving around for two days, chatting, having a nice time. And all the way round you've been thinking, *Here's this black girl and her man; they must've done it for sure.* How could you do that?'

'I didn't. I—'

'I'll tell you something else. When you—'

'Will you shut up a minute? Just for once in your life?'

Atlanta stared at her in surprise.

'I didn't believe it,' Sarah went on, finding herself close to tears. 'I didn't. Not when they started saying all this. When they asked what you were really doing down on Beach Road, I told them that if we had a white witness we wouldn't even think of digging around like that.'

'Too right.'

'And then they showed me the records. You were caught dealing drugs. You got off with a caution, sure, but that's still possession with intent to supply. So what am I supposed to make of that?'

Atlanta stared at her intently, leaning forward, her eyes flicking from side to side as if trying to peer around Sarah's face to see what was behind it. Then, unexpectedly, she smiled.

'If that's what they told you,' she said, 'then I forgive you.'

And, ignoring Sarah's astonished expression, she

settled back again in the sun. This time, though, to tell a story.

'About three years ago, I was living with this guy. I won't tell you his name. Anyway, he was into drugs. Not in a big way. Mainly for himself, and maybe a bit dealing for friends. He'd promised me he wouldn't ever bring any of it to my flat. It's not that I wouldn't smoke weed once in a while, but not when I was training and not anything else. But one day, I got burgled. They smashed in the door, took the video, my computer, and some other stuff. When I got back, the police were already there, checking it out. They were all very sympathetic. They made me some tea. And you know what they found in the cupboard? A little bag of cocaine.

'Well, they weren't so cool about things after that. They had me in the station for hours. They must've believed me when I told them it wasn't mine, but I wouldn't give them a name. And all the time I was waiting for him to come and get me out. To admit it was his. I'd called him, and he said he'd come. But he never did.

'In the end, I said it was mine. It was a deal, really. You know how it works. I admitted it and they gave me a caution. That was that, or would have been. But the papers got hold of it and the athletics board started threatening to suspend me. And I lost my sponsorship deal. So that was me finished. Out.'

Sarah thought about this.

'Is that why you got rid of all your trophies?'

'Yeah, that's right,' Atlanta replied, surprised that Sarah should understand. 'I didn't want anything they'd given me after that. I threw it all away.'

'And what happened to this man?'

'I never saw him again. His stuff went into the dustbin as well. And soon after that I moved house. It was like starting again. I went back to working as a designer and picked up some freelance work straight away. So it all worked out OK, didn't it? I had a lot of time to see my family again. And I saw more of Ed, and we got it together. I knew him from school, and he was just back from the army around then.'

She lay back, staring at the sky, leaving Sarah to wonder if there was anything she could say. She felt cold inside and wondered how badly she had messed things up, and what Morton would say, and whether Atlanta might still cooperate.

Atlanta sat up again, looking puzzled.

'Why did you ask me all of this anyway?' she asked with some of her usual mocking tone.

'How do you mean?'

'I mean, if you thought I was a drug dealer or a killer, why didn't you have me arrested?'

'I don't know,' Sarah admitted. 'Because I didn't believe you had anything to do with it, I suppose. But I thought you might have got yourself caught up in something bad.'

Atlanta thought about this.

'That's really sweet,' she said. 'Maybe if . . . Well, if there was something I needed—'

She broke off as Sarah's phone rang. Automatically, Sarah answered it while still watching Atlanta, still thinking about what she had said and might be about to say. But the message soon distracted her. It was the control room, calling to let her know that they had found a body.

It took them only a few minutes to reach the scene. They parked at the end of a long track that ran from the coast road down to the sea where one of the search team, in a fluorescent jacket, stood waiting for the ambulance. Sarah wanted Atlanta to wait with the car but she insisted on coming. Sarah was surprised; she had thought Atlanta would shy away from anything unpleasant but she didn't want to press the point.

They walked over some low dunes and onto the beach which was empty except for a distant blob of orange where another of the searchers was standing sentry on the body. Sarah was afraid of what she might find and how she would react. She had no idea what Atlanta was thinking. In the end she managed to find something neutral to say.

'You'll be pleased to get back to London, I guess, when this is all over.'

'Yeah, too right.'

'We'll probably be through tonight or tomorrow morning.'

'Whatever.'

The sun was now hidden by a bank of heavy cloud and Sarah regretted leaving her jacket in the car; by the time they reached the edge of the water she was chilled through. The man in the orange jacket looked frozen and hardly nodded at them, in case a dose of the wind should slide down his neck. Atlanta stood to one side.

Close up, the body was every bit as bad as Sarah had expected. It was horribly battered, the face unrecognizable, and only a few tatters of clothes remained, black and stained white, flapping in the breeze. She had a suspicion that parts of the corpse had been gnawed at in the water. Where the skin was not torn or bruised it was a horrible pale colour. Nothing could have persuaded her to touch it.

'Is it him?' The man's words were muffled by his jacket, pulled up around his nose. She nodded her head.

'I think so.'

It was impossible to be sure, with the face smashed and half gone and no chance of finding any identification. But the scraps of cloth around the body looked more like the remains of a dinner suit and shirt than anything else.

She wondered what to think. Sorrow? Not if he was the kind of man she now suspected he had been. Sadness? Perhaps that was closer to it. No one could wish this swollen, ruined end onto anyone.

The wind ebbed and flowed, driving a faint mist of sand across the beach, building a line of tiny dunes along one side of the body, speckling it with grains of gold. Each time the wind rose it pulled back the scraps of shirt, then let them fall again, revealing a particularly lurid bruise just over the heart with a ragged tear in the flesh at its centre.

Sarah heard a faint growl and looked up to see a police van pull up by the edge of the dunes. She doubted Morton would bother calling out the forensics team. Once again they would find the scene scrubbed clean with salt water. She already had the only clue they were going to find: Dr Hannay had been stabbed, just as Mrs Aylmer had said.

*

They left in silence, just as it began to rain. Atlanta had gone off and cried for a bit while Sarah had talked to the police team and then helped carry the body in its thick plastic bag back to the edge of the beach. Atlanta had asked Sarah to drive, saying she felt tired. Even now she was morose, lost in thought, sitting hunched deep in her coat in the passenger seat. When Sarah asked if she was all right she only grunted in reply, then ignored her altogether.

They passed the turning to Yarwell, went past the sign for Atlanta's hotel, but when Sarah asked her if she needed to rest or wanted some time for herself, she shook her head mutely. But Sarah was shocked to see how upset Atlanta was, with reddened eyes and her face crumpled up like a child's. She found a turning to pull into and parked the Jeep. Together they listened to the drumming of rain on the roof and the wash of occasional passing cars.

'Will . . . will his parents have to see him?' Atlanta asked after a while.

'No. There's usually someone else who can make the identification. The morgue people can do a lot, but maybe not this time.'

'Do you think you'll find the . . . the other one? The nurse?'

'I don't know.'

'Will she be like that?'

Sarah shrugged and began fiddling with one of the cassettes lying on the dashboard. It took her a moment to realize it was one of the ones Tom had made for her and Atlanta had picked up. The precise, stylized handwriting was so familiar, though it was three years since she had looked at it. She turned it over, feeling the plastic casing worn like a pebble from the beach.

'Nick told me about your boyfriend,' Atlanta said. 'The one who was drowned.'

For a moment Sarah was awash with anger at the thought of them lying in bed discussing her, exchanging confidences. But the feeling passed as quickly as it had come. She was too tired out. And she had wanted to talk to someone about it since Sunday morning, since she had first been sent to Compton.

'Tom,' she said quietly. 'His name was Tom Strete. We were together for three years. Then one day he went sailing off a sandbank a few miles off the coast. A bank called Dead Sand, would you believe? He must've got the tide wrong or something because he ran the boat straight into the sand and turned it over. The water was only a couple of feet deep.'

'How come?'

'You'd be surprised. The sea's so shallow in places that it shoals at low tide. You can get out and walk about. Anyway, he made it to the sandbank and he waited while the tide rose again, and in the end it covered him up and washed him away and drowned him.'

After a while Atlanta said, 'You weren't with him, were you?'

'No, I wasn't. He was with a girl called Kelly Newsom. She had the only life jacket and he'd broken his arm when the oar went over. So she swam back to shore to get help and left him there.'

I wouldn't have gone, Sarah said to herself. *I would have stayed and waited for help together.*

'She was too late, though. There was too much fog

219

by then for a helicopter. When the lifeboat got there, they found what was left of the boat but he was gone.'

'Nick said it was Tom had the life jacket and this Kelly who didn't, and he gave his life jacket to her. That's an amazing thing to have done. You must've been proud of him.'

'Not really. It's bad enough knowing your boyfriend was screwing someone else without him having to die for the bitch. Or wouldn't you know about that?' she added nastily.

'Who else knew about Kelly?' Atlanta asked, ignoring her comment.

'No one said anything. They wouldn't, would they? I was supposed to be his girlfriend. They didn't want to think about what he was up to. And if anyone knew they weren't going to rub my nose in the fact he was with someone else when he died.'

'But she survived, didn't she?'

'The story was he was giving her some sailing lessons.'

'And that wasn't true?'

'No. He'd been seeing her for months.'

'How do you know?'

'I know.'

Atlanta turned in the seat to face her.

'Did they ever find him?' she asked.

'A week later. I never saw him, though. They buried him in the church at Compton. I went to the funeral, but then I couldn't bear it anymore and I never saw any of them again.'

'So how come you ended up on this case? Don't they know?'

'No. I never told them. They had me working on

another case like this last year. A woman was killed and dumped in a river. It's tidal and the body was carried down towards the sea. I was there when they found her.'

'So you know what it's like?'

'Yes,' she said, swallowing hard to get past the lump in her throat. 'I know.'

She smiled ruefully at the thought that she had started off trying to comfort Atlanta. Now she wanted to cry herself, to release the misery deep within her. It hurt to hold it back.

'You miss him, don't you?' Atlanta said.

'I do,' she said flatly. Then she switched on the engine and glanced in the rear-view mirror to check the road was clear. 'It's time we were going.'

Chapter Twenty-Four

At the station Sarah found there was a briefing about to start so she left Atlanta to go through the last of the mug shots. There were about twenty CID and uniformed officers in the meeting room, some sitting, others perched on the tables. Sarah joined the ones standing at the back, wanting to speak to no one.

The atmosphere was very different to the flatness of the night before. A few people were looking pleased, almost smug, as if they knew what was up but weren't allowed to say. Others sensed the excitement and chatted and laughed more loudly than usual. And everyone had one eye on the door at the far end where Morton would emerge.

He was late, and that only added to the buzz. Sarah wondered if it was deliberate. Perhaps he knew a bit of showmanship would be useful in dispelling some of the rumours floating around at his expense.

'What's going on?' she asked Kevin Sands as he leaned against the wall beside her.

'No idea,' he replied with a shrug.

Another officer, one Sarah didn't know, leaned over.

'We've got a name at last: the man the black girl saw. He lives in Compton, would you believe?'

'How did you find him?'

'The usual. "Information received." One of Blake's contacts, I think.'

'Is there anything in it?' she asked.

'Not sure yet, but he looks a lot like the picture the girl did. And we went through some old paperwork which matches up. This same bloke, Ronald Ellis, was in trouble a few years back for having an illegal hand-gun. Kept it when the law changed after Dunblane. Didn't make much of a secret about it, either. In the end we caught up with him. Maybe it was a tip-off from a neighbour, come to think of it. Anyway, he still had the gun and he got six months suspended.'

'So what's the link?'

'Well, they also reckon—'

But then Morton came in briskly, as smart as ever in his light grey double-breasted suit. And though Morton's face was set Andy Linehan, trailing behind, was smirking. They had certainly made the break-through they were waiting for.

'Right. Now first of all what I've got to say is strictly for your own ears. No one's to say anything to anyone.'

But there was now a smile lurking behind his stern words.

'We've got a lead on a local man, name of Ellis, lives on the outskirts of Compton. He's a known gun nut. He lives with his mother and there's some thought he could fit the profile for someone given to bouts of violence. We've been keeping an eye on him since yesterday while we've been making some discreet enquiries. I'll circulate photos later. If anyone knows him, or thinks they've seen him about, or picks up any rumours, then let me know straight away.'

Morton ran through the outcome of the checks they

had run: background, current circumstances, finances, possible enemies, any record of threats or confrontations or odd behaviour. Then he paused for a word with Linehan. His audience relaxed a bit, exchanged whispers and shifted in their seats. They too had sniffed a good lead at last, and liked it.

'We're planning to bring him in later for an interview and an ID parade this afternoon. But let's not take our eyes off the ball,' Morton finished off. 'It's only a lead, not a whole case. Bill's team'll be working on it, but for now we follow up every other line just as thoroughly.'

Outside, DCI Blake stopped her in the corridor and indicated by a jerk of his head that he wanted a quiet word. He was looking even more unimpressed than usual, though whether it was with her, or someone else, or the world in general she had no way of telling.

'I hear you're looking after our prime witness,' he said, eyeing a couple of their colleagues balefully as they passed by.

'That's right,' she said cautiously.

'And how's it going?' he said with a kind of smile. She suspected that, to him, policing had been a far easier and more satisfying profession when WPCs were there to search female suspects and reunite stray children with their parents.

'Fine. Except that most people here think she's the prime suspect.'

'Do they now?' he said in mock surprise. 'I don't suppose that has anything to do with her being, er, Afro-Caribbean, does it?'

'You tell me.' she said, before wondering if she was being a bit too aggressive.

'I don't like the sound of this,' Blake replied, dropping his bantering tone. 'What's Jeremy said about this?'

'He told me to keep an open mind.'

'Aye, well, that's always good advice.' Blake was lost in thought. 'But I'll give you some advice that's a wee bit more practical, shall I? If anyone,' he said quietly, waving a finger towards her, 'if anyone says anything, you come and tell me. Straight away. You might think I'm an old dinosaur but I've never let racism get in the way of good policing and I don't intend to start now.'

'Sure,' she said, taken aback by his vehemence.

'Good lass. Now sometime soon we should have a wee talk. I've heard you're thinking of promotion.'

It was a strange way of putting it as he had sat on her promotion board and done his best to stop her.

'What you need is a year or two in CID. I might have a vacancy coming up. There'll be a board, of course, but it could be worth your while to apply,' he said with a wink.

Sarah was completely thrown by this. She would never have thought of trying for any job with him, certain that she would not be considered. For a moment she was thankful she hadn't yet posted the application form for the job at Summertons, which still lay in the bottom drawer of her desk.

'Aye, you come and we'll have a chat and maybe a drink too. I like Jeremy, as you know. He's good at his job. These days you need managers; that's the way the service is going. And he's a very good manager.'

'Right,' she agreed, unsure where his change of subject was taking them.

'But there are some old virtues that are dying out. Like looking after the people who work for you.'

He shifted his bulk onto his other foot, leaning forward to emphasize his point.

'You were first on the scene on Sunday, weren't you? I know because I happened to be there in the control room. And you're looking after the key witness. Probably getting her to cough up lots of extra information. Girl talk. That's all very good, but I hope you're getting the credit for it. Some people – some ambitious people – can take that for themselves. Not me. You remember that. So if there's anything you think I should know you give me a call, day or night. OK?'

She nodded, still wondering what lay behind this.

'Good girl,' he said, patting her on the shoulder, as if trying his best to reinforce her perception of him as a well-meaning chauvinist. She watched him head off down the corridor, whistling jauntily.

There was nothing more for Atlanta to do but wait for the identity parade later that afternoon and as she said she was tired Sarah drove her back to the hotel in a spare patrol car. All the way Atlanta sat slumped in her seat, hardly saying a word but instead staring out of the window at the passing countryside. When she said she wasn't interested in lunch, Sarah even began to wonder if she was falling ill. But when she suggested this Atlanta just snorted and shook her head.

'I'm fine. Just tired. OK?'

'Sorry. I was only thinking—'

'I'm fine,' she snapped. 'Stop going on about it.'

Sarah waited by the car as Atlanta walked into the hotel, and she noticed the driver of a delivery van parked opposite by the chemist watching too, as she climbed the stairs, her coat flapping open to show her short skirt and long legs. As Atlanta slipped through the hotel door, the gaze of the van driver followed her and stayed even after the door had closed behind her, as if in his mind he hadn't finished with her. At first, Sarah had assumed it was a casual eyeing up, but there was something about his intentness that made her wonder who the driver was. Could he be there for a reason? Once again, she felt worried that using Atlanta to try to spot the killer had its risks. Atlanta herself had probably told several people and Sarah's colleagues gossiped far too much. Anyone, telling their wife or husband, girlfriend or boyfriend, or mates in the pub, could have given away the information that Atlanta had seen someone and could make an identification. A black woman was all they would need to know; it wouldn't be hard to find her in a town like Yarwell. She was far too conspicuous to be the hunter. But not to be the hunted.

Chapter Twenty-Five

A few minutes later Sarah was still watching the van driver, who had started to eat a sandwich and read his newspaper, when Alban called.

'They said on the news that you'd found a body,' he said in a rush.

Shit, she said to herself. She had promised to let him know, if she could.

'That's right. At Blundell.'

'Do you know . . . can you say who it was?'

'I can't. Not for sure.'

He said nothing for so long that she started to think they had been cut off.

'Can I talk to you? Now?'

She sighed. It was the last thing in the world she wanted to do.

'I wouldn't ask if it wasn't important.'

'I know that. Where are you?'

'At Compton. Down by the beach. Can we meet there?'

'Of course.'

Sarah had decided to tell Alban about the body, as he had asked, but when she began to explain why he mustn't tell anyone else until it had been formally identified, he shook his head.

'It's OK. I don't want to get you into trouble, and in any case it isn't important, is it?'

'I suppose not.'

'They're both dead,' he said in a matter-of-fact voice. 'Both dead, and whether you find their bodies or not doesn't matter.'

'It matters to me. And finding out what happened.'

They had walked onto the last line of dunes. Below, the tide was in and the wind was helping to push the seas high up the beach.

'What was it like when they brought Tom back?'

He spoke in such a simple tone that she found it easy to sit beside him and answer in the same detached way, as if she was watching herself from a distance.

'People said it would be better. Better to have something to mourn and to bury. They were probably right for them, but not for me.'

'I didn't see him.'

'No one did. I don't suppose there was much to see.'

They watched more of the waves roll in, now almost at their feet.

'I never said thank you for looking after me at the funeral,' said Sarah.

'That's OK.'

'You didn't go to the wake afterwards, did you?'

'No.' It had been in the *Mariners* in Yarwell, and afterwards they had gone back to someone's flat, drinking all the time yet without it having any effect. She had been as sober by the end as when she had started, sober enough to realize that Nick was hiding something from her, and sober enough to make him tell her, They had gone outside, walked down to the quay and she had dragged it from him. About Kelly.

'And that was the last time I saw you,' he said.

She had been sober enough, too, to know what she was doing when she went back to Nick's place in the boatyard. The first hours when Tom was missing, the ten long days of the search, and then the wait for the funeral; all that tension left her that night in a few minutes on the floor of Nick's flat above the slipway.

The tension had gone, but not the anger. Screwing Nick had helped. She could still remember the feeling, something like triumph, as they lay only a few feet above the sea. Moving out of the flat had helped too; simply throwing what she needed into a few bags and walking away from it. But most of all her anger had been satisfied by ignoring every one of Tom's friends and family. Ignoring their calls. Returning their letters unopened. If she couldn't hurt Tom then she could hurt those around him. Those who must have known what he was doing behind her back.

'You're cold,' Alban said, and she realized it was true. Or was she shaking as she remembered the violence of her hatred? Had she really been like that? So vicious in taking out her pain on those around her.

'We should go back,' he went on.

'What did you want to tell me?'

'About Chris and Nicola. I've worked out, now I've been interviewed by one of your colleagues, what you're all thinking: that they went out there because they were having an affair and maybe someone killed them because of it. Which is a stupid idea,' he continued with a touch of his old acerbic self, 'and only a total arse could think was at all likely. I mean, people don't do that sort of thing.'

'Some people do. Someone killed them.'

'I know,' he said quietly. 'That's why I wanted to tell you this. About a year ago I went to a party at the hospital and met Nicola. We got chatting, and she told me about her boyfriend, and that was that. But you know how it is? I really fell for her.'

'Oh God, Alban. I'm so sorry. I'd no idea.' Sarah felt stupid that she hadn't guessed; too wrapped up in herself.

'Well, I didn't tell anyone. I still haven't, except you. She knew, of course, though she never said anything. And all I ever did was send her a valentine. Something corny like "If you ever change your mind . . ." '

'But she didn't.'

'She did. She sent me a postcard a few months later saying "maybe". Just that one word. I found out later that she'd got fed up with never hearing from her boyfriend and the last straw was he'd promised to come back over the summer and then said he couldn't afford it. She didn't know if he was hoping she'd cough up, or whether he'd found someone else and didn't want to say. Anyway, she told me about it.'

'What about Hannay?'

'That's the thing. I knew he'd been hanging around her a few months ago. She was really funny about it, partly because she didn't take him too seriously. I wasn't so sure, so I asked him.'

'He must've got a shock.'

'Not really. I mean, I'd met him enough times. We used to go out in a group with lots of people from the hospital. He was quite up front in saying that he had been interested in her, but not any more. He wished me good luck,' Alban added. 'Isn't that funny?'

'So why did they go to the beach?'

'I don't know. But my guess is he wanted to look at the stars, watch the waves, maybe chat to someone he liked. Nothing more than that.'

They sat watching the waves roll in while she tried to work out what she thought of this. And trying, too, to make sense of this side of Alban she wouldn't have expected to see. He wasn't a very kind person – at least not to those he wasn't close to. She wondered what would have happened if he rather than Nick had told her about Tom being unfaithful. Nothing, she guessed. They certainly wouldn't have ended up in bed together, even if she'd wanted it. In fact, he wouldn't have told her in the first place.

'Do you remember a girl called Kelly?' she asked.

'Kelly Newsom? She was with Tom when . . . well, you know. Why do you ask?'

'Did you know they were seeing each other?'

'Are you sure they were?'

'I know they were.'

'Well I didn't know anything about it.'

'Never mind.' She had gone four years without knowing any more about how they had got together, how long it had been going on. There was no need to learn more now.

'She moved away afterwards,' Alban said. 'I thought you'd done the same.'

'I did, for a while.'

She was cold, and zipping up her coat to right under

her chin didn't seem to help. She suggested they go back.

'Who told you about Kelly?' he asked as they stepped down from the dunes.

'It doesn't matter. It was a long time ago. Why?'

'It's just such a horrible thing to have done.'

'Do you think so?'

'Of course. When people say don't speak ill of the dead, they've got a reason. If you find out someone's done you down, there's nothing you can do to get even with them, is there? Plus you never hear their side of the story.'

'What "side" would that be? "I cheated on you because . . ." '

'I suppose so.'

She didn't say any more until they reached her car.

'I won't tell anyone about what you've said unless I need to,' she said, and on an impulse she kissed him. 'If you want to talk any time, just call.'

He nodded. She wanted to keep hold him of him, help him to cry, but the moment passed and he turned and walked away.

Driving back down the lane into Compton, Sarah took Tom's tape from her pocket and fed it into the stereo, and then on an impulse turned off the lane and into the village itself. She passed the church and turned into the narrow rutted lane that ran beside the grave-yard under the massive lime trees. She switched off the engine, cutting off the music. In the sudden still-ness, she remembered Ed standing in the kitchen of Atlanta's flat, eating cereal and grinning at the memory of what he and Atlanta had got up to here. He hadn't been too explicit, but she guessed they had taken advantage of the same warm night that Hannay and Page had enjoyed on the beach. They wouldn't have done it in the car; that had far too little dignity for either of them. But the church was at the edge of the village with no houses within a hundred yards. Under the stars, on the smooth cool grass of these lawns, with plenty of shadows and no chance of anyone disturbing them, it would have been right.

She remembered the last time she had come here. Then, the fierce heat of the sun had even penetrated to the inside of the church, usually so shaded and cool. It had burnt down on them as they stood around outside, no one sure whether they should go in or not, waiting for the cortège. None of them, none of Tom's friends at least, were expert in the ways of funerals. The harsh light had glared back from the grass and the trees in unnaturally bright, surreal shades of green. And afterwards they had come blinking back into the light, to stand around the grave roasting in the heat, dressed in black except for the rector. She remembered the flushed faces, the fingers easing tightly fitting collars, jackets held away from shirts and from skin already damp with sweat; the orders of service used furtively as fans, the women dabbing at their faces with balled handkerchiefs already sodden with tears.

But she hadn't cried. Not then. Nor had she sweated. Instead, despite her woollen jacket and skirt, she had shivered and wondered if she would ever feel warm again.

Now she opened the gate and followed the path to the left, to where there was a sheltered hollow ringed with yew trees. Tom's grave was closer to the church itself, she knew, but she didn't want to go any nearer.

Sarah could picture Ed and Atlanta so clearly. She sat on a wooden bench and listened to the rustle of the leaves. She imagined them leading each other by the hand, nervous, excited, and settling down behind one of the headstones, here in the most secluded part of the churchyard. And then instead of Atlanta it was she who was lying back on the damp grass, looking up to see a face picked out in the light and the shade. Reaching her mouth up towards his hot breath. Feeling his hands running so lightly over her that her skin turned cold and her belly turned to fire.

But it was daylight on a cold September afternoon. No stars, no moonlight, no thick indigo darkness, only a pale cold grey light and the threat of more rain. It was nearer to winter than summer. The cold and the damp were seeping into her clothes, chilling her skin. She stood and then hurried back to the warmth of her car.

Chapter Twenty-Six

Sarah rang the incident room to see if there was any news or anything she could usefully do out at the coast. After her talk with Atlanta, then seeing the body, and now Alban, she was in no mood to go home and relax. There would also be the boxes to have to face.

'There is, actually,' Andy said, and she listened while he tapped at his keyboard and grunted. 'Page's family have a holiday home in Norton Staithe. Could you go and look it over? Page stayed there lots of times before and there's just a chance there'll be something there worth the trip. Letters or something,' he added vaguely.

'Fine,' she said, and took down the address. A waste of time probably, but better than nothing. 'Won't I need a warrant?'

'We've got their permission. If you find anything, you will let me know straight away, won't you?'

The cottage was one of three lost down a side road outside the main village, and surrounded by vast green oaks. All three looked empty, not exactly abandoned but certainly desolate. The clues were the rough lawns dotted with dandelions and daisies, and the absence of flower beds – who'd come for a weekend and spend it weeding? She wondered, as she parked a little further down the quiet lane, whether there were any villagers left at all, or if every last house was now a holiday home.

The door was locked, more for the sake of form than any idea that a thief would be kept out for more than a few seconds by the cheap mortise lock or the single panes of glass. But in any case she knew from Andy that the key was either under a brick by the door or in the shed at the far end of the garden.

A few minutes' searching proved him wrong, although the casually placed brick was there. But fortunately the window above the flat-roofed kitchen was open a crack and it only took a minute to climb up and ease it wide. Better than breaking a windowpane or forcing the lock. Less paperwork.

Inside, the cottage had the faint smell of salt and damp she remembered from her own childhood holidays. The motley furniture, cast-offs from home or from a local dealer. The hard-wearing carpet stained with mud by the door and ash around the fireplace. Watercolours hung at random on the walls. Odd ornaments stood on the window ledges, presumably gifts which might one day need to be produced to show a relative that, however horrible their offering, it had not been thrown away.

The ground floor had been knocked through so that the tiny kitchen, dining room and lounge ran into each other. The Page family was not very tidy. There were books and a blanket lying about, two mugs and a plate sitting in the sink. But even with the small amount of clutter, there was nothing really there to see. Nothing obvious, anyway.

Sarah started on the sideboard in the dining room, first checking that the bottom held only plates, glasses and elderly bottles of vermouth, advocaat and cheap gin, then turning to the drawers. Here were bills, copies of old parish magazines, instructions for the cooker and for lighting the wood-burning stove, and much more of the same. She rooted around for a little longer before admitting defeat, finding in the last handful of jetsam from the back of the second drawer an old stub of pencil, a crumpled letter covered in mysterious numbers which turned out to be scores from cards or maybe Scrabble, and a dusty lump of rock, worn by the sea into weird patterns of white and blue. It was not exactly a thing of beauty, though she could well imagine it would have caught the eye of a child.

She wondered if it was Nicola who had found it on the beach and carried it in triumph back to her parents in her small child's hands. Maybe she'd given it to them and they had moved it stage by stage out of sight, out of the reach of childish fingers or childish memory but never having the will to throw it away.

Sarah pushed the drawer back into place and walked briskly through to the lounge. There was a low coffee table with an under-shelf stuffed with old papers which gave her something to take her mind away from the image of that girl growing up, only to die in a pointless killing. *With her whole life before her.* Someone had used a similar phrase at Tom's funeral.

There had been a visitors' book at the Red House where at the end of each stay they had recorded who had come, what they had done and of course the weather. If the Pages had something similar, there was at least a chance of it revealing who had been the third person on the beach filming Nicola and her boyfriend. She rifled through the piles of board games and magazines and soon found what looked like a small photograph album. She flicked through, reading entries at random: *Excellent time. Many thanks. A marvellous way to unwind.* And the family too had recorded each visit. *Wet walk on Blundell beach. Mended the shower curtain. Saw seals on Sunk Sand. Barbecue – didn't rain!!!*

She turned to the previous month. Nicola's parents had come down at the beginning of August. She'd come herself two weeks ago with Vikki, a friend. No mention of boyfriends. That was the last entry, which might explain the mess. Maybe Nicola had planned to come on here over the weekend so she'd have a chance to clear up before her parents got back from holiday. Sarah started to leaf back, reading entries at random, wondering if any names would stand out, any clue as to her character would seep through the terse entries.

Then she heard footsteps outside, caught sight of a figure hurrying past the window, then a key in the lock.

She stood, frozen, as the door was pushed open. A girl stepped cautiously in, then stopped dead.

'It's all right,' Sarah said. 'I'm from the police.'

She had guessed at once who the girl must be. The family likeness was there, the same dark black hair and pale skin, the same blue eyes.

'Are you Nicola's sister?' she asked.

'I don't have a sister.'

They stood facing each other for a moment, each unsure what to say.

'Did Chris send you?' the girl said at last.

'No. He's . . . Why do you ask?'

'I don't know. Did you say you were police?'

'That's right. I've got a warrant card, if you want to see it.'

'Has something happened?'

Sarah put down the visitors' book, weighing what to say next. There was something here she couldn't fathom.

The girl was so confident that for a horrible moment Sarah was convinced she must have come to the wrong house. Even the names in the visitors' book could be a coincidence.

'Have you not heard about Nicola? Nicola Page? She's dead.'

The girl sat at the dining table, putting a loaf of bread down in front of her and staring at Sarah in shock.

'I don't understand,' she said slowly. 'I'm Nicola.'

Chapter Twenty-Seven

Sarah was in the garden, on the phone to Morton. She watched through the kitchen window as Nicola made herself a sandwich, forking the contents from a tin of tuna and mixing it with mayonnaise from a jar. Meanwhile, Morton continued to fire questions at her.

'Since when?' he demanded. Even though the connection was poor the incredulity in his voice was all too clear.

'Since Sunday morning.'

'Then why the hell's she been hiding? Why didn't she call us?'

'She says she didn't know anything about it. The murder, the search, any of it.'

'Come off it. She must've seen the papers, or listened to the radio.' Morton sounded furious, as if he wished the girl really was dead.

'She's been ill. She had this kidney infection last month and was only just back at work. I think that whatever Hannay gave her may have brought it back on, or maybe she couldn't get it out of her system properly. Anyway, she's been sleeping mainly and only went out today to get some bread and milk because there was nothing left in the freezer.'

Morton had gone very quiet. Sarah realized she

hadn't told him – or any of them – about her suspicions that Hannay might have drugged Nicola, intending to rape her. This was awkward, to say the least.

'OK,' he said in the end. 'Bring her in. No, ask her if she'd like to come down to the station and clear a few things up. See if there's any more to her story. Wait . . .' She could almost hear him having second thoughts. 'Do you think there's any possibility she might have more to do with this than she's saying?'

Sarah had had the same thought only a few minutes before, standing beside Nicola in the kitchen, asking her questions as the girl sliced the bread, suddenly conscious that she could turn and stick the blade into her without anyone being able to help. It was a nasty moment. But it had been nothing more than nerves and strain.

'I don't think so.'

'Do you want me to get you some back-up?'

'No. I'll let her finish her sandwich. We should be with you by seven.'

'Fine. On your way you can check with Mrs Aylmer that it's the same girl she saw. At least we can clear that up. It's only a few minutes out of your way. And for God's sake don't take her straight up to the door. I don't want the old dear to die on us from shock. Tell her first and keep Page in the car. And when you get here, take her to see Andy. He'll have to handle that side of it. I'll be in the briefing room.'

'I'll see you there.'

'No rush,' Morton said drily. 'I still have to think how we'll explain this to the press.'

*

Perhaps because Sarah wasn't facing her, but sitting at her side, her eyes fixed on the road, Nicola was able to begin to talk about what had happened. She was worrying most about her parents, and how soon they could be told that she wasn't missing or dead.

'Are you sure they'll get the message through?' she kept asking.

'It should be fine.' They were due to fly back that evening and Sarah had asked David Tollington to call the airline himself. His pleasant persistent approach would manage it somehow.

'I only went to the ball because I was sick of being ill, if you know what I mean. I was really careful about what I had to drink, but after the dinner I felt a bit funny and Chris suggested a walk along the beach on the way back to clear my head.'

'Just the two of you?'

'Yeah. He made a bit of a game of it. He said if we mentioned it to anyone else they'd all come and it would be a mob. Which is probably true. But I know he wasn't trying anything on.'

'Did you see anything on the beach?' Sarah prompted after a while.

'No. Like I said I woke up when the water reached me. It was just getting light. At first I didn't have a clue what was going on. It was like one of those dreams where you're in the wrong place. D'you know what I mean? Like you're in the middle of a crowd with no clothes on, or taking your exams and you haven't done any revision. I felt awful, and so cold. There was no sign of Chris. I thought he must've gone off and left me. Except that his car was there.

'I felt so scared. I don't know why, but I thought

something awful must have happened. I didn't want to see anyone, or talk to anyone. I couldn't have faced it. All I wanted was to be on my own. I can't have been thinking straight and I felt so weird. I didn't know what to do at first. But I had this coat on me. It was again like part of the dream, because it wasn't mine and it couldn't have been his because it fitted me pretty well. So I put that on, and there was some money in the pocket. Some change. Then I thought about the cottage; it's only a couple of miles from Compton. So I walked into the village and waited for the bus there.'

'How long for?'

'Only a few minutes. There's an early morning bus. There was hardly anyone on it but maybe the driver'll remember me. I must've looked a state.'

'And you didn't see anyone when you got to the cottage? You didn't phone anyone?'

'I went to sleep. I slept pretty much all day. I had something to eat in the evening but then just went back to bed. I was feeling really ill. The same thing I had before. It makes me feel so tired and sort of listless. Nothing's worth the effort. My parents were away and I didn't want to phone anyone from the hospital. Not that there's a phone here anyway. You have to walk into the village.' She thought a bit more. 'But then I started to wonder. About why I felt so ill. It couldn't have been just the wine, I didn't have that much. I was drinking water or orange juice most of the night. And then I wondered if maybe someone'd spiked my drinks. For a laugh. You know, a double vodka in the orange juice.'

'Why would they do that?'

'I don't know. Well I do, of course. I can't believe

it though. I mean, if it wasn't vodka but something else.'

'You mean a sedative?'

'Yes,' she said, surprised. 'I didn't know what to think. And it didn't come to me all at once. It was only that I knew something was wrong.'

'Did anyone give you any pills? Something for your headache, maybe?'

'No, I took some myself. Chris had some so I pinched a couple of those.'

'Were they copraxomol? In a bottle in the glove compartment?'

'That's right. How did you know?'

'We found them in his car.'

'In his car? Is he OK?'

Sarah realized she hadn't even told her Chris Hannay was dead.

Morton and Linehan had taken Nicola off to one of the interview suites and Sarah had been left to type up her report and wonder whether to bother replying to any of the messages left on her desk. There was one from Patrick, and two from Nick. But it seemed too much effort to call any of them, or even to phone Alban and tell him the news about Nicola. She felt drained, left in a strange state of absence, feeling no strong emotion of any kind. The last time she could remember the sensation was after Tom's funeral; the sense that she should be feeling more. Or that it was too over-whelming to feel anything at all.

After a while Andy Linehan came in and suggested a trip to the canteen.

'What's up?' she said guardedly.

'I'm hungry, obviously.'

'How's Nicola?'

'She's fine. We've taken a statement and she's gone off to rest. I think she'll go down to Heathrow to meet her parents.'

'Does what she say make sense?'

'Come on, I'm starving,' he said. 'I'll fill you in while we go.'

He headed off, seemingly as cheerful as ever.

'The thing I can't get over was her just sitting there,' he said as they shuffled forward in the queue. 'Do you think she really didn't know?'

'No reason why not. There isn't a TV or a radio there I could see.'

'It must've given you the shock of your life when she showed up,' he said with a laugh.

'Not at first. I thought it was her sister. She's lost a bit of weight since that photo.'

'Do you reckon she knows more than she's saying?' Andy asked.

'I don't think so,' Sarah replied, watching him choose without enthusiasm a plate of lasagna and salad. 'She looked really out of it. How did she take it when she found out Hannay was dead?'

'Pretty calmly,' he said, pushing aside the salad so he could fit a generous scoop of chips on his plate. 'A bit shaken, obviously, but not really upset. I don't think there was anything between them.'

'Is there still a chance she killed him?'

'It's possible. If he did try to rape her, maybe he had a knife and she got it off him and stabbed him. But I don't think it's likely.'

'It'd be tidier that way,' Sarah said vaguely, looking around for a quiet table. 'No one else to look for.'

'Not as I see it. After all, we've got our main suspect, Ellis. This whole thing will have been a right cock-up if it turns out to be a domestic after all. The nurse bumping off her boyfriend and then hiding in a very obvious place that we still take three days to find.'

'Does anyone really think it wasn't a stalker?'

'No. Pretty much everyone is prepared to accept it was Ellis. He fits the profile, he's got previous convictions for violence and for sexual offences, and Mabbott picked him out from a mugshot. Lucky for Mabbott and Denton he didn't come across them first, and had already had his fun for the night.'

Sarah had a sudden image of what it would have looked like, in the mist of the early morning, if that had been the crime scene she had been called out to attend. Ed lying face down in the road, the sand stained black around him. The door of the Jeep standing open. Atlanta, lying across the passenger seat, the wounds not visible until she was lifted up. Blood spattered across the roof of the car, the windscreen, and soaked into the fabric of the seats.

She pushed her plate of food aside and looked away when Andy started to speak again, his mouth full of lasagna.

'It all seemed to hang together. Maybe it still does. Not everyone finds your witness credible, but I'm sure she'll give a great performance in court. The real problem, though, is Ellis' motive. We thought he must have found Hannah and Page on the beach, and killed them both. Maybe raping her first. But if he didn't kill Page – didn't touch her, presumably didn't even know she was there – then why kill Hannay? It weakens the case, however you look at it. So if you're wondering why you aren't the heroine of the hour, it's because of that.' He waved a forkful of chips at her, amused. 'You were told to find her body, not bring her back alive. A walking, talking Nicola Page is definitely an embarrassment.'

Chapter Twenty-Eight

Sarah returned to her flat, looking forward to a quiet evening and an early night. Rachel was out again and the place was unusually quiet. She turned on the radio for the local news, but there was nothing about the case. Then she remembered to check her phone and found three messages to call Morton, each more urgent than the last. When she got through, she found him spitting blood.

'Your Miss Mabbott is a complete washout. First she says Ellis isn't the man she saw. Then she refuses to sign her witness statement. She can't remember a thing. She says she must've been mistaken.'

'Did she say why she'd changed her mind?' Sarah's first thought was that Atlanta was refusing to cooperate because of the suspicions they harboured about her. But she had seemed all right about that earlier on.

'Nothing,' Morton said. 'She just kept saying she'd made a mistake. Which is bloody right. Then Andy had a go at her and she clammed up completely. She's back at the hotel now but we can't leave it there.'

'Did anyone say anything to her?'

'No. We played it by the book. We got a sergeant up from Norwich to take her to the identity parade, someone nothing to do with the case so he wouldn't even have known about it.'

'What do you want me to do?'

'Get over to her hotel and try talking some sense into her. At least find out what's brought this on. Maybe she's been intimidated, or bought, or something.'

'Right. I'll go straight there.'

'Phone me when you've talked to her. Don't let her go. Hold her if you need to. She's certainly wasted enough of our time for a charge. I'm going to talk to the Met.'

'What's that about?'

'Never mind,' he said, sounding a little evasive. 'You just get her back on side, OK?'

It was after ten when Sarah reached the Royal Oak, and she was surprised when her call up to Atlanta's room from reception went unanswered.

'You've just missed her,' a member of the hotel staff said as she passed. 'She went out, oh, maybe five minutes ago.'

'I must've been fetching some tea,' the girl on reception said, as if she'd been accused of something.

'Did you see which way she went?' Sarah asked.

'No, but she had her coat on. And a scarf.'

Sarah stood on the steps of the hotel, wondering where Atlanta might have gone. Maybe someone had picked her up in a car, but she doubted it. She was much more likely to have gone down towards the harbour. Perhaps she'd arranged to meet Nick there. It wasn't likely she'd gone out for a pleasant evening stroll, even with a coat and scarf. It wasn't that kind of night.

Sarah wondered how to find her in a town the size of Yarwell, but in the event it was pitifully easy. She walked down to the market place, where several kids were hanging about, some sitting on the back of a bench while one of the others tried not to share her chips out. They were absorbed, shrieking and calling out, and didn't hear her until she was almost next to them.

'I'm looking for a friend of mine. Have you seen anyone go past?'

'What's he look like, then?'

'She's a she. Tall, in her twenties, hair cut short and in a big long coat.'

They looked a bit blank, until one of them said doubtfully, 'There was this black woman went past a few minutes ago. She had a long coat on.'

'That's her. Which way did she go?'

They gave her several different answers, with some laughter, but she picked one of the quieter kids and asked him directly. He pointed down Church Street, towards the harbour, and she thanked him, ignored the comments thrown after her and hurried on.

An old man in a cap and coat, dragging a shivering Scottie dog along, also pointed the way. The black girl had passed by not more than five minutes before, almost by the harbour, he told her, and this was confirmed by the proprietor of the Friars Delight, who was standing by his doorway, perhaps hoping that his impressive beer belly would draw in some custom on a quiet night.

Reaching the lower town Sarah decided to start at

the Mariners. She thought about phoning the station to ask for some help but decided to try to sort things out herself without making things even worse for Atlanta, or maybe for both of them. She quickly looked into the two bars, checking the couple of snugs and quiet corners, but the place was quiet and there was no sign of her.

She caught the landlord's eye. 'Have you seen a black woman come in here this evening?'

'Black?' He looked blank. 'No. I'd have remembered.'

'A coloured girl, you said?' One of the men at the bar, not one she'd seen before, turned to her.

'That's right. My age but taller.'

'That's her. Saw her down by the marina, oh, say, ten minutes ago. A minute or two before I got here. Was it ten minutes?' he said, turning to the rest of the group at the bar.

'If that,' said one of the others.

'Yes, she was climbing down onto the pier. Didn't seem to know where she was going. Like you said, black. Tall. Good looker, too.'

'Thanks.'

She ran down to the edge of the harbour, then slowed as she came to the start of the jetty. There was just enough light to show that no one was moving about. There was no noise either, apart from the slapping of water against the boats and the pier and the distant roar of the sluices. She stood for a moment and wondered what to do. If she waited here Atlanta would have to come back this way. There was no other way off the jetty, now that the walkway over the sluices was closed. But she was anxious to find out what

Atlanta was up to and the harbour wasn't a safe place to wander around at night if you didn't know it.

Sarah walked slowly to avoid making too much noise and so she could look over each of the boats as she passed. Nothing seemed out of place – no lights, no voices – though without a torch it was impossible to be sure. After a minute or two she could see the end of the jetty, where it turned towards the river and the sluices.

Then she saw Atlanta. She was sitting on the rail at the end of the jetty, her legs hooked around the lower rung, staring fixedly out to sea. She was quite still, so that despite the lights Sarah almost missed her.

The sound from the sluices drowned out her footfalls as she approached.

'Atlanta!' she called out.

Atlanta turned and froze for a moment. Then she jumped onto the walkway and started to walk quickly the other way, her coat flapping behind her. Instinctively, Sarah ran after her, only for Atlanta to start to run as well. Sarah knew in a second or two she wouldn't catch her. But then she didn't need to; it was a dead end.

After a few seconds Atlanta reached the steel-mesh fence. It was more than ten feet high and extended out beyond the walkway over the swiftly flowing water beneath, to end in a row of wicked spikes. She tugged at the gate which was set into the fence, but though it rattled and the fence shook, it stayed fast.

'Atlanta!'

She stepped back, glanced at Sarah, and then climbed calmly over the handrail and stepped onto one of the spikes at the side of the fence. With this single foothold, she swung herself around the spikes and climbed back safely onto the far side, to walk off into the dark without a backwards glance.

Sarah called out to her but there was no reply. She told herself she would have to go after her. The sluices were closed off for a good reason: they were treacherous enough in the daylight, let alone at night. Without waiting for fear to freeze her, she followed Atlanta's example, suspending herself for a moment above the rushing water, then scrambling gratefully onto the far side. The water beneath was flowing straight into the harbour and joining the currents leading out to sea. Once caught by them, there would be little chance of reaching land again. And if no one saw her go in, there would be no hope of rescue.

Atlanta had walked on and was standing at the far end of the narrow wooden catwalk which ran above the sluices. There was scaffolding all around and Sarah remembered that the whole structure was being rebuilt as part of improvements to the town's flood defences. Atlanta could go no further.

'Atlanta!' she screamed above the noise of the water. 'You've got to come back. It's not safe.'

'I'll come back. Just leave me alone.'

Sarah inched towards her. Spray made the planks beneath her feet slippery and she grasped the handrail grimly until she could hold Atlanta's sleeve instead.

'Whatever's happened, you've got to come back.'

The other woman shook herself free.

'You don't know what I've done.'

'It doesn't matter,' Sarah said patiently. 'It's not safe.'

In the end, something about the place – the dark, the rushing water beneath – seemed to convince her.

Atlanta nodded and started to come back along the walkway. Sarah relaxed and turned too, only for one of the planks beneath her to twist, tipping her backwards against Atlanta. She grabbed at the handrail but that gave way. And then there was nothing beneath them.

It was further to fall than she would have believed. The water was harder too, and colder. Sarah struggled back to the surface gasping, her ears ringing. A wave washed almost over her head and she started to tread water, looking about. One of the legs of the jetty was only a few feet away and she swam towards it, only for the next wave to throw her against it, scraping the skin off the back of one hand. The wood was slimy and encrusted with razor-sharp barnacles, but she hung on as the waves washed by.

Sarah was scared but the bulk of the post was a comfort. She could probably climb back up to the landing stage from there if she started now, before her fingers got too cold. Or she could work her way along from pier to pier until she reached the harbour wall. But it was still a dangerous place, with a wicked current that dragged at her as she clung on, trying to pull her free. She thought of the man who had drowned here last year.

Looking around for Atlanta she saw her a few yards away, already a little downstream of where they had fallen in. She was further away from the sluices, in a patch of deceptively calm water. Atlanta wouldn't know about the current; she would probably think, with the lights and the boats nearby, that there was no more danger here than swimming in an indoor pool.

Sarah let go of the post and struck out towards her, and at once the rushing of the current was gone, making it seem calm, safe. But she knew this was only an illusion and that the current was carrying them both along at six knots or more.

'Atlanta!' she shouted. 'Swim towards me!'

Atlanta must have had heard but she carried on swimming away from the pier and into the current. Not knowing the harbour, she wouldn't notice how quickly they were being swept away. But Sarah could tell. It frightened her. Every instinct told her to turn back and head for the safety of the jetty, but she swam on.

Atlanta had stopped, and though it was hard to see with the lights bouncing off the waves, Sarah thought she was laughing.

'Atlanta!'

'You've come in for a swim too?'

'It's no joke.' Sarah grabbed hold of her. 'We're being swept out to sea.'

'No way. Look at the lights over there.'

'Listen to me. We have to swim for that line of boats.'

Atlanta laughed again.

'You do that if you want. We're no distance from the pier.'

She shook herself free and began to swim back, against the current. Sarah swam after her, telling her to look at the lights.

They went on like this for a few moments until Atlanta had stopped laughing and Sarah had fallen further behind. Sarah told herself she had to give up, there was nothing she could do for the other woman and soon she would be beyond help herself.

She trod water, looking around to try to get her bearings. In front of her were the lights of the town, perhaps only a quarter of a mile away but seeming much further in the dark with her head only inches above the inky water. Away to one side but hidden by the dark would be the far bank of the harbour and to her right, by now, the sandbank which lay to one side of the main channel.

There was no sign of Atlanta. She couldn't be more than fifty feet away. Unless she had gone under.

A few dozen yards from her was a buoy rocking gently on the waves, its green marker light flashing every few seconds. Helped by the current, Sarah struck out towards it, trying to stay calm, to avoid rushing her strokes, until it towered over her, a vast steel cone, painted green but flecked with rust and fringed with weed.

She sighed with relief and floundered the last yard or two only to find that the steel was too smooth to hold. Cursing, she scrabbled at the side, but was already past it and carried away. The last she saw of the buoy was the marker light winking from the top.

Sarah tried not to panic but she knew there was every chance she would soon be dead. The buoy was at the edge of the harbour. There were only a few boats moored away to her left, then the lifeboat station and then the open sea.

Then she saw a red plastic marker buoy, hardly bigger than a football, a few feet from her. She managed to flail across to it and wove her fingers into the links of the chain which moored it firmly to the seabed. At low tide it would be left high and dry on the beach, which meant the water below was no more than ten or fifteen feet deep, but that was no comfort; it only meant that the tide ran that much faster. She could feel it dragging at her again. And it was cold, so cold that it was eating into her, numbing her fingers, her legs, and making her breath come in shallow gasps.

She tried to think where she must be in the harbour, what she should do next. It seemed incredible that she could be facing death within sight of land, of the town itself, of her old flat. But she knew she had to do something. Another few minutes and she would have no strength left. It wouldn't take long for the cold to reach deep into her, tear her fingers from their precious hold and carry her away.

She rested her cheek against the float. Out of the water it felt warm. She wanted to rest her head on the plastic pillow, until her strength returned.

Sarah thought of how she had been out in this same sea the day before, looking for the bodies. Now she would be the corpse floating putrid in the still water at low tide, bashed into pieces by the breakers on a far shore or beached, a piece of carrion, tatters of clothes fluttering, scaring away the crows. But she knew there were boats moored no more than a hundred yards from her. If she let go and swam slowly towards them, not fighting the current but going with it, she should make it.

But she was too tired, too cold.

Someone called her name, screamed it.

A wave washed into her mouth.

Sarah woke, retching, scared almost out of her wits,

to find that Atlanta was beside her, holding on to the buoy, and to her.

'I thought I'd had it,' Atlanta gasped. 'I thought I was dead for sure.'

Atlanta held her close while they caught their breath, but she was chilled too; there was no warmth in her. Sarah told her about the boats nearby and what they had to do and Atlanta nodded as if she understood. Neither of them was ready but they had no time to wait.

They let go and at once the dragging fingers of the current were gone. Sarah swam a little away from the current but mainly let it carry them. It felt very calm and quiet and at first Sarah felt she could carry on. But she soon tired, and Atlanta swam back to her and held her head clear of the water.

They swam on and soon after they saw the first boat, only a few yards away. She knew they would be carried past but there would be more further on so she shook her head when Atlanta tugged at her sleeve. They swam a few more strokes and then the current washed them past the gleaming hull of a small yacht.

The two of them hung onto the side, feeling the full strength of the current trying to pull them away. The side of the boat was only a couple of feet above the water but with their sodden clothes Sarah knew it would be beyond her to climb up without help. She told Atlanta to go first, helped push her up and over, and then waited as the other woman picked herself up.

It was then that she realized what she had done. Now that she was safely on board what was to stop Atlanta leaving her here? Or even prising her fingers from the side of the boat, or attacking her with the tiller or winch arm or some other weapon lying about on the deck? She listened, but there was no sound from above. She looked about in case there was another boat within sight.

Then Atlanta leaned over.

'You plannin' staying in there?'

Chapter Twenty-Nine

It was horrible moving about, out of the water. The cold was intense and Sarah started to shiver violently. With every movement her wet clothes chilled a different part of her skin. And the cold made her clumsy. Stumbling in the dark, she bashed herself on the tiller and swore viciously until she felt better.

Sarah knew that the boat must have a fair-sized cabin and she found the hatch more by feel than sight. But it was fastened with a padlock. She felt the lock and hinge for a moment, tapped the wood to check it was not unusually thick and gave the hatch a kick, then several more, until it split in the middle.

'Very neat,' Atlanta said between chattering teeth, looking at the mess of smashed wood.

Sarah knocked away the wreckage without saying anything and then crept through into the cabin. There was a torch hanging near the door and with this she could see exactly what she'd expected. The cabin bowed out in the middle and narrowed towards the bow, which was blocked off to form a locker for the sails. There were benches along each side, which presumably doubled as bunks, with lockers underneath. There was a stove, a couple of overhead lockers and a table in the centre of the cabin which could be used as a chart table. Everything was made of brown chipboard and brown fabric, and the whole effect was hardly more nautical than the inside of a caravan.

She found some matches by the cooker and tried to light the lantern which swung above the table, but her fingers were numb and she was shaking too much to manage. She heard Atlanta come into the cabin behind her and saw she too was in a bad way.

'Are you all right?'

'I've never been so cold,' Atlanta replied, stumbling over the words. 'We should've stayed in the water.'

'We'd have died.'

Sarah wedged the torch so that it shone upwards, lighting the cabin with a weak glow. She then turned back to the lockers, pulling out brightly coloured wet weather gear, and then a vast sweater which she threw over to Atlanta. Further down there was a pile of blankets, dusted with salt and sand, another sweater and a sleeping bag.

Another locker held a tin box with tea, a packet of stale crackers and half a bottle of rum. Tea was too much effort but the rum was like swallowing a radiator. Fortified, she started on the other lockers as Atlanta unrolled the sleeping bag. Out of the water, she seemed to have made a quick recovery. She chatted away while Sarah looked through the rest of the lockers for more food, a radio, a signalling lamp or some flares she could use to attract some attention. But there was nothing there. In any case, trying to be rescued would mean going up on deck again, and she had only just managed to create some illusion of warmth in the cabin.

'What are you going to do, then?' Atlanta asked.

'How do you mean?'

'To get us off.'

Sarah was amazed by the other woman's calm acceptance that everything could be left to her. It wasn't the rum, though. Atlanta had a couple of sips, then seemed to think better of it and refused the offer of any more.

'It'll be low tide in a couple of hours,' Sarah said. 'Then we can walk back to the harbour.'

'Walk?' Atlanta was incredulous. 'How do we do that, then? I thought we were halfway to the sea.'

'We are. But the tide goes out that far,' Sarah said. 'Like at Blundell. This boat'll be lying on bare sand by then.'

Atlanta started to laugh.

'You're telling me we were going to drown, and a few hours later people could've been making sand castles and flying their kites and stuff in the same place?'

'I suppose so.'

She lay back in her bunk, shaking with laughter, gasping for breath. And then, quite suddenly, she wasn't laughing any more but was crying.

'Come on. Drink some more of this.' Sarah wasn't sure it was a good idea but there was nothing else she could think to do, and when Atlanta had swallowed a huge gulp of the rum, had coughed most of it out again and caught her breath, she seemed a little recovered. She looked at the back of her hand, beaded with drops of spirit, and laughed.

'How low can I get? I can't even keep a drink down.'

'It's the shock.'

Atlanta wrapped her blanket closer around her.

'When I saw him today,' she said, 'that was the first

time I'd ever seen anything like it.' She held her own hands out, turning them over, studying them intently. 'He was coming to pieces. You know what I mean? There were pieces hanging off him.'

'I know.'

'I'd thought about dying before. You do, don't you? Especially when people you know die. But then if you saw them they'd be all laid out, neatly done, like they were asleep. Or in a coffin. Not like that. Not rotting.'

Atlanta wrapped her arms around her knees, staring quietly at the pool of light from the torch, following her own thoughts.

'That night, I didn't know what Ed was up to,' she said in the end, and Sarah felt the mood change, a sudden tension. She was conscious of everything, from the slap and gurgle of the waves along the hull to the expression on Atlanta's face, half-hidden in the shadows, as she began to talk. Now, after the days of waiting, Sarah was about to hear some answers, perhaps to learn what had really happened. She didn't feel surprise, or elation, or regret that Atlanta was involved. Maybe that would come later. For now, she only wanted to know.

'He said he was going to drop something off with a friend of a friend. I knew there was something funny about it. I'm not stupid, right? He was supposed to go round to see him in the evening. I didn't fancy sitting in a pub on my own very much, so I went with him.'

'Who was it he was seeing?'

'I don't know; I never saw them. They'd given him some directions so, like they said, we parked near the church, by the gate. Ed went off and I had to stay there waiting for him.'

Atlanta paused and Sarah thought about whether she should caution her. But Atlanta wanted to talk. Maybe she felt she had to. Cautioning her might break her flow. The worst of it was Sarah knew there were rules, but she couldn't remember what they were.

'What did you do?'

'It was OK at first. I had the light on, and I read a magazine. But then I thought that if there was anyone around they'd see me, right? They'd see I was sitting there on my own. So I switched out the light. I felt safer then. I tried to get some sleep but I couldn't. I was nervous, I suppose. It was so quiet. Well, not really quiet because you could hear the wind, but no real noise. Nothing human.

'Then I went for a walk down the path. I wanted to see if there was anything to see, but it was really dark and there were all kinds of rustling and stuff. I got as far as where there's a big tree by the right and I could hear this stream running alongside, and the noise of the water scared me more than anything. I don't know why. There was an owl, too,' she said, half-smiling. 'Like in a horror film. I'd never heard one before. Not a real one. And screams too.'

'Screams?'

'Not human. I could tell it was an animal. Screeches, more like. But it was scary all the same so I went back to the car.'

She sipped the rum, then passed it back to Sarah.

'It was about then that this guy appeared out of nowhere. Just like I said. A face against the window. I screamed my head off, and he must've had a bigger fright than me and headed off down the road.

'After a bit, I got out again and walked up and down. It was strange but I felt safer being out in the open than sitting in the car. I could see or hear anyone coming.'

She smiled but Sarah could see she could still remember the fear.

'When did Ed come back?'

'Not long after. He was gone about half an hour in all, maybe a bit more. I was cussing him too for leaving me there, and thinking about how he'd have to make it up to me big time. How I wouldn't speak to him the whole way back or something. In the end he came back really quickly. I didn't hear him. I'd walked along the path and then turned back to the car a couple of times. You know, I wanted to see if he was coming but he'd said I shouldn't leave the car. So I was walking back when he grabbed my arm; had his hand over my mouth. I tell you, I almost died of fright. I was going to kill him for messing about like that, but then I could see he was serious. Anyway, we went back to the car and we went off. I knew something had happened. He was all tensed up and he had his head down. He wouldn't look me in the eye, like he was a guilty little boy.'

'What did you do next?'

'We went home,' Atlanta replied, matter of fact. 'We got back about four and straight off we had a big row. I really went for him. Shouted at him. I called him all kinds of things. I don't know what I was thinking of. I told him I didn't want to see him again. So he went off and I went to bed. I wished I hadn't done it. He went off without complaining, without saying anything back to me, really. Like he knew he deserved it. It was only later I worked out he was trying to protect me, to keep me out of it.

'The next day Ed came round to see me. He made out like it wasn't a big deal but he was really shook up, and there's not much that makes him like that. I hadn't seen him like that before, except when his mother was ill and they thought she might die. It was like he didn't want to talk, didn't want me saying anything at all, didn't want me there except to hold. I said I was sorry and he did the same, and then it was back like it was.'

Atlanta lay back and stared at the deck above her head.

'It was then I told him about you lot phoning up and he had no choice but to tell me what had really happened. Someone Ed knew, someone he trusted, wanted him to deliver something for him. A letter. It was supposed to be simple and Ed agreed because he owed this guy a favour and he thought there couldn't be that much wrong in it, even if it was a bit suspicious.

'Then he told me that the man he'd done the favour for had called him and told him someone had got killed on the beach the same night and that he should keep quiet about being there. I said we should tell the police but Ed said they'd never believe we weren't involved, and anyway he'd have to say what he'd been doing and who else was involved and he couldn't do that. Not to someone he knew.'

Sarah could believe it; she'd seen how it was in the police. That kind of loyalty – to the service but most of all to your colleagues. That was why it was so difficult to prove anything if everyone stuck together. If you broke ranks and spoke out, then they'd make your life a misery.

'Later, he told me there were others involved. Serious people. If he said anything, then something bad would happen to him. Or to me.'

'So you knew all the time it wasn't Ellis?'

'Yeah.' She smiled, thinking about it, shamed, embarrassed but clearly still pleased with how she'd managed to fool the police. 'When Ed told them what I'd told your man Linehan, they were really pleased. They thought it would help point the police in the wrong direction.'

'You were taking a real risk.'

'I suppose so. But there wasn't anything else to do. I wanted to tell you, you know. But they'd told Ed they had someone on the inside, in the police. So if we went to them, they'd know straight away.'

Sarah was surprised they'd both fallen for such an obvious lie.

'Anyway,' Atlanta went on, 'I wanted to do something that helped. For Ed. To help him out. It was kind of exciting too, at first. It was my idea to do the picture. I made him look really evil, didn't I? Years ago, there was this man – I don't remember his name – shot a load of people somewhere. I could still remember the picture they had on the news so I gave the guy the same expression. And he looked right, didn't he?'

Sarah had to agree. That was why she had thought it was the face of the killer. Because that's what Atlanta had meant to draw.

'So why didn't you identify him?'

'I couldn't. Seeing the body – well I'd enjoyed it

until then, pissing you lot about – but after that I knew it was for real.'

They sat in silence, listening to the water lapping about them. Sarah was still wondering whether to say anything about Nicola or whether that would break the flow, when Atlanta said, 'Are you going to be in trouble about this?'

'No, I don't think so. Not as much as you, anyway,' she couldn't help adding.

'Yeah, too right.' Atlanta laughed but then looked more sombre. 'There's nothing I can do, is there?'

'If you make a statement, help get the others convicted, then there's every chance you'll get off. Maybe a suspended sentence at worst,' she added confidently, though she had no idea if it were true.

'And Ed?'

Sarah decided to assume that Ed was innocent as well. She could hardly suggest otherwise.

'It's the same for him. More so, really. He knows who did this. He could help us reel them in. Then he'd be . . . well, not exactly in the clear but pretty nearly. And you should get a lawyer, too. A good one. Not one from the list at the station.'

'Won't I have to pay?'

'Don't you think it's worth it?'

Atlanta thought about it.

'You got a Yellow Pages on you?'

'I can do better than that,' Sarah replied, and on a scrap of paper jotted down the name and address of the solicitor she had sent her application to. As she did so, she noticed that the torch battery was fading, and once Atlanta had the piece of paper folded away Sarah switched it off to save the last of the power. She sat with her back to the locker, feet braced instinctively against the chart table to counter the faint pitch and roll of the ebbing tide. She wondered about Atlanta's story. She was sure there was more: probably the name of at least one of the people Ed had gone to see and what they were up to, although that wasn't hard to guess. It had to be landing something on the beach, maybe weapons or perhaps illegal immigrants, but most likely it was drugs.

'I never asked why you chased after me,' Atlanta said, her voice heavy with tiredness.

'You ran away when I called.'

'Yeah. I was a bit on edge. I was trying to think what to do. What to say to Ed.'

They fell silent again. Sarah listened to Atlanta's breathing become deeper and more regular as she drifted off to sleep, rocked by the gentle movement of the boat. Sarah, who was trying to massage some warmth into her feet, watched her enviously. She was surprised that Atlanta could ignore the cold and the damp so completely.

Which made it more of a surprise for Sarah when she woke herself an hour or so later, when the boat began to ground. She was dazed at first, piecing together the last few hours until she could understand where she was, and that the deep grating noise was the hull of the boat settling on a gravel bank as the tide receded. Then the boat came to a sudden stop which jolted her forward. Atlanta, who had slept through the noise and bumps, rolled off the bunk in a heap. She sat up, cursing and looking around.

'It's the tide going out. We're sitting on the bottom now.'

She didn't know if Atlanta had understood, but the other woman pulled the blanket about her again against the chill in the cabin and sat glaring around her as the boat lifted off the bottom and then dug into the sand again, and began to lean to one side.

'We'll be steady in a minute or two.'

Sure enough, the growling soon stopped altogether, leaving them canted at an angle.

'What do we do now?' Atlanta asked.

'If you want, we can walk ashore.'

Atlanta gathered together her blanket and sweater and boots, and stuffed the rest of the packet of crackers into the pocket of the oilskin coat she had borrowed. She looked at Sarah with an anxious miserable expression, as if realizing what returning to land would mean for her.

'Cheer up,' Sarah said.

'You think tonight's going well, do you?'

'You're alive, aren't you? Anyway, we're not the only ones back from the dead. We've found Nicola Page.'

Chapter Thirty

They climbed over the rail and slid down to the ground, their feet sinking in up to their ankles. At first Sarah wondered if they would be able to move at all, as she dragged one foot free of the sticky mud only to push her other in deeper. But Atlanta staggered over, pulled at her arm and helped her free.

'I'll carry you ashore,' she said, the smile she had worn since the moment Sarah had told her about Nicola still with her, 'if you swear there's a bath and a hot drink at the end of it.'

'It's not far,' Sarah said. 'It's sand most of the way. We'll be there in half an hour.'

She didn't mention that they might have to wade or even swim through some of the larger pools left by the retreating tide or that there were huge patches of slimy weed to get past. But there were still enough lights shining in the town to show them the way, even though they couldn't see the ground beneath them so clearly.

They stumbled on, taking the most direct route they could towards the lights, through a vast flat landscape of sand dotted with pools of inky black where seaweed lay in great patches. After a while Atlanta pointed to a shape away to their right. Without thinking they veered towards it, to find it was a lump of concrete half buried in the sand. A chain led away from it for a few yards to end in a red plastic float, like the one they had rested on when the tide was flowing out to sea, trying to take them with it. Atlanta breathed in sharply as if about to say something, but in the end they looked at it in silence for a moment and then headed towards the lights of the town.

A few minutes later they reached the wall of the quay and looked up at the edge, twenty feet or more above their heads. They walked along the base of the quay until they came to an iron ladder set into the wall, each rung crusted with weed, shards of rusty iron and barnacle shells. Sarah wondered how she would ever climb up. It was tempting to sit for a while, and rest. But she could hear the water trickling back behind them as the tide started to come in again. In a few hours the water would be far over their heads. There was no other way up.

'You go first,' Atlanta said. 'I'll try and catch you if you fall.'

Sarah sighed and began to climb.

At the hotel Atlanta walked up to reception with surprising dignity, ignoring the water dripping from her. But the night porter only grunted as he passed the key over, hardly looking up from the TV. In Atlanta's room, Sarah made her go first for a shower while she phoned the incident room and then Andy Linehan's mobile, but got no reply on either.

'Could you eat some breakfast?'

'I would love some breakfast,' Atlanta replied above the sound of the shower.

It was almost six o'clock, probably still too early for any chance of something to eat in the hotel but there was always the Harbour Café.

When Atlanta had finished in the bathroom, Sarah stripped off her sodden clothes and turned the shower on full. She looked down at the clothes, streaked with mud and twined with green weeds, and thought of the scraps of clothing on Hannay's body, of what they had found in the river last year. She decided to throw them straight in the bin but almost at once thought again: how much did Levi's cost these days?

'I'm going to look for some food,' Atlanta called to her. 'I'll see you down there. I've left some stuff out for you.'

After her shower Sarah sat on the bed, and winced at her aching muscles. She hadn't realized how tired she was, or how battered either. Her hands were covered in tiny cuts from the barnacles on the piers of the landing stage, and there was a long scrape along one shin which she had probably picked up when she was scrambling into the boat. She had several other bruises, the worst of which was on her right hip, about the size of a cigarette packet and already turning a lurid shade of yellowy-green. She couldn't remember when or where this had happened but it was painful to the touch and promised to get much worse before it went.

Sarah found the pile of clothes Atlanta had left for her, noting wryly that every stitch was black. Next to them lay Atlanta's sketching book which Sarah flicked through. There was a drawing of the church in

274

Compton, which Sarah wished she had had the time to finish, and another of the sands at Blundell, where she had given up on the pines and drawn palm trees instead. There was a page of sketches – almost caricatures – of Sarah's colleagues which she guessed Atlanta had done while being interviewed. But the two or three scenes from Compton Spit were not so light-hearted. The waves she had drawn were hard and spiky, and the clouds were piled up threateningly. Though she might have walked along the beach confidently enough, on a deeper level Atlanta had hated or feared the place.

She dressed quickly, still thinking of breakfast, and then rinsed the grit from her shoes and put them on again with a grimace, wondering if she could find time to stop off at her own flat before appearing at the station. She knew she ought to go straight there, or at least try to phone in again. But food had to come first.

As she came down the stairs to reception, she saw Morton and Linehan, and two PCs she didn't recognize. One was holding Atlanta tightly by the arm, while the other was fitting handcuffs onto her. They all looked up at Sarah. As did the porter, staring in amazement from behind his counter, and a couple more staff peering around a door at the far end of the lobby.

Linehan started towards her then stopped himself. But they all stared, as if they expected her to turn and run.

'Sarah,' Morton said quietly. 'Would you come here, please?'

She walked over to them, babbling about what had happened the night before and what she had found out, trying to ignore Atlanta's pleading look. Morton interrupted her. 'You'll come back to the station, you'll wait until I've cleared this mess up, and then you'll answer my questions. And if you try and leave, I'll have you arrested.'

He turned back to Atlanta.

'Atlanta Mabbott,' he began in a formal tone, so that she looked up at him in surprise, 'I am arresting you on suspicion of conspiracy to pervert the course of justice. You do not have to say anything, but it may harm your defence if you do not mention when questioned something which you later rely on in court. Anything you do say may be given in evidence. Do you understand?'

She stood stock-still, gazing at him unbelievingly.

'Sergeant Pascoe and PC Weir will take you to the police station. You'll have a chance to make a single phone call to a friend or relation or lawyer. I wouldn't bother trying to call Mr Denton. He's just been arrested by my colleagues at the Met. Then we'll have you in the cells for a while. That'll give you the chance to think about what you want to tell me when we have a chat later on. Because this conspiracy charge could be only the start. You've fucked me around; you've fucked us all around. But now we're going to find out what really happened, and if you and your boyfriend didn't do it you'd better come up with some names.'

Morton nodded to Linehan, who came forward and took Atlanta gently by the elbow. But she shook him off and continued to face Morton, as if trying to find some words. She brushed a tear away with the back of her hand and swallowed hard.

'If there's something you want to say now, that's fine with me,' Morton said, his voice so cold it was like

an insult. After a moment, Atlanta shook her head and
let herself be led to the door. But once there she looked
back not at Morton but at Sarah, just as she had feared
she would.

She didn't say anything. She didn't even have a
particular expression that Sarah could read. In a way
that was the worst thing, She was a blank, as far away
as when Sarah had first met her.

Chapter Thirty-One

They left Sarah in one of the interview rooms for most of the morning; to write up her report and to 'think things over', as Andy Linehan put it coldly. No one had said she couldn't go outside, to her own office or to the canteen, but she couldn't face any of her colleagues. There was no window in the room to look out of, so once the report was finished there was now nothing to do except think about what she was supposed to have done wrong. Taking Atlanta back to her hotel rather than straight to the station? Talking to her without making sure she was properly cautioned or charged? Stupid maybe, but not enough to explain Morton's cold rage.

At first Sarah had been sure that, once he had read her report and Atlanta had explained what had happened, Morton would realize his mistake. She had enjoyed thinking of the elegant scathing phrases she would use when he came to apologize to her. But then she began to wonder exactly what Atlanta would say; she might invent all kinds of stories, make up accusations to muddy the waters or to try to entangle Sarah deeper in the conspiracy. Atlanta was so convincing, so persuasive. She had fooled them all for days.

The door opened, but instead of Morton it was

David Tollington who backed in, holding two mugs of tea.

'I thought you'd need some of this.' He checked that the door was shut. 'Morton doesn't know I'm here,' he said in a conspiratorial voice, 'so I'd better not hang around. But if there's anything you want to tell me, or ask me, you only have to say.'

'I'm fine, thanks.'

'I don't think so,' he said, sitting opposite her. She looked at his worried face, his anxious eyes, and she had to breathe deep to stop her tears. It would be so easy to let go, to be comforted with a hug and some meaningless reassurance.

'David, why am I here?'

'You really don't know?'

'No. I mean, yes. It must be something to do with the murders, but I don't know what.'

'I don't know that much myself,' he said, glancing at the door. 'Morton hasn't told me, obviously, but they've got three or four CID up from Norwich and a couple more from the Met as well. But the upshot of it all is that they think you've been passing on information about the inquiry.'

'But that's ridiculous.'

'I know that but Morton's convinced they've been getting information from the inside somehow. And there's this evidence going missing: that stuff from the beach which vanished on the way to the lab. He thinks someone on the inside got rid of them.'

'This is crazy. Who is it I'm supposed to have given this stuff to?'

'The killers,' he said, and she went cold. 'They've been discussing how deep you're in. There's one camp saying you must be involved in some way. That's led by Lisa Ross – I don't know what you've done to her but she's got it in for you for certain – and I think Andy Linehan's half convinced.'

She remembered the way Andy had refused to talk to her as they drove back to the station.

'Morton had me in,' David was saying, with another glance towards the door. 'He asked me straight off if I thought you were on the take. I told him absolutely not. But I don't think he was convinced. After all, you've had access to all the information. You were first on the scene.'

'I didn't volunteer Collins sent me.'

'Then there's you getting on so well with Mabbott.'

'But that's what I was supposed to do. They said look after her, make sure she's all right. I liked her, sure. But I didn't tell her anything; it was she told me. She admitted being there on the night, she and her boyfriend. They knew more than they were saying and I'd persuaded her to come in and make a statement.'

'That's not how Morton sees it. You didn't bring her back to the station and you were still at the hotel when he arrested her.'

'That's true,' she said, deflated. 'I don't know what I was thinking of. It seemed to make sense at the time.'

'How much of your side of it does Morton know?' David asked after a while.

'I don't know. Not much. I haven't had much of a chance.'

'Will you let me talk to him?'

'If you want.'

He stood and made for the door.

Morton himself arrived a few minutes later, taking a chair and placing it carefully on the opposite side of the table. Andy Linehan closed the door quietly and took his place at Morton's right hand, his chair slightly back from the table. Morton, without saying anything, took the sheets of paper from the table and began to read in silence, passing them one by one to Linehan as he finished. Sarah tried to read his expression, but there was nothing there except the barely contained anger he had shown from the moment he had come in and, before that, at the hotel. Towards the end he was skimming the pages and shifting impatiently in his seat.

'Is this it?' he said, waving the final sheet before passing it on.

She nodded.

'So what am I supposed to make of this?'

'What did Atlanta say?'

'Mabbott,' he said coldly, 'has said not one word. She seems to have no intention of saying anything until her solicitor arrives – a solicitor you appear to have recommended to her, by the way – and probably not even then. Denton has been arrested in London and is also not saying anything. So when he gets here I'll probably have the pleasure of wasting my time interviewing him too.'

'Maybe she's scared about what'll happen. I mean, if there's someone on the inside passing on information, then she—'

'You don't still believe she's innocent, do you?'

'Yes, I do. Look,' she went on, suddenly desperate to be believed. 'A friend of Ed's asked him for a favour. All he had to do was deliver an envelope. No questions asked. So he follows their instructions, leaves Atlanta in the car, meets them, hands over whatever it is and that's that. But then, later, there's trouble. Hannay stumbles in on whatever they're doing – landing drugs, I guess – or maybe he's part of it. I don't know. But when they kill him, they realize Ed could be a problem. Even more so once they know we know Ed and Atlanta were there that night.

'Ed and Atlanta don't come to us because they don't think they'll be believed, and we can't blame them, can we? So Atlanta comes up here and plays her part, and we all get very excited. But then she sees Hannay's body, and she realizes it's not a game. There's a man dead, and she and Ed are in deep. So she tells me about it.

'And because I like her and feel sorry for her, and I want her to be all right, and Ed too, I say she should come in and make a statement. Maybe I should have arrested her but I didn't. Instead I took her back to her hotel to have some breakfast and pull herself together so she could face having to come into the station to tell us that she'd helped cover up for a gang of killers.'

She'd come to an end and had nothing left to say, though she carried on glaring at the table as if it was going to argue with her.

After a while, Morton laughed wryly.

'Sarah, you are even more stupid than I thought.'

She looked at him, shocked. She had expected anger but his voice was filled with contempt.

'Can't you see? What she's done is spin together what actually happened that night with a pack of lies. She's admitting she and Denton were there. But instead of this drugs gang *they* were the ones meeting up with

Hannay. He wanted to sell drugs stolen from the hospital, and they wanted to buy. And one or other of them killed him.'

She wanted to laugh in his face. The idea of either of them doing anything of the kind was a joke. Although she didn't know Ed that well he seemed very calm and relaxed; not someone to lose control, not someone with the kind of overwhelming arrogance who would kill someone else because they were inconvenient, or he didn't want to pay a debt.

'Of course Denton is the most likely suspect,' Morton said. 'Mabbott was probably covering up for him. Either way, one of them stabbed Hannay.'

Sarah couldn't imagine Atlanta wielding a knife but she could imagine her covering up for Ed just as she had defended him so fiercely to Sarah on Blundell Sands the day before. And she had seen the two of them together, the way Atlanta would like to touch him from time to time even as she made fun of him and pretended to be so ironic and detached.

'You're wrong about them,' Sarah said shakily. She could see Atlanta holding Hannay, pinning his arms while Ed lined up the fatal blow; the two of them standing over the corpse, grabbing an attaché case full of money or drugs. She told herself it was nonsense.

'We'll know more when we get all the forensic tests back,' Linehan said cheerfully.

'But it doesn't make sense. Why would Hannay go there with Nicola Page?'

'We're still not sure that she isn't part of it,' Morton said. 'After all, she had as much access to drugs as he did.'

'But why would they kill him?'

'Why not? Perhaps he had a load of drugs on him. He's got no back-up so they kill him and don't have to pay him. It might have been a spur of the moment thing. Or maybe there was an argument.'

'But last night, Atlanta told me—'

'Don't start about last night. Please. The less I think about that, the better. I'm telling you we've found the killers, right? But I'm probably going to have to let them go. Mabbott by this evening and Denton tomorrow. Unless some new and pretty watertight evidence comes in we can't hold them any longer than that.'

'But if you haven't got any evidence,' she said, close to tears, 'why are you so sure they did it?'

'It's not stuff I can use in court but I know they did it. I needed to get the evidence and that meant surveillance, spending time building up a case, all of that. Because of you, that's all gone by the board.'

'If I could speak to her, maybe I could—'

'Can you still not see what you've done? She's told you a load of stuff about the case – half a confession if you like – and you didn't even caution her. If it ever gets to court, the defence will have so much fun at our expense. But it probably won't, now, because the CPS will piss themselves when they see the papers. A chief suspect and one of the investigating officers sipping rum on a yacht together; they won't believe it. And, to be honest, neither can I.'

He stood up and gathered together the pages of her statement.

'You know,' he said, 'I thought you were quite good. That's what people said. A bit green, maybe a bit naive, but very bright and conscientious. That's what makes this so funny. You fucking up the whole case like this.'

'If that's what I've done, give me a chance to sort it out.'

'You're joking, aren't you?' he snorted.

'If I could talk to her . . .'

Morton was about to turn away. Then his eyes flickered past Sarah, catching a signal from Linehan standing behind her.

'OK. You have your chat. Twenty minutes.'

Chapter Thirty-Two

Atlanta was curled up on the bed, apparently asleep. Everything around – the walls, the floor and even the ceiling – was covered in stark white tiles. It made the place as cold and clean and menacing as a abattoir.

Sarah had brought a mug of tea; she set it down next to the bed and gently shook the other woman by the shoulder.

'Fuck off.' The words were muffled by the sweater pulled up over her face.

'Atlanta?'

She rolled over so sharply, that Sarah stepped back in surprise.

'Oh God, it's you.' She sat up, hugging her knees. 'All that stuff last night? None of it was true, you know. None of it.'

'You know they've arrested Ed?'

'Yeah. Can I see him? Speak to him?'

'No.'

She hung her head, swearing under her breath.

'You're not going to tell him what I said, are you?'

'Atlanta, if he's got any sense he'll tell us anyway. It's too late for thinking you can end up in the clear. You have to choose which side you're on. Both of you do.'

'I'm not going to say anything.'

'Think about it.'

'Let me speak to Ed. Then maybe I will. But that's all I'm saying now.'

Sarah waited but Atlanta wouldn't say any more. There was nothing Sarah could promise and she knew Morton could be listening in, perhaps even recording their non-conversation.

In the end she got up to go. With Atlanta now a suspect rather than a witness Sarah would have no reason to return to the cells or play any more part in the investigation. It seemed incredible, after all that had happened since Sunday, but the next time she saw Atlanta would probably be from the witness box at her trial.

'Will you come back later?' Atlanta asked. 'I want to hear how Ed is.'

'Someone will but it probably won't be me.'

'Right.' Atlanta nodded, working it out for herself. She looked angry, but Sarah knew her well enough by now to know she was upset.

'I'm sorry,' Sarah said. 'I really am. I'll do what I can for you both.'

'Yeah,' Atlanta replied without looking at her. But as Sarah headed for the door she called her back.

'If I don't see you again, there's something I should tell you. About Nick.'

Sarah didn't want to hear. If Nick and Atlanta had slept together, that was one thing. To know any more, to have to listen to an apology or a justification, would be worse by far.

'Nick was the one who told you about Kelly, wasn't he?' Atlanta said.

Sarah stared in surprise.

'No one else did, right?' She waited for Sarah to reply, and when she didn't went on. 'You wouldn't ask anyone, because you were too proud. And no one told you because it wasn't true.'

'What are you going on about?' Sarah said, mystified.

'It wasn't true. About Kelly. She and your Tom weren't seeing each other.'

'What do you know about it?'

'Nick made it all up.'

It was like reaching out and finding a handrail was gone, Sarah thought. Like falling into darkness. Like trying to stand on shifting sands only for the tide to sweep you away.

'That's rubbish,' she said quietly. But the words didn't convince her.

Atlanta shrugged.

'It doesn't matter to me. I just wanted you to know.'

'But it doesn't make any sense. Tom was his cousin. They were friends, really close. Why would he say it if it wasn't true?'

'So he could screw you,' Atlanta replied as if it was obvious. 'Or maybe so he could get back at Tom in some way. Or at you. I don't know; I wasn't there. You work it out.'

It wasn't like that. Sarah remembered the night: sitting on the sofa, listening to the records Tom had liked, talking about him. She had sensed Nick was holding something back but he was too simple a soul to lie to her properly. In the end she had wheedled it out of him. First he had said she had to forget Tom. Then he had told her about Kelly, so that her suspicions, her unacknowledged jealousies, came flooding out. Then, without knowing how, she had ended up in his bed. She had cried herself to sleep in his arms, drained by it all.

Sarah sat down. She still couldn't believe that Nick had lied.

'You're just saying this to get back at me. And him. I don't know why. Maybe because he only wanted a one-night stand.'

'What do you mean?'

'I know about you and him. I saw him coming out of your room in the morning.'

But Atlanta was laughing.

'You think I did it with him? He came round because I'd left my address book in the pub. Jeez, girl, you've got a lot to learn. The man's a wanker. I wouldn't do it with him if you put a gun to my head. No offence,' she added, thinking better of what she'd just said, 'but he's not for me. I've already found the man I want, and it ain't him.'

Sarah looked at the floor. She felt calm. For now, all she wanted was to be sure.

'How do you know?' she asked Atlanta quietly.

The other woman counted the answers off on her fingers.

'First, it's obvious. Second, Nick as good as told me that night we went out. Third . . . well, I don't think I need a third, do you?'

Sarah had heard her colleagues say that the deeper the wound, the less you felt it. She'd never believed it and had hoped she would never find out for herself. But maybe it was true for emotional wounds too. You didn't feel them at first.

Atlanta's look had too much pity in it. Sarah turned away and rapped on the door. She heard the duty sergeant heave himself off his chair behind the custody desk and lumber down the corridor.

'Hey,' Atlanta said. 'There's something else.'

Sarah looked at her warily.

'It's only to say good luck,' Atlanta went on. 'And to take care of yourself,' she said with more meaning. 'Don't do anything stupid, will you?'

'I won't,' Sarah replied as the door opened.

'Yeah, well, make sure you don't,' Atlanta said, looking away.

Linehan was further down the corridor, talking to the duty sergeant, but he looked up and came over to her.

'Any luck?' he said quietly. She shrugged.

'No. She's feeling bad enough about saying what she did last night.'

Using what Atlanta had already told her, they might be able to convince Ed that she was cooperating with the police. They could say that Atlanta had sold him to save herself, in the hope that he would accuse her in return out of fear or spite. Between the two of them, playing one against the other, they could probably get all the information they needed. Sarah suspected it was how most of her colleagues would handle it, but if she could make Ed see how much trouble they were both in, he might be prepared to admit his part to put Atlanta in the clear. But perhaps she was being romantic. Was there anyone who would do the same for her? Who would admit to their part in a crime and a cover-up out of loyalty to her? Family, perhaps but Nick? Or Alban?

RIPTIDE

Tom would have, she told herself.

'Maybe it doesn't matter,' Andy said. 'Morton reckons Denton'll talk.'

'How come?'

'He knows his girlfriend's in deep shit. So in return for letting her go he'll tell us the lot.' He broke off as the sergeant reappeared and told him there was a call waiting.

'Get yourself some rest,' Andy said to her, smiling a little uncertainly. 'I'll call you later if we need you.'

Sarah sat at her desk, unable to think or do anything except stare at the computer screen and feel again all the shame and anger of the morning. She hardly heard David as he came in.

'Is everything OK?' he asked uncertainly, noticing her strained face.

'No. No it isn't. I would very much like it,' she added, close to tears, 'if you would buy me a sandwich.'

They sat in the canteen, the plastic sandwich wrappers pushed to one side and two cups of vile coffee from the vending machine cooling in front of them, while Sarah tried to find the right words.

'Do you ever find it all too much?' she said at last. 'The job? All of it?'

'I suppose so,' he said placidly.

'So much that you couldn't face doing it any more?'

David thought about this. Meanwhile, Sarah could hear some of her colleagues discussing the case at the table behind her, laughing as one of them had to pay up on a bet.

'There are times like that,' he said. 'The Julie

291

Stanforth case was one. There was one thing about that which really got to me; I've never forgotten it.'

Sarah tried to close her mind to the talk behind her. Someone was saying in a loud assertive voice that they'd been slow not to get straight onto the black couple.

'It was a couple of days before we found her body. The bastard dumped her handbag in a litter bin. Only a couple of hundred yards from here, just off the market place somewhere. He must've got a real kick out of that.'

He was fiddling with a packet of sugar from the bowl that stood between them, rolling it into a tight ball then letting it go again.

'Anyway, once they'd done all the usual tests, I got the job of telling the boyfriend we'd got it. Returning it to him. Inside, as well as the usual stuff like keys and make-up, there was a bundle of photos, a couple of letters and a diary. They were all soaking wet and covered in grit. He looked at it all and then he said he didn't want it. At first I couldn't understand. I thought he might be about to confess, or something. After all, you always do suspect the husband or the boyfriend, don't you? Even though he had a cast-iron alibi. But it wasn't that.

'I found that out later, when we found the body. You were there, weren't you? Well, then I knew why he didn't want it back. Having those letters and stuff around would be like living with a corpse. It was evidence of how she'd died. It was like the . . . I don't know. She was all bloated and swollen, just like the pages of her diary. And covered in muck, like the photos.'

He sipped his coffee. At the next table, someone was asking if any of them had ever slept with a black woman. A week before, it would have gone straight past her.

'When I go home after something like that,' David was saying, 'and pretend I've just had another day in the office, that's when I wonder if I'm asking too much of Helen, of myself. Of the kids. You know. You take so much anger into yourself, working on stuff like that. You only ever solve a few cases. Even then, you can't make things the way they were before. People are still hurt. They've still lost whatever was stolen. They still can't face going out any more. They still won't trust others the way they used to.

'You either stop caring, or it starts to eat you up inside.'

He pushed the coffee away from him.

'Anyway, this isn't helping. You should go and get some rest. It'll look better in the morning.'

'Will it?'

'It always does,' he said confidently, as they headed for the door.

'So do you think I should stay?' she said. 'Stay in the force?'

He stopped, annoyed for a moment to be put on the spot.

'I wish you would. I really do. You're not, if you don't mind me saying so, a natural for the work. But that's a good thing. We don't want everyone to be like Blake. Or Morton.' He shrugged. 'But I can't say you should stay. You've got to do what's best for you.'

Chapter Thirty-Three

Sarah spent a wasted afternoon pretending to be interested in her other work, until David insisted she go home. She had hoped to leave unnoticed but Graham Blake was hanging around the reception area, chatting to the desk sergeant, leaning on the main counter and fiddling with a pack of cigarettes he wasn't supposed to smoke.

'Ah, Miss Delaney,' he said loudly. 'I hear you are to be congratulated.'

'Really?' she replied cautiously.

'Oh yes. Anyone who can provoke Chief Inspector Morton into the stream of expletives I heard him utter earlier today must have hidden depths I had not begun to suspect. Jeremy worked for me for five years, as you well know. I never got so much as a flying fuck from him, so to speak.'

She stood patiently, waiting for him to tire of the game.

'I'm sorry,' he said unexpectedly. 'Not the time and place, I know. But I hope you've learned your lesson.'

'How do you mean?'

'You're only in this mess, lassie,' he said in an undertone, 'because you didn't listen to what I said. I told you to come and tell me what was going on. I said it doesn't matter who else you've told, I want to hear it from you.'

He smiled, trying to release the tension.

'Come on in here,' he said, leading her back to his office where he sank back into his leather chair and gestured to her to take the seat opposite. 'Tell me all about it. What have you got to lose?'

So she did. And by the time she had finished her tired and flat account of what had happened, which to her own ears would convince no one, he was nodding wisely, pulling at his moustache and allowing himself a faint smile.

'If you're telling the truth,' he said cautiously, 'then we've got some thinking to do. You, me, Haydon, all of us. If not, you're in deeper than I could ever believe.'

'I did just what I was told to,' she said. 'I looked after Atlanta. I kept an open mind. I know I should have told Morton straight away after getting back to the shore but we were both in a state.'

'Or maybe you thought it would be nice to be the one to solve the murder all on your own?'

'No, it wasn't like that.' She felt herself blushing. 'There was a bit of that, sure. More that I wanted to show I could follow up a lead properly. That I could do more than look for bodies. And I got Atlanta to talk.'

He ignored her and began to doodle on his notebook, the pen making a series of circles and loops, as far as she could make out like the scrollwork on a banknote. Then he started on something more elaborate made up of circles and arrows and tiny symbols.

'It's very difficult for me,' he said pensively. 'It's not my case. If I interfere people will say I'm bitter at being passed over, sour that it's Jeremy who's taken the job. There's only so much I can do.' He put his hands behind his head and looked at the ceiling. The mood had changed again. He was plotting something and she was enjoying the way he seemed to treat her more like an equal. She too began to relax a little.

'You know, don't you, that Mabbott is lying?'

'That's what everyone says.'

'Ah, but what I've learned in my all too many years in the force is that just because you find out someone is lying, it doesn't mean you've found the truth. I don't believe Mabbott or Denton had anything to do with Hannay's killing but the answer isn't out at Compton Spit, like you think. It's in the life of the victim – this time anyway. Probably at the hospital. So your best bet is to go home, forget all about this and let me sort it out in my own way.'

He leant back, the slightly surreal smile returning.

'Drink?' he said expansively, pulling out a bottle of whisky and waving it towards her.

'No thanks. I've got to drive.'

'Fair enough,' he said, putting the bottle away without filling his own glass. 'Another time, then.'

Outside the station the wind was stronger, tearing at the trees and sending papers and leaves skidding around the station car park. A ten-minute walk to her flat and then she could sleep like the dead – if she could forget what Morton had said to her in his cold, angry voice during their brief and unpleasant final interview. He had explained that Ed had changed his mind; neither of them would talk and unless something turned up quickly they would have no choice but to let Mabbott go that night, and Denton the next day. Morton had refused to listen to her arguments that the couple were only marginal to the case. Anyway she had nothing to go on except a frail trust in Atlanta, itself fading as she thought more about the facts and her own gut feeling that the answer lay not in the hospital in Norwich or in London but at Compton Spit.

As she unlocked her car, she glanced back at the police station. One of her colleagues came out, followed by Alban and Nicola. They were over to a patrol car parked on the other side of the compound and she guessed they were being driven to the airport to meet her parents. Sarah quickly got into her car, glad that neither of them had seen her. There were something so intimate and contained about the way they had walked down the steps, Alban holding Nicola's arm to steady her, she leaning towards him. Sarah had no wish to intrude.

She let them leave first, then followed a short distance behind as they drove through the town centre. But they soon turned off the ring road onto the Norwich Road, while she carried straight on, towards the coast.

The wind buffeted the car on the more exposed parts of the road. And once she had reached Compton and parked by the entrance to Beach Road, she could hear it driving the sea hard onto the beach.

Sarah had no idea what she was looking for. She left her car by the church, where Atlanta and Ed had parked that night. From here, the footpath to Compton crossed the iron bridge and ran through the fields. The path continued the other way onto the dunes and to the sea itself, just out of sight but an ever-present sound, while the track continued out along the spit towards the Red House, curving until it was lost from sight among the gorse and the pine trees.

She paused for a moment outside Rosemary's house, wondering if she should stop and go in. Wondering too if she should ask her advice about what she planned to do. The idea of sinking into Rosemary's armchair, looking around the room, so familiar although she had only been there once, was seductive. Sarah knew, too, she would probably receive wise advice. So she walked the other way, onto the dunes, and faced the wind coming off the sea. The sky and sea seemed to merge; the scene was vague, ill-defined, from the wind which backed and veered to the confusion of the breaking waves. The only clarity was in the line of breakwaters, marching into the sea and disappearing beneath the waves, their ends marked with tall steel poles.

'Sarah!'

She turned to see Andy Linehan waving from below, by the road. She waited while he climbed up to join her.

'What are you doing here?' he shouted above the wind. 'I thought you'd gone home.'

'There's something I've got to do.' She spoke so bleakly that he quickly changed the subject.

'I hope Jezza wasn't too hard on you. It's only that he's under a lot of pressure, especially now he's got them in the bag and might have to let them go. There are some who'd have been a lot more brutal, believe me. But Jezza brought you in on this and if you hadn't got the right experience . . . well, then that's his responsibility. Some people aren't cut out for plainclothes work,' he said with a sideways glance at her. 'Better to find out sooner rather than later.'

'Perhaps you're right,' she said, not believing a word of it and not really caring. She was thinking of the first time that she and Tom had stood there, looking out across the breaking seas. She had been amazed by the simplicity of the scene: no cafés, no crowds of sunbathers, no houses or bathing huts. The land simply ended, the water began, and the only traces of humanity were the futile rotting breakwaters trying to hold back the tides.

'I must admit that Mabbott was very convincing,' Andy was saying. 'She had me fooled all the way along. I don't think I can remember a suspect who was so plausible. So relaxed about stringing us along.'

'She had nothing to do with the murder,' Sarah said simply.

'Come on, love. You might like to think it was just Denton but she must have known all along what was going on. Or maybe she did it,' he said with a slight edge. 'Maybe it was your friend Atlanta who stabbed him, left him bleeding to death like that.'

He was trying to provoke her, perhaps annoyed that she was staring out to sea, seemingly unconcerned by what he had to say.

'No.' She turned to him. 'What she told me out there on that boat, was exactly what happened. Which means something else took place here.'

He looked at her more closely.

'Are you sure you're OK? You look a bit out of it.'

'I'm fine. It's just that someone I know is dead.'

'I'm sorry,' he said, taken aback. 'I'd no idea. I'm really sorry. Was it someone close?'

'Yes.'

She looked away again.

'You should go home,' he said in the end.

'I'm going to have a walk. Clear my head.'

He watched her as she followed the path along the top of the dunes towards the line of pine trees further down the spit.

Chapter Thirty-Four

The storm had if anything grown stronger but it was still a warm wind and the rain had held off. The shredded clouds let through patches of light from the setting sun and Sarah almost enjoyed the walk. A single gull flew past, skimming the waves and then rising up on the wind, shrieking triumphantly. Sarah felt some of the same exhilaration as she watched it. After a while, she cut inland through the line of pines until she picked up the faint path that ran towards the Red House.

Once there, Sarah could feel the wind dragging at the roof and battering at the walls. She could hear it moaning around the eaves and rattling the shutters. But it had stood through much worse storms than this, and the dunes gave it a little shelter. Walking around it, her feet made no sound on the springy turf. She remembered how Tom had shown her the way to climb in using the roof of the scullery and the loose catch in the bathroom window. The window slid up with only the faintest sound, as it had always done: enough to set the heart racing but not enough to wake Tom's parents sleeping further down the corridor.

Sarah explored the house as if in a dream, not sure what she was looking for; walking silently down the landing and glancing into the clean, bare rooms, finding nothing of the present, no sign of recent occupation, nothing out of place. But there were a thousand memories of the past. Tom's bedroom, the creaks of each floorboard in the corridor the room she had used. She turned the tap in the washbasin and it still made the gurgling, frothing noise she remembered so clearly.

She sat on her old bed, fingering the counterpane, sniffing at the faint traces of dust in the air. She picked books at random from the shelf beside her, turning them over. There were several she could remember Tom reading. In one of them, folded up as a bookmark, she found an old order of service. It was for Nick's brother Andrew's wedding, and the she remembered the day so clearly. Tom in full morning dress, the immaculate tailoring, the fresh carnation and expertly polished shoes making such a contrast with his thatch of brown hair and his manic grin.

Downstairs, the kitchen was tidy, silent except for the quiet hum of the fridge. The carpets and furniture were all exactly as they had been except a little more threadbare, a little more faded from the sunlight. At first it was unsettling, as if she had truly returned to an earlier time or to a house kept unchanged as a memorial to the dead. But she knew that there was a pragmatic explanation for the neglect. If the place had only a few years left before being lost to the sea, then there was no point in spending money on it.

She thought about calling Nick and telling him she knew what he had done, but she wanted to face him in person. In any case the phone had been disconnected. She held the receiver to her ear, listening to the dead silence, as quiet and as expectant as the rest of the house.

Sarah found the key to the boathouse in its usual place and opened the scullery door. It was the same route she and Tom used to take to leave the house at night, going out to lie together on the dunes. Soft, warm evenings of indigo and silver, or nights where they would huddle in front of a fire of driftwood, at the edge of warmth and cold.

The boathouse was even more crammed than she remembered. From the roof hung masts and spars, a row of oars, two surfboards, coils of rope, nets and floats. The shelves held tins of varnish, packets of screws, boots and deck shoes, and cans of fuel – red for petrol, black for diesel. There were oilskins, wet-suits and life jackets hanging up, and logs stacked in the far corner. The catamaran which had stood in the centre of the boathouse had been replaced by a Zodiac inflatable in grey and red, sitting on a gleaming new launching trolley. Sarah was sad about that; she had learnt to sail in the cat, with Tom, launching it on calm days through the surf and sailing far out to sea, as far as Coldharbour Sand, Seal Sand, Dead Sand.

Beside her, on another shelf, stood a pile of games: two table tennis bats with their rubber facing peeling off; a box of tennis balls, grey and scuffed; a football sitting in an upturned frisbee; a baseball bat. She picked it up, feeling its weight and balance, the smooth perfection of the finish except where, punched neatly into the wood just below the handle, it carried Tom's name. The bat she had bought for him for his eight-eenth birthday.

Still holding it, she switched off the light, and closed and locked the door.

Sarah returned to the house. Her plan had been no more clear than a feeling that the answer must lie here on Compton Spit, and probably at the Red House, and that by being here she might come across it. But she was sure now that there was nothing here to discover about the murder of Chris Hannay. That no longer mattered.

She looked around the sitting room, remembering doing the same in Nicola's cottage the day before. Here, the guest book was where it had always been, under the coffee table in the sitting room, alongside the old magazines and battered board games. She recognized the soft red cover, padded like a steakhouse menu. Inside there were years of entries in different hands, some a few words, other small essays interspersed with drawings and maps. She began flicking through the pages as she went upstairs to her old room, where she lay on the bed, looking for the entries in Tom's handwriting. Staying with friends from school or with his family. Trips along the coast or out in the catamaran.

Sarah read about the times they had stayed there together and even found entries she had written, so self-consciously. Then came the time, four years before, when the sequence was broken. Nothing was said: only no one had come for several weeks and the entries afterwards were shorter and less light-hearted. And none of them had been made by Tom or by her. Occasionally, after that, someone would allude to

Tom's death. *Drank to Tom* one entry read, a year after he died. Another mentioned going to the service held at the local church each year for seafarers.

She switched off the light and let herself remember the past.

As she lay there in the darkness, one hand behind her head, the other warm between her thighs, hearing the rising wind and the waves pounding the shore, feeling the drafts of cool air eddy through the house, odd thoughts came to her.

Tom sitting beside her in the church while she savoured the sight of Andrew sitting nervously a few rows in front of her, uncomfortable in his best Army uniform, complete with braid and even a sword, anxious at the delay, the absence of his bride, turning around every now and again, leaning forward to whisper to his best man to be reassured that she was going to come after all. And Tom asking her what she thought of it all. Asking her in a tone of voice she had found strange at the time though she had given it little thought. She could recall her reply: how silly it all was, as if a service to a God no one believed in could make any difference; how if you loved someone, that was what mattered. Now she understood: he wanted to ask her to marry him. Not then perhaps but maybe later; perhaps at the reception, or walking home afterwards. And what would she have said?

She would have waited; not to tease but to make sure he was sure, and then she would have hugged him and told him a thousand times *yes*.

Another thought. Another moment of understanding. Nick, that night; above her, inside her, smiling at her, almost laughing, but not sharing the joke as Tom would have done. The way he had ignored her until Tom's death, but ignored her in a meant way. Nick must have fancied her even then, but never had the chance to do anything about it. And when Tom had died, his own cousin, the first thing he had thought of was to comfort her. He had been the first to come to tell her. Had he always hated her as well? Had he wanted to see her suffer? To inflict more pain on her than he could ever have done with a blow or a weapon? Or did he, even then, in the first moments of realizing his cousin and friend was dead, think of a way of turning it to his advantage? And when he had done so – when she was spread beneath him, opened up by his lies – had he laughed about it?

Sarah felt no anger. Nick had come and gone. For now, for these strange moments, she had Tom back again.

Her mind drifted on, close to sleep, thinking of her shame and anger at seeing Nick emerge from Atlanta's room; the certainty that they had lain on the floor, he driving into her in just the same way, his lips glistening in the faint light as he smiled. But it was all a mirage, it had never happened; so now there was no jealousy, only anger at her own weakness years before. Maybe she had always known that she had been sold a lie, even before Atlanta had told her so.

And Atlanta herself; she had laughed at the idea of screwing Nick. She had said that he was a prick; that she was already going out with the only man she had ever wanted. And one reason she wouldn't give.

But Sarah now knew, with sleep helping to steer

the pieces into place. The way Atlanta picked at her food one moment, and devoured plates of stodge the next. The way she wanted to sleep in the afternoon, and planned to sell her flat and move closer to her mother. The way she wouldn't drink, even after being caught in the tide and almost drowned.

I may have got everything wrong so far, Sarah thought. I may have missed what was right in front of me but this I know. She's pregnant.

Would it be a boy, strong and proud but still in awe of his mother? Or a girl, with the same mischievous mocking attitude, an uncomfortable prospect for some future head teacher? She smiled at the thought of Atlanta waddling into a maternity ward; Ed changing the baby's nappy, laughing as he did so; Atlanta, singing it songs, rocking it to sleep.

Sarah slept.

Chapter Thirty-Five

Sarah woke at the sound of a key in a lock. She sat up, dazed, staring around the darkened room. The front door opened, someone coughed and scuffed their feet on the mat. They weren't being cautious. They knew the place. Grabbing her shoes, Sarah scurried to the top of the stairs, ready to run if they came up. But whoever it was went straight into the kitchen. They began crashing about, slamming cupboard doors, filling the kettle. She smelt a faint waft of cigarette smoke. Sarah started to inch down the stairs, but then the man – surely it was a man – returned and she had to scuttle back out of sight. He went on into the living room, settling himself heavily on the sofa with an appreciative grunt. She heard the sound of a cap being twisted off, the neck of a bottle clink against a glass and a surprising amount poured out.

She wondered how long he would be there, whether he might come upstairs for any reason, and if there was any way she could get past him safely. She guessed not. From the sofa he would be able to see the foot of the stairs. She looked out of one of the windows at the car the man had come in. It was parked slightly oddly, not in front of the porch but further round the side of the house, and backed in so that the boot was only a couple of feet from the door of the boathouse.

Then she recognized the car. It didn't make any sense. He wouldn't behave like he was at home; he'd start a search or wait quietly, as she had done, to see who would come. It didn't make any sense.

It was Graham Blake's car.

She tried to work it out. Could Blake really be the senior police officer Ed's 'friends' had boasted of owning? It was ridiculous, of course. He had all those years in the force, all those arrests to his credit.

But if he was, then there was nothing he didn't know. He could run his own mirror image of the investigation – laying false leads, destroying evidence, undermining any attempt to find the truth. He could have set up Ellis, making sure that information was received that pointed to his intended scapegoat. And when that plan started to fall apart, he could have helped switch the focus of the investigation to Ed and Atlanta.

Sarah heard a faint beeping noise from the sitting room below. She paced cautiously back to the top of the stairs, just in time to hear Blake making a phone call.

'It's me. I'm at the house. I've got her.'

Her? Could Blake know she was here? She paused for a while, listening, while she tried to work out what he meant and who was on the other end of the call.

'No problem,' Blake continued after a moment. 'We waited at her car and told her we wanted to ask a few more questions.'

So it must be Atlanta. But not going willingly. Tricked.

'Not with a gun in the back of her head,' Blake guffawed. 'I think she knew, though,' he added more soberly. 'I think she knew what it meant. I mean, she's pretty sharp. She must've known that once she'd seen us, we weren't going to be letting her go.'

Sarah crouched down, feeling sick. They must have driven Atlanta somewhere lonely and quiet. Perhaps into Colman's Wood or one of the old gravel pits.

'I know what I'm doing, son. People want a story. That way, we can wrap this all up. The story is Denton meets the doctor, there's a fight – who knows why – and he kills him. His girlfriend backs him up, of course, and makes up this story about a psycho. Then, when that falls apart, they both disappear, who knows where. Probably off to Africa on false passports one step ahead of the poor old plod. And only we know that in fact they're . . . well, let's say elsewhere.'

Listening to Blake describing their murder so cheerfully, being so matter of fact, made Sarah's skin crawl. She could see Atlanta being dragged from the car, struggling, trying to escape. There would be at least two of them, so she had no chance. One would hold her while the other put the gun to her head.

'There wasn't any choice,' Blake said sharply. 'I had to pick her up before she went back to London. We couldn't have done anything there, could we? We agreed. Anyway, as long as Denton thinks we've got her, he won't talk. I've made sure of that.'

But they wouldn't want the noise and the mess of a shot, Sarah thought. Instead, they'd have choked or smothered her. It would have been hard work. She could imagine them grunting with the effort of holding her down, but in the end she would have weakened, struggled less. And they'd have carried on to make sure.

'The weather's not my problem, son. You come and take over here, and when the conditions are right, we'll do it then. She's not going anywhere,' he added.

Her body must be in the car. In the boot. Probably already wrapped in plastic, ready to be taken out to sea and dumped overboard. That was the only thing Blake could mean: the weather was certainly too bad to use the Zodiac. If they chose the right place, somewhere like Missel Hole, there would be little chance of anyone ever finding any trace of the bodies – for surely they planned to kill Ed too.

'Well, as soon as you can, then,' Blake said, slightly mollified. 'And tell your old man he owes me for this. Owes me big time.'

He rang off. Sarah heard him pour another drink. Then he began to whistle.

Sarah sat at the top of the stairs, cold, shivering, overwhelmed by what she had done. She had talked to Blake. She had assured Atlanta it would be fine. She had managed, in the end, to make Atlanta trust her. And now this.

What would Atlanta have felt in those last few minutes? She must have known what was to come. Perhaps she tried to talk him out of it. Or pleaded for her life. Or maybe defied him. Sarah hoped it had been that way. Then bundled into the boot of his car. Nothing more than a bag of rubbish to be dumped.

For a moment Sarah thought of going down to confront him, or attack him with Tom's baseball bat. Or better still, standing in the witness box at Blake's trial, telling them every word he had spoken. She took out the wedding programme and scrawled down what he had said while she could still remember each word, tipping the card so that it caught the moonlight. But she would have to see Atlanta, to make sure. The last thing to do before she left.

She went to the top of the back stairs and looked down into the darkness. Still there was no sound from Blake. Sarah wondered how long it would be before whoever it was he had spoken to turned up. She began to plan which way she would go. The road or the path? The road would be more exposed but she would hear a car coming and could hide in the ditch.

Step by step, placing each foot carefully as close to the wall as she could, she went down the stairs, the same route she had first taken with Tom. Sarah felt he was close as she placed her feet so there was no creak from the floorboards, as he had shown her. She felt the same sensations: sick with anticipation, her breath shallow, her heart beating fiercely, her skin sensitive to every movement.

Sarah paused on the last step, listening. There was no sound from the sitting room; it was as quiet and as frightening as a wild animal's lair. In front of her, on the tiled floor, lay a band of moonlight. She would have to step through it to reach the welcoming darkness of the scullery. To her right was the kitchen. Was it worth the risk? Another weapon, as well as the bat? Hardly daring to breathe, she crossed to the worktop and felt for the wooden block she remembered, touched the array of handles and drew out a long, thin-bladed filleting knife.

Was that how they had killed Atlanta? How they planned to kill Ed? A knife? Or would Blake have risked blood staining the carpeting in the boot of his car or splattering the cuffs of his jacket? No, she was sure they would have strangled her.

She thought about Blake. He might be asleep or dozing. She could creep into the room, come up behind him, stick the knife into him before he had a chance to react. She could already taste the satisfaction at the sight of his blood, see the look on his face.

Sarah leant against the door frame, waiting for the tide of hate to recede. She headed for the scullery, too fast, skidding on the tiles, only to regain her balance in a couple of rushed steps. The bolt of the pantry door slid back without a sound; perhaps it was the same coating of oil which Tom had given it. She held her breath but the silence was complete, so much so that the scrape of the door, its wood swollen with damp, made her wince and the breeze coming through the door seemed bound to bring Blake out to investigate. She eased the knife carefully into the waistband of her skirt, suddenly afraid of the narrow blade, and the pleasure she might have found in using it. Then she stepped into the night.

Chapter Thirty-Six

Sarah stood in the shadows, looking across the lawn to the fence and the dunes beyond. She could make for the welcoming darkness of the bushes and the trees, walk to Rosemary's house, call Morton from there and ask for help; but first there was Blake's car. She needed to go and see for herself. It was the only way to be sure what had happened. And now she was outside, she was free from the trap. She would be fine.

It was easy enough to work her way round the back of the house, avoiding the sitting room window. The back of the car was only a few feet from the boathouse. Her feet made no noise on the turf.

Blake had left the car open. And the key in the ignition. For a moment she thought she would be able to drive away, but when she turned the key, nothing happened. She realised it was protected by an immoboliser, and she would need to enter a code. So instead she reached across to scrabble under the dashboard for the handle which released the boot. The clunk it made didn't worry her; the wind was making enough noise as it lashed the trees and rattled the windows to cover it. But she had to wait a minute before she could screw up the courage to look in the boot. She hoped the body would be wrapped up. She didn't want to have to see her face.

The low beams of moonlight left the inside of the boot in a pool of darkness. Still sheltering out of sight beside the car, Sarah swallowed hard and reached in. She felt plastic sheeting, moved her hand, passed over cloth and brushed against skin. She snatched her hand back, then looked in again, easing back the sheeting. Atlanta's arms were tied behind her, and her feet bound together too. There was a long scarf wrapped around her head and tied at the back. There was dried blood on her neck.

Sarah couldn't leave her there like that, like a worthless thing. She slid out the knife and cut through the ropes but left the scarf in place. She pulled her to the edge of the boot, shifted her onto her shoulders and lifted her clear. Sarah staggered a little, regained her balance and looked back towards the house. Still no sound. No sign of life. Blake would be on his second whisky, used to the odd sounds from the battering wind. If she could reach the back of the house, keeping out of the moonlight, then she could find some bushes where she could hide the body.

Then something grabbed her throat. The body twisted, throwing her off balance. It took her precious seconds to realize it was Atlanta, pulling her down to the ground, wrapping one of the trailing ends of rope around her neck. Sarah tried to call out, but already the air was gone from her lungs, the rope frighteningly tight. She tried to slip her fingers underneath but the rope had dug in too deep. She was pressed against the car, her feet slipping on the damp grass. She tried to hit out but Atlanta ignored her blows.

It wasn't real. The face wasn't a real face but a cloth mask. The suddenness of it, the fear as she couldn't breathe gave her no chance to think.

Atlanta tore away the scarf. And when she saw it was Sarah she was killing, she stopped. Relaxed. Sarah waved an arm feebly and felt the pressure at her neck ease.

'Where are the others?' Atlanta hissed, still holding her tightly.

'I'm not . . .' Sarah croaked. 'Not me. Blake. He's in there.'

The rage was still in Atlanta's eyes but Sarah could see some doubt as well.

'I came to get you,' she said. 'Trust me.'

She watched Atlanta, resisting the voice inside her telling her to run, that Blake must have heard, that he would be coming after them. Then Atlanta nodded and, relaxed her grip.

'We've got to get away,' Sarah said. 'Blake will have heard. We've—'

Atlanta was looking past her at the house, and froze when the door opened and a torch snapped on. The beam swung across the lawn and fixed on the car, the open boot. They could see the figure behind the light fumbling with something – a gun, Sarah guessed.

She pushed Atlanta away, telling her to run, and ran herself. But she'd forgotten about the fence. At the last moment she swerved to her left and slithered to the bottom of a ditch. It was damp and dark and she felt safe, like an animal gone to ground. But she needed to know what was happening.

She crawled as quietly as she could to the top of the ditch. The tree above cast a deep shadow and the longer grass and a pile of logs gave some cover. She looked about but Atlanta was nowhere to be seen.

Blake had walked into the centre of the lawn, flicking the torch around him. Sarah pressed herself as close to the ground as she could. Broken stems tickled her face and she could smell the damp earth as well as the sweet crushed grass. She remembered the earth falling on Tom's coffin, running through her fingers onto the polished wood; rich brown earth breaking into a powder, brushed from her hands but the smell lingering.

Blake stood uncertain. He must be wondering whether Atlanta had escaped on her own, whether he should try to hunt her down, or wait for the others or make his escape. He circled the car, always keeping the beam of light moving. Twice it skimmed over Sarah and she ducked her head just in time, grateful for her black clothes.

Sarah wondered where Atlanta could be; she couldn't have made it to the house or crossed the lawn. Blake must have realized this and was approaching cautiously, checking around and under the car and then heading towards the road. He began to play the beam of light along the line of the fence, working his way towards her. She knew she should break cover now, before he got too near, but couldn't make herself move. Then she sensed Atlanta somewhere behind her.

Perhaps Blake heard something, because he flicked the light around suddenly. Atlanta was caught in the light, almost at the top of the fence. Blake fired twice, and she twisted one arm outstretched, her fingers grasping at the dark. Sarah was close enough to hear her cry, even over the sound of the shot. Then she fell backwards to the ground.

She didn't move or make another sound. She lay, a dark heap, a bundle of blacks and grey and silvers.

The sound of the shots had been deafening. The silence that followed seemed to subdue even the wind and the sea. Blake walked cautiously forward, the gun held out in front of him in his right hand, rubbing an ear with his left.

Atlanta stirred, and scrabbled at the ground with one hand.

Blake stood over her, the gun pointing at the ground. He stared at Atlanta for a long moment. He must never have shot anyone, Sarah thought. He must be preparing himself for it. Perhaps he's scared. Or perhaps he's savouring the moment.

He raised the gun so it was pointing at Atlanta's back.

I'm going to watch him kill her.

He thought again, and crouched down.

Unless I do something now.

Blake placed the gun against the back of her head, then stopped. He examined it, fiddled with it. Then, with a grunt of satisfaction, he replaced the gun and readied himself again.

By then, though, Sarah was only a few feet behind, expecting at every moment for him to hear her, to turn and fire. But he didn't hear her footsteps, quiet on the soft grass. Perhaps he was deafened a little by the shots. Or concentrating too much on his first kill.

Sarah brought the baseball bat down on the back of his head. She knew at once it wasn't hard enough. He grunted, staggered, but managed to keep upright, still holding the gun. She swung the bat again, knocking him to one side. He lurched forward, dazed, growling, and she swung a third time, almost overbalancing. She winced at the sensation, both resisting and giving. He fell and she hit him again, and again, until he stopped moving.

Sarah knelt beside Atlanta, felt the pulse at her neck and then touched the dark glistening stain on her back. She wiped her fingers on the sleeve of her jacket and called her name, but there was no response.

'Atlanta? Listen to me. You're going to be fine, I promise you.'

Sarah held her hand, remembering how Atlanta had talked about the plane breaking up in mid air, imagining the passengers hitting the ground, lying like this for a moment or two, broken-backed, staring at the dark.

There was a movement behind her, a groan. Blake coughed, choked; a small stream of vomit spread on the ground beside him. She could smell the whisky.

Sarah took the gun and flung it into the bushes, then ran to the car to fetch the rope to tie up Blake and got the first-aid box from the house to do what she could for Atlanta. But when she returned Atlanta was conscious, and had even managed to prop herself up against the gatepost. The shot must have missed anything vital, for although the wound was torn and bleeding, Atlanta could breathe easily.

'Atlanta? Can you hear me?'

She nodded. Sarah leant her forward, pulled up

her sweater and shirt and sprayed the wound with antiseptic. Atlanta winced.

'Am I going to die?' she asked, suddenly lucid from the pain of the spray, and almost managing a smile.

'No. it's fine. But you're bleeding a bit so I'm going to have to bind this up.'

She nodded, already starting to slip back into oblivion.

'We've got to get away from here,' Sarah said. 'Now.'

'I can't move,' she said, shaking her head.

'You can. You've got to.'

'A minute,' she said, leaning back, closing her eyes. 'Be OK in a minute.'

'No, now!'

'Phone someone,' Atlanta muttered.

'I can't. The bloody phone doesn't work.' She thought of going to look for Blake's phone, but she didn't want to waste any time. 'Look, the others are coming. If we're still here they'll kill us. Can you hear me?'

'You go.'

'Atlanta! If they get us, they'll get Ed too. Like you, as soon as he's released. Then we'll all be killed. Do you believe me?'

Atlanta stared at her, then nodded. 'Have you got the gun?'

'I threw it away,' Sarah said lamely. 'Over there somewhere.'

'Brilliant.' Atlanta closed her eyes in pain. 'Can you help me?'

'I can try. I'll carry you.'

But in the end, there wasn't time.

In the distance, on the coast road, she heard a car. The headlights shone faintly. The engine noise faded, then returned as it turned off the main road and into the village.

Chapter Thirty-Seven

Sarah managed to carry Atlanta as far as the side of the house and from there, hidden by the shadows, she watched the car drive up to the gate and stop, the engine ticking over. Whoever was inside must be surveying the scene: Blake lying on the grass, the house quiet in the headlights, no noise but a sense of waiting.

The engine died. Again a wait. Then the door opened and a figure climbed over the gate and walked over to where Blake lay. When Sarah saw it was Nick she sighed with relief and almost skipped across the lawn towards him.

'Nick! Nick!' she called. She wanted to hold him, to hear him tell her everything was going to be all right. For a moment she could forgive him everything, even Tom.

He looked up, surprised, puzzled, wary. His leather jacket, his jeans and desert boots were all familiar but his expression was different.

She thought how it must look.

'It's all right. There's no one here.'

'Who did this?' he asked, pointing at Blake.

'I did.'

'Is he dead?'

'I don't think so. I don't know.' It hadn't occurred

to her that she might have killed him, or that she would
have to explain or justify herself. She remembered the
way Blake had talked about Atlanta on the phone, what
he had in mind for all of them.

'How much do you know?' he asked quietly.

It took her a moment to work out what he'd said.
What it meant. But most of all, it was his look, the
same one she remembered from the café four years
before. So that the words didn't matter. *It's Tom* . . . A
few words and she knew it all. Or thought she did.

He was still watching her.

She was surprised how clearly she could think.
How the pattern was clear, as it always had been. Ever-
present, like the sound of the sea, except that because
it was familiar she had missed it. If only she had looked
in the right way.

'I know enough,' she said, slowly and quietly.
'About you. About Blake. The drugs, or whatever it
was. Your brother and your father. Using the boatyard
as cover. About what you were going to do to Ed and
Atlanta. That's enough, isn't it?'

She shivered. It was cold, with the wind washing
around her legs like the pull of the sea, cutting through
her sweater. Atlanta's sweater.

'Where's the black girl?' he asked.

'She's gone. Gone to get the police.'

Nick looked pained. The blood had drained from
his face.

'Why are you here?' he asked.

'To give you a chance.'

'Yeah?' He laughed. 'You want a cut? Is that it?
That's really funny, you know. They said to bring you

in. It was me that told them there wasn't any point; you weren't like that.'

'No. You were right. I'm not.'

'So why are you here?' he asked again, this time with more edge in his voice. He stepped forward slowly. She wanted to run, but she couldn't.

'Like I said, to give you a chance. They'll be on their way. Morton, the rest of them. You've got a few minutes, though.'

'To do what?'

'You can't drive; they'll have the road sealed off by now. But you could get away by sea.'

'You're joking. It's blowing a gale.'

'You don't need to go far, only to Yarwell or Martlesham. Anyway, if anyone can do it, you can. You know these seas better than anyone.'

He shifted uneasily, glancing behind him. 'I can't see anything.'

'They won't come with flashing lights and sirens.'

He glanced down at Blake. He would have told Nick what to do. He would have been thinking three moves ahead, just as he'd played the investigation all the way along. Manufactured evidence, suppressed the truth. But Blake's eyes were closed.

'Where's his phone? I need to call the boatyard. Warn them.'

'The one in the house doesn't work. I tried Blake's, but it needs a code to make it work,' she lied. 'You could be back at Yarwell in half an hour if you go now.'

'Why are you doing this for me?' he asked.

'We haven't got time for this,' she said, desperation creeping into her voice.

'No,' he said musingly. 'Pity.'

He smiled, a hungry smile, the same as the way he was looking at her. Looking her over. Thinking of the times he had screwed her, with the sound of the sea beneath them. Thinking that she still wanted him, still loved him. That she was doing this for love.

The prick, she thought to herself. The conceited, arrogant prick.

'Come on,' she said, turning away. 'I'll give you a hand.'

He followed her to the boathouse. There the sound of the storm was if anything more intimidating, as it tore at the roof and rattled the doors facing the sea like a restless animal. She helped him fit the outboard onto the inflatable, checked the fuel, adding some diesel quickly while he shrugged his way into a drysuit. She was desperate to get him gone before the whole monumental bluff came to pieces in her hands. But there was one question she had to ask.

'I want you to tell me about Tom,' she said abruptly.

'What's to tell?' he said, still fiddling with the outboard motor.

'He wasn't seeing Kelly, was he?'

'What does it matter? It's all old history.'

'It matters to me.'

He shrugged. She remembered how he hated being put on the spot.

'Why did you make it all up?' she went on. 'He was your cousin. Your friend.'

'He was dead. Besides, I was doing you a favour.'

'How could you think that?'

'You were all broken up about it,' he said reasonably, standing close in front of her. 'I thought it'd make it easier if you thought he'd been screwing around. Sort of good riddance.'

He touched her shoulder gently. She flinched.

'Not that I didn't enjoy it.' Though she couldn't see his expression, she could hear the smirk in his voice. 'I did. If you want to know, I'd always fancied you. From when you and Tom first got together. But you'd go on like I didn't matter. Flirting. Deliberately touching and kissing him right in front of me. So maybe it was a chance to pay you back for that too.'

The sudden violence in his voice frightened her. She tried to back away, but the boat was right behind her.

'Anyway,' he said reflectively, the anger fading again. 'The funny thing is, after the first night I became quite fond of you.'

Sarah wondered what to do or say next. She had what she had come for. Now all she wanted was for him to be gone.

'I still am, you know,' he went on. 'We should never have split up.'

He leant towards her and held her tightly, pressing her back against the hull of the inflatable. His hand stroked her cheek, then roamed down to her breasts. Desperate, she tried to respond, to turn revulsion into the illusion of passion. But when he tried to kiss her, she held her against his mouth.

'I'm doing this for Tom,' she said quietly.

He stopped, then nodded as if he understood. He stepped back, letting her go. Without another word they opened the doors that faced the sea, and the wind that had been breaking on the sides of the hut came pouring in, laden with a fine spray thrown up from the crashing waves beyond. He switched off the lights and at once they could see that the dark had lifted a little with the approaching dawn. The breakers gleamed white like bones in black earth.

Together they pushed the trolley down the ramp and onto the beach. The wheels moved surprisingly easily over the sand and in seconds it stood at the sea itself. He took the painter and held it while she rolled the trolley forward, so that the foam boiled around the frame, lifting the boat a little, and washed around her legs, so cold it made her gasp. She felt the backwash of the waves, dragging the sand from beneath her feet.

Nick climbed past her onto the boat and her heart lurched when the outboard motor failed to catch. But he tried again, it spluttered and then caught and ran sweetly. He lowered it into the sea and the boat began to edge away from the beach. Sarah tugged the trolley clear, then turned back to see the boat already twenty yards out, turning to face the incoming waves. In the half light she could see Nick struggling to keep the boat upright as the seas passed beneath it, tipping the nose high in the air.

He gunned the throttle and turned the head of the boat further round. He glanced back to the beach, but whether at her or not she couldn't tell.

Slowly, the boat battered its way through the oncoming waves and beyond the line of the breakwater. It turned towards the running sea, into the wind, and the movement became easier, each wave passing beneath the prow rather than slamming into the side. It seemed he was past the worst.

And then the engine cut. For a few moments he tugged desperately at the starting rope. The engine

whined but wouldn't catch. The boat slewed side-on to
the waves. Then it turned over. In seconds it was
driven onto the breakwater. The prow showed for a
moment, pointing to the sky, then disappeared into
the foam. And within a few minutes all that remained
in sight was a single red petrol can, bobbing on the
waves like a marker.

Chapter Thirty-Eight

Sarah stood by the window in the waiting room, watching the trees outside the hospital sway and bend in the wind. Inside it was quiet, except for footsteps passing in the corridor, the occasional rattle of a trolley and the faint hum of the air conditioning.

One of her colleagues had agreed to give her a lift back to the station where she was due to have another interview with Jeremy Morton. She had no idea what she would say. The truth, of course; but could she face telling it?

She had gone with Atlanta in the ambulance, slipping away from the questions and bafflement and accusing stares of the police. Of her colleagues. She had sat calmly during the drive through the deserted early-morning roads knowing everything would be fine, even when Atlanta had drifted into unconsciousness again. It was only at the end that she had broken.

One of the doctors was already standing, syringe in hand, watching a clear liquid spray from the end of the needle, when she remembered to tell them that Atlanta was pregnant. He had looked surprised, felt along his patent's side and said something to the nurse beside him about it being very early and easy to miss. But when he told Sarah that if she hadn't spoken up

Atlanta might have lost the baby, she sat down and cried.

Since then Sarah had slept fitfully, the police had come and gone, happy to leave her there now they had her statement. Ed too had arrived, coming straight from the police station, and was now in with Atlanta, insisting he wouldn't leave her until she was out of hospital and back in London.

One of the nurses put her head around the door and smiled brightly at her.

'She's asking for you.'

Ed was standing outside the ward, on the phone, trying to reassure someone that Atlanta was fine. He smiled at her, waved his hand and made some kind of dumb show she couldn't understand.

Atlanta was sitting up in bed, wreathed in smiles. She grabbed Sarah's hand, thanking her for everything, saying she owed her more than she could ever repay.

'They told me what you did, you know.'

'What was that?' Sarah replied, not wanting to think of Blake. Or of Nick.

'About my being pregnant. They said you told them just in time.'

'They'd have realized soon enough.'

'Well, maybe. But it's still so early. And we . . .' For a moment, to Sarah's great surprise, Atlanta seemed lost for words. But she soon regained her natural, ironic poise.

'We've so much to thank you for, Ed and I,' she said in a serious tone which didn't match the look in her eyes.

'We thought we'd ask you to be one of the god-parents.'

'I couldn't do that,' Sarah said quickly.

'Sure, you can,' Atlanta said, pleased by Sarah's reaction, and dismissing her objections with a wave of her hand. 'I've seen you with your nephews. You're great with kids.'

'I can't,' Sarah insisted desperately.

'You think about it at least. You have to do that because I'm ill and I may have a relapse.' She pulled a pitiful face.

'How are you feeling?' Sarah asked, not sure that Atlanta was entirely joking, and happy to change the subject.

'It really, really hurts. My head, mainly. They've given me an injection for my back so that just feels really odd. Itchy, but nothing more than that. But nothing for my head.'

Sarah lost the thread of what Atlanta was saying, thinking back to the Red House, until she heard a name.

'What?'

'Nick. If I hadn't made it plain enough, the man gave me the creeps.'

'He's dead.'

Atlanta stared. 'I'm sorry,' she said after a moment. 'I shouldn't have been making fun like that. I thought he'd gone off in a boat.'

'He did. He drowned.'

'Shit. I mean, I know—'

'I killed him.'

'What do you mean? There was a storm. He didn't have to go out in it.'

'No. You don't understand. He would have made it. But I killed him. I put diesel in the fuel tank for the

331

outboard instead of petrol. Deliberately, so it would clog the engine up. Cut out. And then he didn't have a chance.'

'You had to, though. He'd have killed you for sure.'

'But that wasn't why I did it. It was because . . .' But she couldn't find the words.

'It was self-defence, wasn't it?'

'I wanted to kill him. I hated him. I'd have smashed his face, shot him, stabbed him, anything.'

Atlanta lay back on the pillow, looking at the ceiling as if trying to find sugared words to make everything better, but all she said was, 'Forget it.'

'I can't.'

'You should get your fucking head sorted out,' Atlanta said in sudden fury. 'Stop hurting yourself. Can't you see how fragile it all is? You could have been dead. All of us, Ed too. They'd have killed us, dumped us at sea. You know what they did to me, Blake and the other one? They told me what they were going to do before they put me in the boot. So I'd know, so I could think about it for all the hours I was in there. You know the little one? Ray? He told me he wanted to fuck me. Because he'd never done it with a dead woman before. Great joke, yeah?'

Atlanta blinked away a tear. 'So are you telling me any one of them is worth a moment of your life, worrying about what you've done?'

Sarah shrugged.

'If you tell anyone,' Atlanta said slowly, 'a word of what you've told me now, I'll never speak to you again. Yeah? You hear me, Sarah Delaney?'

Sarah had to smile. She had an inkling of what Atlanta would be like as a mother.

'All right.'

Sarah made to go, and then asked a final question.

'Do you know if it's a boy or a girl?'

'Ed thinks it's a boy,' Atlanta said, smiling broadly, 'but I *know* it's a girl.'

As soon as she entered the police station Sarah could tell that the place was in shock, even in mourning. The corridors and offices were filled with groups talking in hushed tones, trying out different theories on each other and on themselves. It must all be some great cock-up, and Blake would be cleared and back on duty in a week. He must have got into something too deep. They'd always known there was something wrong.

No one would look at her as she passed. Some mumbled things, others looked away. She felt conspicuous in her black clothes, like a spectre. She thought about changing into the spare uniform hanging in her locker downstairs but she couldn't face it. She wanted to be herself now, not a police officer.

She went up to see Morton, and as she passed glanced in through the open doorway of Blake's room, then stopped to take it in. Everything was as it usually was: the photo frames on the desk, the old-fashioned leather-bound blotter, the computer, never used, pushed to one side, the piles of files on the shelf behind, and the cupboard which would still house a collection of malt whiskies which Blake used to produce when there was anything to celebrate – even if only the end of the week or the day.

Morton was on the phone but he waved her to a chair. She studied him while he finished his call. He looked washed out, drained and a lot older. But she guessed a few days' rest was all he would need to recover; he was that kind of man.

'How is your witness?'

'She'll be all right. They won't keep her in long.'

Sarah was pleased he had asked. He'd told her to look after Atlanta and she'd done so. That was something.

'I'd like you to come back to Compton Spit,' Morton said wearily. 'I need to know exactly what happened.'

'Am I under arrest?' She wondered if she should find a lawyer. Perhaps the Federation could provide one. Or Summerton's. She smiled at the idea of following up her job application with a request to represent her on a murder charge.

'No. I'd have had you arrested last night, though. Everyone thought you'd gone mad and attacked Blake for no reason. But luckily for you we'd already picked up Ray Hall. He got pulled over on the Cromer Road with a defective brake light, would you believe, and tried pulling a knife on one of the officers. The same one he used on Hannay is my guess. Once we got him back here he said he wouldn't talk to anyone but Blake. Claimed he was one of his informants. And that started me thinking about who it could be on the inside.'

'How is he?'

'Blake? He's in a coma. Too early to say how he'll be. But I take it you hit him in self-defence.'

She nodded. Neither of them mentioned Nick Walton.

'Are you ready to go now?'

*

As they drove Sarah began to doze, lulled by the warmth of the heater and the drone of the engine. She found it hard to concentrate on what Morton was telling her.

'When I told Ray Hall we'd got Blake, he decided to come clean. It turns out there were three of them, plus Blake. Normally, Andy Walton would handle the arrangements on shore while Nick Walton and Ray Hall would pick up the stuff from a boat out at sea. That was very neat. The boat would put out a distress signal, saying it had engine trouble, and the lifeboat would be called out. Walton and Hall would take the drugs, and then the boat would manage to "fix" the engine trouble and carry on. Or the lifeboat would escort it in to Yarwell. If anyone was suspicious, they'd watch the yacht, not the lifeboat, wouldn't they?

'But they couldn't do it very often. Someone might start to wonder why there were so many call-outs to broken-down yachts when Ray Hall and Nick Walton were on duty. So once in a while, like last Saturday, they'd pick up the stuff in the Zodiac and take it back to Compton Spit. They waited to pick up the letter from Denton and then set off to walk to the Red House.

'Ray Hall's story is that Hannay's death was all an accident. He says this man came from nowhere, in a complete state. I suppose Nicola had just collapsed in a coma and he was trying to get help. He must've thought they would help him, which was his bad luck. Ray said they thought he must be police, even though he was going on like a maniac. When they grabbed him he started lashing out. That's when Ray says he pulled the knife. He didn't mean to stab him, but in the struggle he did. He didn't think he'd done him any harm because Hannay broke free and ran off. They did the same and legged it the other way. It was only when Ray got home and saw the blood on him he started to get worried. And then the next day there's two bodies. That must've been a shock for them.'

He waited, as if expecting Sarah to say something. She remembered how Blake had said there was only one body at the beach when he'd called from the control room that morning. He must already have had a call from Nick or one of the others and gone there to see what was going on. He was first on the scene, before Morton or even Sarah herself. But she couldn't find the energy to explain this to Morton.

'You won't believe the stuff we've found at the boat-yard,' he went on. 'They'd even got a couple of machine guns hidden away in there. Andrew Walton was in the army, so that's probably where they got them from.'

It was a final irony, she thought, that she had assumed Ed was doing a favour for a friend of his, a black drugs dealer. And now it turned out he was helping out Nick's brother, an old comrade from the army. Loyalty to the regiment. Just like loyalty to the force. She wondered how many of her colleagues had suspected Blake.

'So what was in the letter Ed had?' she asked.

'I don't know,' Morton admitted. 'Denton says he didn't open it, and I believe him. It must've been something like directions to collect the money or deliver the drugs. Maybe the code for a left luggage locker. But I don't suppose Walton or Hall are going to say, so we'll probably never know.'

They turned off the main road into the village. Sarah could picture the Red House, sealed off with striped plastic tape, surrounded by police and scene of crime officers, a few bemused residents watching from a distance. Amongst the brambles and dunes and on the beach, squads of police would be forming up to begin their searches.

And at sea a red petrol can would be bobbing on the waves, swept along by the same currents that had left Chris Hannay's body on the shore. And carried Tom away.

They drove in silence past the village sign, the pub, the old stables. The church. She sat up, wide awake.

'Could you pull over?' she said suddenly. 'Now. Here.'

Morton stopped the car, leaving the engine running. He looked at her expectantly.

'You go on,' she said. 'I'll meet you there. I'll walk over the fields.'

'We need to sort this out,' he said gently. 'We can't waste any time.'

'Don't worry, I'll see you there,' she said, getting out of the car. 'There's something I have to do first.'

Sarah crossed the road and opened the gate to the churchyard. Morton watched as she walked uncertainly between the headstones, looking about her. Then she stopped, having found what she was looking for.

She crouched down by one of the graves, her head bowed, a small dark figure in the autumn sunlight.